DATE DUE		1984
OHP AUG 2 0 1984		

Something Out There

Something Out There

Stories
by

NADINE GORDIMER

THE VIKING PRESS   NEW YORK

Acknowledgment is made to the following periodicals in which some of the stories in this book originally appeared: *Boston Globe:* "Blinder"; *Cosmopolitan:* "Sins of the Third Age"; *Harper's:* "Rags and Bones"; *Index:* "Crimes of Conscience"; *Mother Jones:* "At the Rendezvous of Victory"; *The New Yorker:* "A City of the Dead, A City of the Living" and "A Correspondence Course"; *Salmagundi:* "Something Out There."

LIBRARY OF CONGRESS CATALOGING IN PUBLICATION DATA
Gordimer, Nadine.
Something out there.
I. Title.
PR9369.3.G6S66   1984   823   83-40250
ISBN 0-670-65660-7

The author acknowledges with thanks the following sources for 'Letter from His Father': *A Biography of Kafka*, Ronald Hayman, Weidenfeld & Nicolson, 1981; *Wedding Preparations—and other pieces*, Franz Kafka, translated by Eithne Wilkins and Ernst Kaiser, Definitive Edition, Secker & Warburg, 1954. From the contents of *Wedding Preparations* I have quoted from the following: *Reflections on Sin, Suffering, Hope and the True Way; The Eight Octavo Note-books; Letter to His Father; Fragments from Note-books and Loose Pages; Paralipomena*; Max Brod's *Notes. Letter to His Father* is among the Kafka manuscripts housed in the Schocken Library at Jerusalem.

Printed in the United States of America
Set in Aldus

For Reinhold

Contents

A City of the Dead,
A City of the Living

You only count the days if you are waiting to have a baby or you are in prison. I've had my child but I'm counting the days since he's been in this house.

The street delves down between two rows of houses like the abandoned bed of a river that has changed course. The shebeen-keeper who lives opposite has a car that sways and churns its way to her fancy wrought-iron gate. Everyone else, including shebeen customers, walks over the stones, sand and gullies, home from the bus station. It's too far to bicycle to work in town.

The house provides the sub-economic township planner's usual two rooms and kitchen with a little yard at the back, into which his maquette figures of the ideal family unit of four fitted neatly. Like most houses in the street, it has been arranged inside and out to hold the number of people the ingenuity of necessity provides for. The garage is the home of sub-tenants. (The shebeen-keeper, who knows everything about everybody, might remember how the house came to have a garage—perhaps a taxi owner once lived there.) The front door of the house itself opens into a room that has been subdivided by greenish brocade curtains whose colour had faded and embossed pattern worn off before they were discarded in another kind of house. On one side of the curtains is a livingroom with just space enough to crate a plastic-covered sofa and two chairs, a coffee table with crocheted cover, vase of dyed feather flowers and oil lamp, and a radio-and-cassette-player combination with home-built speakers. There is a large varnished print of a horse with wild orange

10

mane and flaring nostrils on the wall. The floor is cement, shined with black polish. On the other side of the curtains is a bed, a burglar-proofed window, a small table with candle, bottle of anti-acid tablets and alarm clock. During the day a frilly nylon nightgown is laid out on the blankets. A woman's clothes are in a box under the bed. In the dry cleaner's plastic sheath, a man's suit hangs from a nail.

A door, never closed, leads from the livingroom to the kitchen. There is a sink, which is also the bathroom of the house, a coal-burning stove finned with chrome like a 1940s car, a pearly-blue formica dresser with glass doors that don't slide easily, a table and plastic chairs. The smell of cooking never varies: mealie-meal burning, curry overpowering the sweet reek of offal, sour porridge, onions. A small refrigerator, not connected, is used to store margarine, condensed milk, tinned pilchards; there is no electricity.

Another door, with a pebbled glass pane in its upper half, is always kept closed. It opens off the kitchen. Net curtains reinforce the privacy of the pebbled glass; the privacy of the tenant of the house, Samson Moreke, whose room is behind there, shared with his wife and baby and whichever of their older children spends time away from other relatives who take care of them in country villages. When all the children are in their parents' home at once, the sofa is a bed for two; others sleep on the floor in the kitchen. Sometimes the sofa is not available, since adult relatives who find jobs in the city need somewhere to live. Number 1907 Block C holds—has held—eleven people; how many it could hold is a matter of who else has nowhere to go. This reckoning includes the woman lodger and her respectable succession of lovers behind the green brocade curtain, but not the family lodging in the garage.

In the backyard, Samson Moreke, in whose name tenancy of Number 1907 Block C is registered by the authorities, has put up poles and chicken wire and planted Catawba grapevines that make a pleasant green arbour in summer. Underneath are three metal chairs and matching table, bearing traces of white paint, which—like the green brocade curtains, the picture of the horse with orange mane, the poles, chicken wire and vines—have been discarded by the various employers for whom Moreke works in

11

the city as an itinerant gardener. The arbour is between the garage and the lavatory, which is shared by everyone on the property, both tenants and lodgers.

On Sundays Moreke sits under his grapevine and drinks a bottle of beer brought from the shebeen across the road. Even in winter he sits there; it is warmer out in the midday winter sun than in the house, the shadow of the vine merely a twisted rope—grapes eaten, roof of leaves fallen. Although the yard is behind the house and there is a yellow dog on guard tied to a packing-case shelter, there is not much privacy. A large portion of the space of the family living in the garage is taken up by a paraffin-powered refrigerator filled with soft-drink cans and pots of flavoured yoghurt: a useful little business that serves the community and supplements the earnings of the breadwinner, a cleaner at the city slaughter-house. The sliding metal shutter meant for the egress of a car from the garage is permanently bolted down. All day Sunday children come on errands to buy, knocking at the old kitchen door, salvaged from the city, that Moreke has set into the wall of the garage.

A street where there is a shebeen, a house opposite a shebeen cannot be private, anyway. All weekend drunks wander over the ruts that make the gait even of the sober seem drunken. The children playing in the street take no notice of men fuddled between song and argument, who talk to people who are not there.

As well as friends and relatives, acquaintances of Moreke who have got to know where he lives through travelling with him on the buses to work walk over from the shebeen and appear in the yard. He is a man who always puts aside money to buy the Sunday newspaper; he has to fold away the paper and talk instead. The guests usually bring a cold quart or two with them (the shebeen, too, has a paraffin refrigerator, restaurant-size). Talk and laughter make the dog bark. Someone plays a transistor radio. The chairs are filled and some comers stretch on the bit of tough grass. Most of the Sunday visitors are men but there are women, particularly young ones, who have gone with them to the shebeen or taken up with them there; these women are polite and deferential to Moreke's wife, Nanike, when she has time to join the gathering. Often they will hold her latest—fifth living—baby while she goes back into the kitchen to cook or hangs her washing on the fence. She takes a beer or two herself, but although she is in her early thirties and knows she is still pretty—except for a missing front tooth—she does not get flirtatious or giggle. She is content to sit with the new baby on her lap, in the sun, among men and women like herself, while her husband tells anecdotes which make them laugh or challenge him. He learns a lot from the newspapers.

She was sitting in the yard with him and his friends the Sunday a cousin arrived with a couple of hangers-on. They didn't bring beer, but were given some. There were greetings, but who really hears names? One of the hangers-on fell asleep on the grass, a boy with a body like a baggy suit. The other had a yellow face, lighter than anyone else present, narrow as a trowel, and the irregular pock-marks of the pitted skin were flocked, round the area where men grow hair, with sparse tufts of black. She noticed he wore a gold ear-ring in one ear. He had nothing to say but later took up a guitar belonging to someone else and played to himself. One of the people living in the garage, crossing the path of the group under the arbour on his way to the lavatory with his roll of toilet paper, paused to look or listen, but everyone else was talking too loudly to hear the soft plang-plang, and the after-buzz when the player's palm stilled the instrument's vibration.

Moreke went off with his friends when they left, and came back, not late. His wife had gone to bed. She was sleepy, feeding the baby. Because he stood there, at the foot of the bed, did not begin to undress, she understood someone must be with him.

'Mtembu's friend.' Her husband's head indicated the other side of the glass-paned door.

'What does he want here now?'

'I brought him. Mtembu asked.'

'What for?'

Moreke sat down on the bed. He spoke softly, mouthing at her face. 'He needs somewhere to stay.'

'Where was he before, then?'

Moreke lifted and dropped his elbows limply at a question not to be asked.

The baby lost the nipple and nuzzled furiously at air. She

13

guided its mouth. 'Why can't he stay with Mtembu. You could have told Mtembu no.'

'He's your cousin.'

'Well, I will tell him no. If Mtembu needs somewhere to stay, I have to take him. But not anyone he brings from the street.'

Her husband yawned, straining every muscle in his face. Suddenly he stooped and began putting together the sheets of his Sunday paper that were scattered on the floor. He folded them more or less in order, slapping and smoothing the creases.

'Well?'

He said nothing, walked out. She heard the voices in the kitchen, but not what was being said.

He opened their door again and shut it behind him. 'It's not a business of cousins. This one is in trouble. You don't read the papers. . .the blowing up of that police station. . .*you* know, last month? They didn't catch them all. . . It isn't safe for Mtembu to keep him any longer. He must keep moving.'

Her soft jowls stiffened.

Her husband assured her awkwardly. 'A few days. Only for a couple of days. Then—(a gesture)—out of the country.'

He never takes off the gold ear-ring, even when he sleeps. He sleeps on the sofa. He didn't bring a blanket, a towel, nothing— uses our things. I don't know what the ear-ring means; when I was a child there were men who came to work on the mines who had ear-rings, but in both ears—country people. He's a town person; another one who reads newspapers. He tidies away the blankets I gave him and then he reads newspapers the whole day. He can't go out.

The others at Number 1907 Block C were told the man was Nanike Moreke's cousin, had come to look for work and had nowhere to stay. There are people in that position in every house. No one with a roof over his head can say 'no' to one of the same blood—everyone knows that; Moreke's wife had not denied that. But she wanted to know what to say if someone asked the man's name. He himself answered at once, his strong thin hand twisting the gold hoop in his ear like a girl. 'Shisonka. Tell them Shisonka.'

'And the other name?'

Her husband answered. 'That name is enough.'

Moreke and his wife didn't use the name among themselves. They referred to the man as 'he' and 'him'. Moreke addressed him as 'Mfo', brother; she called him simply 'you'. Moreke answered questions nobody asked. He said to his wife, in front of the man, 'What is the same blood? Here in this place? If you are not white, you are all the same blood, here.' She looked at her husband respectfully, as she did when he read to her out of his newspaper.

The woman lodger worked in the kitchen at a Kentucky Fried Chicken shop in the city, and like Moreke was out at work all day; at weekends she slept at her mother's place, where her children lived, so she did not know the man Shisonka never left the house to look for work or for any other reason. Her lover came to her room only to share the bed, creeping late past whatever sleeping form might be on the sofa, and leaving before first light to get to a factory in the white industrial area. The only problem was the family who lived in the garage. The man had to cross the yard to use the lavatory. The slaughter-house cleaner's mother and wife would notice he was there, in the house; that he never went out. It was Moreke's wife who thought of this, and told the woman in the garage her cousin was sick, he had just been discharged from hospital. And indeed, they took care of him as if he had been—Moreke and his wife Nanike. They did not have the money to eat meat often but on Tuesday Moreke bought a pluck from the butchery near the bus station in the city; the man sat down to eat with them. Moreke brought cigarettes home—the man paid him—it was clear he must have cigarettes, needed cigarettes more than food. And don't let him go out, don't ever let him go to the shop for cigarettes, or over to Ma Radebe for drink, Moreke told his wife; *you* go, if he needs anything, *you* just leave everything, shut the house—go.

I wash his clothes with our things. His shirt and pullover have labels in another language, come from some other country.

15

Even the letters that spell it are different. I give him food in the middle of the day. I myself eat in the yard, with the baby. I told him he should play the music, in there, if he wants to. He listens to Samson's tapes. How could I keep my own sister out of the house? When she saw him I said he was a friend of Samson—a new friend. She likes light-skinned. But it means people notice you. It must be very hard to hide. He doesn't say so. He doesn't look afraid. The beard will hide him; but how long does it take for a beard to grow, how long, how long before he goes away.

Every night that week the two men talked. Not in the room with the sofa and radio-and-cassette-player, if the woman lodger was at home on the other side of the curtains, but in the room where the Morekes slept. The man had a kitchen chair Moreke brought in, there was just room for it between the big bed and the wardrobe. Moreke lay on the bed with a pillow stuffed under his nape. Sometimes his wife stayed in the kitchen, at other times she came in and sat with the baby on the bed. She could see Moreke's face and the back of the man's head in the panel mirror of the wardrobe while they talked. The shape of the head swelled up from the thin neck, a puff-ball of black kapok. Deep in, there was a small patch without hair, a skin infection or a healed wound. His front aspect—a narrow yellow face keenly attentive, cigarette wagging like a finger from the corner of his lips, loop of gold round the lobe of one of the alert pointed ears—seemed unaware of the blemish, something that attacked him unnoticed from behind.

They talked about the things that interested Moreke; the political meetings disguised as church services of which he read reports but did not attend. The man laughed, and argued with Moreke patiently. 'What's the use, man? If you don't stand there? Stand with your feet as well as agree with your head. . . Yes, go and get that head knocked if the dogs and the *kerries* come. Since '76, the kids've showed you how. . .You know now.'

Moreke wanted to tell the man what he thought of the Urban Councils the authorities set up, and the Committees people themselves had formed in opposition, as, when he found himself in the company of a sports promoter, he wanted to give his opinion of the state of soccer today. 'Those Council men are nothing to me. You understand? They only want big jobs and smart cars for themselves. I'm a poor man, I'll never have a car. But they say they're going to make this place like white Jo'burg. Maybe the government listens to them. . .They say they can do it. The Committees—eh?—they say like I do, *those Council men are nothing*—but they themselves, what can they do? They know everything is no good here. They talk; they tell about it; they go to jail. So what's the use? What can you do?'

The man did not tell what he had done. 'The police station' was there, ready in their minds, ready to their tongues; not spoken.

The man was smiling at Moreke, at something he had heard many times before and might be leaving behind for good, now. 'Your Council. Those dummies. You see this *donga* called a street, outside? This place without even electric light in the rooms? You dig beautiful gardens, the flowers smell nice. . .and how many people must shit in that stinking hovel in your yard? How much do you get for digging the ground white people own? You told me what you get. "Top wages": ten rands a day. Just enough for the rent in this place, and not even the shit-house belongs to you, not even the mud you bring in from the yard on your shoes. . .'

Moreke became released, excited. 'The bus fares went up last week. They say the rent is going up. . .'

'Those dummies, that's what they do for you. You see? But the Committee tells you don't pay that rent, because you aren't paid enough to live in the "beautiful city" the dummies promise you. Isn't that the truth? Isn't the truth what you *know*? Don't you listen to the ones who speak the truth?'

Moreke's wife had had, for a few minutes, the expression of one waiting to interrupt. 'I'll go to Radebe and get a bottle of beer, if you want.'

The two men gave a flitting nod to one another in approval.

Moreke counted out the money. 'Don't let anybody come back with you.'

His wife took the coins without looking up. 'I'm not a fool.' The baby was asleep on the bed. She closed the door quietly

17

behind her. The two men lost the thread of their talk for a moment; Moreke filled it: 'A good woman.'

We are alone together. The baby likes him. I don't give the breast every time, now; yesterday when I was fetching the coal he fed the bottle to her. I ask him what children he has? He only smiles, shakes his head. I don't know if this means it was silly to ask, because everyone has children.

Perhaps it meant he doesn't know, pretends he doesn't know—thinks a lot of himself, smart young man with a gold ring in his ear has plenty of girl-friends to get babies with him.

The police station was never mentioned, but the man spent one of the nights describing to the Moreke couple foreign places he had been to—that must have been before the police station happened. He told about the oldest city on the African continent, so old it had a city of the dead as well as a city of the living—a whole city of tombs like houses. The religion there was the same as the religion of the Indian shopkeepers, here at home. Then he had lived in another kind of country, where there was snow for half the year or more. It was dark until ten in the morning and again from three o'clock in the afternoon. He described the clothes he had been given to protect him against the cold. 'Such people, I can tell you. You can't believe such white people exist. If our people turn up there. . .you get everything you need, they just give it. . .and there's a museum, it's out in the country, they have ships there their people sailed all over the world more than a thousand years ago. They may even have come here. . .This pullover is still from them. . .full of holes now. . .'

'Look at that, *hai!*' Moreke admired the intricately-worked bands of coloured wools in a design based upon natural features he did not recognize—dark frozen forms of fir forests and the constellation of snow crystals. 'She'll mend it for you.'

His wife was willing but apprehensive. 'I'll try and get the same colours. I don't know if I can find them here.'

The man smiled at the kindness of his own people. 'She shouldn't take a lot of trouble. I won't need it, anyway.'

No one asked where it was the pullover wouldn't be needed; what kind of place, what continent he would be going to when he got away.

After the man had retired to his sofa that night Moreke read the morning paper he had brought from an employer's kitchen in the city. He kept lowering the sheets slowly and looking around at the room, then returning to his reading. The baby was restless; but it was not that he commented on.

'It's better not to know too much about him.'

His wife turned the child onto its belly. 'Why?'

Her face was innocently before his like a mirror he didn't want to look into. He had kept encouraging the man to go on with his talk of living in foreign places.

The shadows thrown by the candle capered through the room, bending furniture and bodies, flying over the ceiling, quieting the baby with wonder. 'Because then. . .if they question us, we won't have anything to tell.'

He did bring something. A gun.

He comes into the kitchen, now, and helps me when I'm washing up. He came in, this morning, and put his hands in the soapy water, didn't say anything, started cleaning up. Our hands were in the grease and soap, I couldn't see his fingers but sometimes I felt them when they bumped mine. He scraped the pot and dried everything. I didn't say thanks. To say thank you to a man—it's not man's work, he might feel ashamed.

He stays in the kitchen—we stay in the kitchen with the baby most of the day. He doesn't sit in there, anymore, listening to the tapes. I go in and turn on the machine loud enough for us to hear it well in the kitchen.

By Thursday the tufts of beard were thickening and knitting together on the man's face. Samson Moreke tried to find Mtembu to hear what plans had been made but Mtembu did not come in response to messages and was not anywhere Moreke looked for him. Moreke took the opportunity, while the woman in whose garden he worked on Thursdays was out, to telephone Mtembu's place of work from her house, but was told that workshop employees were not allowed to receive calls.

He brought home chicken feet for soup and a piece of beef shank. Figs had ripened in the Thursday garden and he'd been given some in a newspaper poke. He asked, 'When do you expect to hear from Mtembu?'

The man was reading the sheet of paper stained with milky sap from the stems of figs. Samson Moreke had never really been in jail himself—only the usual short-term stays for pass offences—but he knew from people who had been inside a long time that there was this need to read every scrap of paper that might come your way from the outside world.

'—Well, it doesn't matter. You're all right here. We can just carry on. I suppose Mtembu will turn up this weekend.'

As if he heard in this resignation Moreke's anticipation of the usual Sunday beer in the yard, the man suddenly took charge of Moreke and his wife, crumpling the dirty newspaper and rubbing his palms together to rid them of stickiness. His narrow yellow face was set clear-cut in black hair all round now, like the framed face of the king in Moreke's worn pack of cards. The black eyes and ear-ring were the same liquid-bright. The perfectly-ironed shirt he wore was open at the breast in the manner of all attractive young men of his age. 'Look, nobody must come here. Saturday, Sunday. None of your friends. You must shut up this place. Keep them all away. Nobody walking into the yard from the shebeen. That's *out*.'

Moreke looked from the man to his wife; back to the man again. Moreke half-coughed, half-laughed. 'But how do I do that, man? How do I stop them? I can't put bars on my gate. There're the other people, in the garage. They sell things.'

'*You* stay inside. Here in this house, with the doors locked. There are too many people around at the weekend. Let them think you've gone away.'

Moreke still smiled, amazed, helpless. 'And the one in there, with her boy-friend? What's she going to think?'

Moreke's wife spoke swiftly. 'She'll be at her mother's house.'

And now the plan of action fell efficiently into place, each knew his part within it. 'Oh yes. Thank the Lord for that. Maybe I'll go over to Radebe's tonight and just say I'm not going to be here Sunday. And Saturday I'll say I'm going to the soccer.'

His wife shook her head. 'Not the soccer. Your friends will want to come and talk about it afterwards.'

'*Hai, mama!* All right, a funeral, far away. . .' Moreke laughed, and stopped himself with an embarrassed drawing of mucus back through the nose.

While I'm ironing, he cleans the gun.

I saw he needed another rag and I gave it to him.

He asked for oil, and I took cooking oil out of the cupboard, but then I saw in his face that was not what he wanted. I went to the garage and borrowed Three-in-One from Nchaba's wife.

He never takes out the gun when Samson's here. He knows only he and I know about it.

I said, what happened there, on your head at the back—that sore. His hand went to it, under the hair, he doesn't think it shows. I'll get him something for it, some ointment. If he's still here on Monday.

Perhaps he is cross because I spoke about it.

Then when I came back with the oil, he sat at the kitchen table laughing at me, smiling, as if I was a young girl. I forgot—I felt I was a girl. But I don't really like that kind of face, his face— light-skinned. You can never forget a face like that. If you are questioned, you can never say you don't remember what someone like that looks like.

He picks up the baby as if it belongs to him. To him as well, while we are in the kitchen together.

That night the two men didn't talk. They seemed to have nothing to say. Like prisoners who get their last mealie-pap of the day before being locked up for the night, Moreke's wife gave them their meal before dark. Then all three went from the kitchen to the Morekes' room, where any light that might shine from behind the curtains and give away a presence was directed only towards a blind: a high corrugated tin fence in a lane full of breast-high khakiweed. Moreke shared his newspaper. When the man had read it, he tossed through third-hand adventure comics and the sales promotion pamphlets given away in city supermarkets Nanike Moreke kept; he read the manual 'Teach Yourself How to Sell Insurance' in which, at some stage, 'Samson Moreke' had been carefully written on the fly-leaf.

There was no beer. Moreke's wife knew her way about her kitchen in the dark; she fetched the litre bottle of coke that was on the kitchen table and poured herself a glass. Her husband stayed the offer with a raised hand; the other man's inertia over the manual was overcome just enough to move his head in refusal. She had taken up again the cover for the bed she had begun when she had had some free time, waiting for this fifth child to be born. Crocheted roses, each caught in a squared web of a looser pattern, were worked separately and then joined to the whole they slowly extended. The tiny flash of her steel hook and the hair-thin gold in his ear signalled in candlelight. At about ten o'clock there was a knock at the front door. The internal walls of these houses are planned at minimum specification for cheapness and a blow on any part of the house reverberates through every room. The black-framed, bone-yellow face raised and held, absolutely still, above the manual. Moreke opened his mouth and, swinging his legs over the side, lifted himself from the bed. But his wife's hand on his shoulder made him subside again; only the bed creaked slightly. The slenderness of her body from the waist up was merely rooted in heavy maternal hips and thighs; with a movement soft as the breath she expelled, she leant and blew out the candles.

A sensible precaution; someone might follow round the walls of the house looking for some sign of life. They sat in the dark. There was no bark from the dog in the yard. The knocking stopped. Moreke thought he heard laughter, and the gate twang. But the shebeen is noisy on a Friday, the sounds could have come from anywhere. 'Just someone who's had a few drinks. It often happens. Sometimes we don't even wake up, I suppose, ay, Nanike.' Moreke's hoarse whisper, strangely, woke the baby, who let out the thin wail that meets the spectre in a bad dream, breaks through into consciousness against a threat that can't be

22

defeated in the conscious world. In the dark, they all went to bed.

A city of the dead, a city of the living. It was better when Samson got him to talk about things like that. Things far away can't do any harm. We'll never have a car, like the Councillors, and we'll never have to run away to those far places, like him. Lucky to have this house; many, many people are jealous of that. I never knew, until this house was so quiet, how much noise people make at the weekend, I didn't hear the laughing, the talking in the street, Radebe's music going, the terrible screams of people fighting.

On Saturday Moreke took his blue ruled pad and an envelope to the kitchen table. But his wife was peeling pumpkin and slicing onions, there was no space, so he went back to the room where the sofa was, and his radio-and-cassette-player. First he addressed the envelope to their twelve-year-old boy at mission school. It took him the whole morning to write a letter, although he could read so well. Once or twice he asked the man how to spell a word in English.

He lay smoking on his bed, the sofa. 'Why in English?'

'Rapula knows English very well. . .it helps him to get letters. . .'

'You shouldn't send him away from here, *baba*. You think it's safer, but you are wrong. It's like you and the meetings. The more you try to be safe, the worse it will be for your children.'

He stared quietly at Moreke. 'And look, now I'm here.'

'Yes.'

'And you look after me.'

'Yes.'

'And you're not afraid.'

'Yes, we're afraid. . .but of many things. . .when I come home with money. . .Three times tsotsis have hit me, taken everything. You see here where I was cut on the cheek. This arm was broken. I couldn't work. Not even push the lawnmower. I had to pay some young one to hold my jobs for me.'

23

The man smoked and smiled. 'I don't understand you. You see? I don't understand you. Bring your children home, man. We're shut up in the ghetto to kill each other. That's what they want, in their white city. So you send the children away; that's what they want, too. To get rid of us. We must all stick together. That's the only way to fight our way out.'

That night he asked if Moreke had a chess set.

Moreke giggled, gave clucks of embarrassment. 'That board with the little dolls? I'm not an educated man! I don't know those games!'

They played together the game that everybody knows, that is played on the pavements outside shops and in factory yards, with the board drawn on concrete or in dust, and bottle-tops for counters. This time a handful of dried beans from the kitchen served, and a board drawn by Moreke on a box-lid. He won game after game from the man. His wife had the Primus stove in the room, now, and she made tea. The game was not resumed. She had added three completed squares to her bed-cover in two nights; after the tea, she did not take it up again. They sat listening to Saturday night, all round them, pressing in upon the hollow cement units of which the house was built. Often tramping steps seemed just about to halt at the front or back door. The splintering of wood under a truncheon or the shatter of the window-panes, thin ice under the weight of the roving dark outside, waited upon every second. The woman's eyelids slid down, fragile and faintly greasy, outlining intimately the aspect of the orbs beneath, in sleep. Her face became unguarded as the baby's. Every now and then she would start, come to herself again. But her husband and the man made no move to go to bed. The man picked up and ran the fine head of her crochet hook under the rind of each fingernail , again and again, until the tool had done the cleaning job to satisfaction.

When the man went to bed at last, by the light of the cigarette lighter he shielded in his hand to see his way to the sofa, he found she had put a plastic chamber-pot on the floor. Probably the husband had thought of it.

All Sunday morning the two men worked together on a fault in Moreke's tape-player, though they were unable to test it with the volume switched on. Moreke could not afford to take the player to a repair shop. The man seemed to think the fault a simple matter; like any other city youngster, he had grown up with such machines. Moreke's wife cooked mealie-rice and made a curry gravy for the Sunday meal. 'Should I go to Radebe and get beer?' She had followed her husband into their room to ask him alone.

'You want to advertise we are here? You know what he said.'

'Ask him if it matters, if I go—a woman.'

'I'm not going to ask. Did he say he wants beer? Did I?'

But in the afternoon she did ask something. She went straight to the man, not Moreke. 'I have to go out to the shop.' It was very hot in the closed house; the smell of curry mixed with the smell of the baby in the fug of its own warmth and wrappings. He wrinkled his face, exposed clenched teeth in a suppressed yawn; what shops—had she forgotten it was Sunday? She understood his reaction. But there were corner shops that sold essentials even on Sundays; he must know that. 'I have to get milk. Milk for the baby.'

She stood there, in her over-trodden slippers, her old skirt and cheap blouse—a woman not to be noticed among every other woman in the streets. He didn't refuse her. No need. Not after all this past week. Not for the baby. She was not like her husband, big-mouth, friendly with everyone. He nodded; it was a humble errand that wouldn't concern him.

She went out of the house just as she was, her money in her hand. Moreke and the baby were asleep in their room. The street looked new, bright, refreshing, after the dim house. A small boy with a toy machine-gun covered her in his fire, chattering his little white teeth with rat-a-tat-tttt. Ma Radebe, the shebeen-keeper, her hair plaited with blue and red beads, her beautiful long red nails resting on the steering wheel, was backing her car out of her gateway. She braked to let her neighbour pass and leaned from the car window. '*My dear* (in English), I was supposed to be gone from this place two hours ago. I'm due at a big wedding that will already be over. . .How are you? Didn't see your husband for a few days. . .nothing wrong across the road?'

Moreke's wife stood and shook her head. Radebe was not one who expected or waited for answers when she greeted anyone.

Something Out There

When the car had driven off Moreke's wife went on down the street and down the next one, past the shop where young boys were gathered scuffling and dancing to the shopkeeper's radio, and on to the purplish brick building with the security fence round it and a flag flying. One of her own people was on guard outside, lolling with a sub-machine-gun. She went up the steps and into the office, where there were more of her own people in uniform, but one of *them* in charge. She spoke in her own language to her own kind, but they seemed disbelieving. They repeated the name of that other police station, that was blown up, and asked her if she was sure? She said she was quite sure. Then they took her to the white officer and she told in English—'There, in my house, 1907 Block C. He has been there a week. He has a gun.'

I don't know why I did it. I get ready to say that to anyone who is going to ask me, but nobody in this house asks. The baby laughs at me while I wash her, stares up while we're alone in the house and she's feeding at the breast, and to her I say out loud: I don't know why.

A week after the man was taken away that Sunday by the security police, Ma Radebe again met Moreke's wife in their street. The shebeen-keeper gazed at her for a moment, and spat.

At the Rendezvous of Victory

A young black boy used to brave the dogs in white men's suburbs to deliver telegrams; Sinclair 'General Giant' Zwedu has those bite scars on his legs to this day.

So goes the opening paragraph of a 'profile' copyrighted by a British Sunday paper, reprinted by reciprocal agreement with papers in New York and Washington, syndicated as far as Australia and translated in both *Le Monde* and *Neue Züricher Zeitung*.

But like everything else he was to read about himself, it was not quite like that. No. Ever since he was a kid he loved dogs, and those dogs who chased the bicycle—he just used to whistle in his way at them, and they would stand there wagging their long tails and feeling silly. The scars on his legs were from wounds received when the white commando almost captured him, blew up one of his hideouts in the bush. But he understood why the journalist had decided to paint the wounds over as dog-bites—it made a kind of novel opening to the story, and it showed at once that the journalist wasn't on the side of the whites. It was true that he who became Sinclair 'General Giant' Zwedu was born in the blacks' compound on a white man's sugar farm in the hottest and most backward part of the country, and that, after only a few years at a school where children drew their sums in the dust, he was the post office messenger in the farmers' town. It was in that two-street town, with the whites' Central Hotel, Main Road Garage, Buyrite Stores, Snooker Club and railhead, that he first heard the voice of the brother who was to become Prime Minister and President, a voice from a big trumpet on the top of a shabby van. It summoned him (there were others, but they didn't become anybody) to a meeting in the Catholic Mission Hall in Goodwill Township—which was what the white farmers called the black shanty town outside their own. And it was here, in Goodwill Township, that the young post office messenger took away the local Boy Scout troop organized by but segregated from the white Boy Scout troop in the farmers' town, and transformed the scouts into the Youth Group of the National Independence Party. Yes—he told them—you will be prepared. The Party will teach you how to make a fire the government can't put out.

It was he who, when the leaders of the Party were detained for the first time, was imprisoned with the future Prime Minister and became one of his chief lieutenants. He, in fact, who in jail made up defiance songs that soon were being sung at mass meetings, who imitated the warders, made pregnant one of the women prisoners who polished the cell floors (though no one believed her when she proudly displayed the child as his, he would have known *that* was true), and finally, when he was sent to another prison in order to remove his invigorating influence from fellow political detainees, overpowered three warders and escaped across the border.

It was this exploit that earned him the title 'General Giant' as prophets, saints, rogues and heroes receive theirs: named by the anonymous talk of ordinary people. He did not come back until he had wintered in the unimaginable cold of countries that offer refuge and military training, gone to rich desert cities to ask for money from the descendants of people who had sold Africans as slaves, and to the island where sugar-cane workers, as his mother and father had been, were now powerful enough to supply arms. He was with the first band of men who had left home with empty hands, on bare feet, and came back with AKM assault rifles, heat-guided missiles and limpet mines.

The future Prime Minister was imprisoned again and again and finally fled the country and established the Party's leadership in exile. When Sinclair 'General Giant' met him in London or Algiers, the future Prime Minister wore a dark suit whose close weave was midnight blue in the light. He himself wore a bush outfit that originally had been put together by men who lived less like men than prides of lion, tick-ridden, thirsty, waiting in thickets of thorn. As these men increased in numbers and boldness, and he rose in command of them, the outfit elaborated into a combat uniform befitting his style, title and achievement. At the beginning of the war, he had led a ragged hit-and-run group; after four years and the deaths of many, which emphasized his giant indestructibility, his men controlled a third of the country and he was the man the white army wanted most to capture.

Before the future Prime Minister talked to the Organization of African Unity or United Nations he had now to send for and consult with his commander-in-chief of the liberation army, Sinclair 'General Giant' Zwedu. General Giant came from the bush in his Czech jeep, in a series of tiny planes from secret airstrips, and at last would board a scheduled jet liner among oil and mineral men who thought they were sitting beside just another dolled-up black official from some unheard-of state whose possibilities they might have to look into sometime. When the consultation in the foreign capital was over, General Giant did not fidget long in the putter of official cocktail parties, but would disappear to find for himself whatever that particular capital could offer to meet his high capacities—for leading men to fight without fear, exciting people to caper, shout with pleasure, drink and argue; for touching women. After a night in a bar and a bed with girls (he never had to pay professionals, always found well-off, respectable women, black or white, whose need for delights simply matched his own) he would take a plane back to Africa. He never wanted to linger. He never envied his brother, the future Prime Minister, his flat in London and the invitations to country houses to discuss the future of the country. He went back imperatively as birds migrate to Africa to mate and assure the survival of their kind, journeying thousands of miles, just as he flew and drove deeper and deeper into where he belonged until he reached again his headquarters—that the white commandos often claimed to have destroyed but could not be destroyed because his headquarters were the bush itself.

The war would not have been won without General Giant. At the Peace Conference he took no part in the deliberations but was there at his brother's, the future Prime Minister's side: a deterrent weapon, a threat to the defeated white government of what would happen if peace were not made. Now and then he cleared his throat of a constriction of boredom; the white delegates were alarmed as if he had roared.

Constitutional talks went on for many weeks; there was a cease-fire, of course. He wanted to go back—to his head-quarters—home—but one of the conditions of the cease-fire had been that he should be withdrawn from the field' as the official term, coined in wars fought over poppy-meadows, phrased it. He wandered about London. He went to nightclubs and was invited to join parties of arabs who, he found, had no idea where the country he had fought for, and won for his people, was; this time he really did roar—with laughter. He walked through Soho but couldn't understand why anyone would like to watch couples making the movements of love-making on the cinema screen instead of doing it themselves. He came upon the Natural History Museum in South Kensington and was entranced by the life that existed anterior to his own unthinking familiarity with ancient nature hiding the squat limpet mines, the iron clutches of offensive and defensive hand-grenades, the angular AKMs, metal blue with heat. He sent postcards of mammoths and gasteropods to his children, who were still where they had been with his wife all through the war—in the black location of the capital of his home country. Since she was his wife, she had been under police surveillance, and detained several times, but had survived by saying she and her husband were separated. Which was true, in a way; a man leading a guerrilla war has no family, he must forget about meals cooked for him by a woman, nights in a bed with two places hollowed by their bodies, and the snuffle of a baby close by. He made love to a black singer from Jamaica, not young, whose style was a red-head wig rather than fashionable rigid pigtails. She composed a song about his bravery in the war in a country she imagined but had never seen, and sang it at a victory rally where all the brothers in exile as well as the white sympathizers with their cause, applauded her. In her flat she had a case of special Scotch whisky, twelve years old, sent by an admirer. She said—sang to him—Let's not let it get any older. As she worked only at night, they spent whole days indoors making love when the weather was bad—the big man, General

Giant, was like a poor stray cat, in the cold rain: he would walk on the balls of shoe-soles, shaking each foot as he lifted it out of the wet.

He was waiting for the okay, as he said to his brother, the future Prime Minister, to go back to their country and take up his position as commander-in-chief of the new state's Defence Force. His title would become an official rank, the highest, like that of army chiefs in Britain and the United States—General Zwedu.

His brother turned solemn, dark in his mind; couldn't be followed there. He said the future of the army was a tremendous problem at present under discussion. The two armies, black and white, who had fought each other, would have to be made one. What the discussions were also about remained in the dark: the defeated white government, the European powers by whom the new black state was promised loans for reconstruction, had insisted that Sinclair 'General Giant' Zwedu be relieved of all military authority. His personality was too strong and too strongly associated with the triumph of the freedom fighter army for him to be anything but a divisive reminder of the past, in the new, regular army. Let him stand for parliament in the first peace-time election, his legend would guarantee that he win the seat. Then the Prime Minister could find him some safe portfolio.

What portfolio? What? This was in the future Prime Minister's mind when General Giant couldn't follow him. 'What he knows how to do is defend our country, that he fought for', the future Prime Minister said to the trusted advisers, British lawyers and African experts from American universities. And while he was saying it, the others knew he did not want, could not have his brother Sinclair 'General Giant' Zwedu, that master of the wilderness, breaking the confinement of peace-time barracks.

He left him in Europe on some hastily-invented mission until the independence celebrations. Then he brought him home to the old colonial capital that was now theirs, and at the airport wept with triumph and anguish in his arms, while schoolchildren sang. He gave him a portfolio—Sport and Recreation; harmless.

General Giant looked at his big hands as if the appointment were an actual object, held there. What was he supposed to do with it? The great lungs that pumped his organ-voice failed; he spoke flatly, kindly, almost pityingly to his brother, the Prime Minister.

Now they both wore dark blue suits. At first, he appeared prominently at the Prime Minister's side as a tacit recompense, to show the people that he was still acknowledged by the Prime Minister as a co-founder of the nation, and its popular hero. He had played football on a patch of bare earth between wattle-branch goal posts on the sugar farm, as a child, and as a youth on a stretch of waste ground near the Catholic Mission Hall; as a man he had been at war, without time for games. In the first few months he rather enjoyed attending important matches in his official capacity, watching from a special box and later seeing himself sitting there, on a TV newsreel. It was a Sunday, a holiday amusement; the holiday went on too long. There was not much obligation to make speeches, in his cabinet post, but because his was a name known over the world, his place reserved in the mountain stronghold Valhalla of guerrilla wars, journalists went to him for statements on all kinds of issues. Besides, he was splendid copy, talkative, honest, indiscreet and emotional. Again and again, he embarrassed his government by giving an outrageous opinion, that contradicted government policy, on problems that were none of his business. The Party caucus reprimanded him again and again. He responded by seldom turning up at caucus meetings. The caucus members said that Zwedu (it was time his 'title' was dropped) thought too much of himself and had taken offence. Again, he knew that what was assumed was not quite true. He was bored with the caucus. He wanted to yawn all the time, he said, like a hippopotamus with its huge jaws open in the sun, half-asleep, in the thick brown water of the river near his last headquarters. The Prime Minister laughed at this, and they drank together with arms round one another—as they did in the old days in the Youth Group. The Prime Minister told him—'But seriously, sport and recreation are very important in building up our nation. For the next budget, I'll see that there's a bigger grant to your department, you'll be able to plan. You know how to inspire young men. . .I'm told a local team has adapted one of the freedom songs you made up, they sang it on TV.'

The Minister of Sport and Recreation sent his deputy to officiate at sports meetings these days and he didn't hear his war song become a football fans' chant. The Jamaican singer had arrived on an engagement at the Hilton that had just opened conference rooms, bars, a casino and nightclub on a site above the town where the old colonial prison used to be (the new prison was on the site of the former Peace Corps camp). He was there in the nightclub every night, drinking the brand of Scotch she had had in her London flat, tilting his head while she sang. The hotel staff pointed him out to overseas visitors—Sinclair 'General Giant' Zwedu, the General Giap, the Che Guevara of a terrible war there'd been in this country. The tourists had spent the day, taken by private plane, viewing game in what the travel brochure described as the country's magnificent game park but—the famous freedom fighter could have told them—wasn't quite that; was in fact his territory, his headquarters. Sometimes he danced with one of the women, their white teeth contrasting with shiny sunburned skin almost as if they had been black. Once there was some sort of a row; he danced too many times with a woman who appeared to be enjoying this intimately, and her husband objected. The 'convivial Minister' had laughed, taken the man by the scruff of his white linen jacket and dropped him back in his chair, a local journalist reported, but the government-owned local press did not print his story or picture. An overseas journalist interviewed 'General Giant' on the pre-text of the incident, and got from him (the Minister was indeed convivial, entertaining the journalist to excellent whisky in the house he had rented for the Jamaican singer) some opinions on matters far removed from nightclub scandal.

When questions were asked in parliament about an article in an American weekly on the country's international alliances, 'General Giant' stood up and, again, gave expression to convictions the local press could not print. He said that the defence of the country might have been put in the hands of neo-colonialists who had been the country's enemies during the war—and he was powerless to do anything about that. But he would take the law into his own hands to protect the National Independence

Party's principles of a people's democracy (he used the old name, on this occasion, although it had been shortened to National Party). Hadn't he fought, hadn't the brothers spilled their blood to get rid of the old laws and the old bosses, that made them *nothing*? Hadn't they fought for new laws under which they would be men? He would shed blood rather than see the Party betrayed in the name of so-called rational alliances and national unity.

International advisers to the government thought the speech, if inflammatory, so confused it might best be ignored. Members of the cabinet and Members of Parliament wanted the Prime Minister to get rid of him. General Giant Zwedu? How? Where to? Extreme anger was always expressed by the Prime Minister in the form of extreme sorrow. He was angry with both his cabinet members and his comrade, without whom they would never have been sitting in the House of Assembly. He sent for Zwedu. (He must accept that name now; he simply refused to accommodate himself to anything, he illogically wouldn't even drop the 'Sinclair' though *that* was the name of the white sugar farmer his parents had worked for, and nobody kept those slave names anymore.)

Zwedu: so at ease and handsome in his cabinet minister's suit (it was not the old blue, but a pin-stripe flannel the Jamaican singer had ordered at his request, and brought from London), one could not believe wild and dangerous words could come out of his mouth. He looked good enough for a diplomatic post somewhere. . . Unthinkable. The Prime Minister, full of sorrow and silences, told him he must stop drinking. He must stop giving interviews. There was no mention of the Ministry; the Prime Minister did not tell his brother he would not give in to pressure to take that away from him, the cabinet post he had never wanted but that was all there was to offer. He would not take it away—at least not until this could be done decently under cover of a cabinet reshuffle. The Prime Minister had to say to his brother, you mustn't let me down. What he wanted to say was: What have I done to you?

There was a crop failure and trouble with the unions on the coal mines; by the time the cabinet reshuffle came the press hardly noticed that a Minister of Sport and Recreation had been

replaced. Mr Sinclair Zwedu was not given an alternative portfolio, but he was referred to as a former Minister when his name
was added to the boards of multinational industrial firms instructed by their principals to Africanize. He could be counted
upon not to appear at those meetings, either. His director's fees
paid for cases of whisky, but sometimes went to his wife, to
whom he had never returned, and the teen-age children with
whom he would suddenly appear in the best stores of the town,
buying whatever they silently pointed at. His old friends blamed
the Jamaican woman, not the Prime Minister, for his disappearance from public life. She went back to England—her reasons
were sexual and honest, she realized she was too old for him—
but his way of life did not recover; could not recover the war, the
third of the country's territory that had been his domain when
the white government had lost control to him, and the black
government did not yet exist.

The country is open to political and trade missions from both
East and West, now, instead of these being confined to allies of
the old white government. The airport has been extended. The
new departure lounge is a sculpture gallery with reclining
figures among potted plants, wearily waiting for connections to
places whose directions criss-cross the colonial North–South
compass of communication. A former Chief-of-Staff of the
white army, who, since the black government came to power,
has been retained as chief military adviser to the Defence
Ministry, recently spent some hours in the lounge waiting for a
plane that was to take him on a government mission to Europe.
He was joined by a journalist booked on the same flight home to
London, after a rather disappointing return visit to the country.
Well, he remarked to the military man as they drank vodka-and-
tonic together, who wants to read about rice-growing schemes
instead of seek-and-destroy raids? This was a graceful reference
to the ex-Chief-of-Staff's successes with that strategy at the
beginning of the war, a reference safe in the cosy no-man's-land
of a departure lounge, out of earshot of the new black security
officials alert to any hint of encouragement of an old-guard
white coup.

At the Rendezvous of Victory

A musical gong preceded announcements of the new estimated departure time of the delayed British Airways plane. A swami found sweets somewhere in his saffron robes and went among the travellers handing out comfits with a message of peace and love. Businessmen used the opportunity to write reports on briefcases opened on their knees. Black children were spores attached to maternal skirts. White children ran back and forth to the bar counter, buying potato crisps and peanuts. The journalist insisted on another round of drinks.

Every now and then the departure of some other flight was called and the display of groups and single figures would change; some would leave, while a fresh surge would be let in through the emigration barriers and settle in a new composition. Those who were still waiting for delayed planes became part of the permanent collection, so to speak; they included a Canadian evangelical party who read their gospels with the absorption other people gave to paperback thrillers, a very old black woman dry as the fish in her woven carrier, and a prosperous black couple, elegantly dressed. The ex-Chief-of-Staff and his companion were sitting not far behind these two, who flirted and caressed, like whites—it was quite unusual to see those people behaving that way in public. Both the white men noticed this although they were able to observe only the back of the man's head and the profile of the girl, pretty, painted, shameless as she licked his tiny black ear and lazily tickled, with long fingers on the stilts of purple nails, the roll of his neck.

The ex-Chief-of-Staff made no remark, was not interested—what did one *not* see, in the country, now that they had taken over. The journalist was the man who had written a profile, just after the war: *a young black boy used to brave the dogs in white men's suburbs. . .* Suddenly he leant forward, staring at the back of the black man's head. 'That's General Giant! I know those ears!' He got up and went over to the bar, turning casually at the counter to examine the couple from the front. He bought two more vodka-and-tonics, swiftly was back to his companion, the ice chuntering in the glasses. 'It's him. I thought so. I used to know him well. Him, all right. Fat! Wearing suède shoes. And the tart. . .where'd he find her!'

The ex-Chief-of-Staff's uniform, his thick wad of campaign

37

ribbons over the chest and cap thrust down to his fine eyebrows, seemed to defend him against the heat rather than make him suffer, but the journalist felt confused and stifled as the vodka came out distilled once again in sweat and he did not know whether he should or should not simply walk up to 'General Giant' (no secretaries or security men to get past, now) and ask for an interview. Would anyone want to read it? Could he sell it anywhere? A distraction that made it difficult for him to make up his mind was the public address system nagging that the two passengers holding up flight something-or-other were requested to board the aircraft immediately. No one stirred. 'General Giant' (no mistaking him) simply signalled, a big hand snapping in the air, when he wanted fresh drinks for himself and his girl, and the barman hopped to it, although the bar was self-service. Before the journalist could come to a decision an air hostess ran in with the swish of stockings chafing thigh past thigh and stopped angrily, looking down at the black couple. The journalist could not hear what was said, but she stood firm while the couple took their time getting up, the girl letting her arm slide languidly off the man; laughing, arranging their hand luggage on each other's shoulders.

Where was he *taking* her?

The girl put one high-heeled sandal down in front of the other, as a model negotiates a catwalk. Sinclair 'General Giant' Zwedu followed her backside the way a man follows a paid woman, with no thought of her in his closed, shiny face, and the ex-Chief-of-Staff and the journalist did not know whether he recognized them, even saw them, as he passed without haste, letting the plane wait for him.

Letter from His Father

My dear son,

You wrote me a letter you never sent.

It wasn't for me—it was for the whole world to read. (You and your instructions that everything should be burned. Hah!) You were never open and frank with me—that's one of the complaints you say I was always making against you. You write it in the letter you didn't want me to read; so what does *that* sound like, eh? But I've read the letter now, I've read it anyway, I've read everything, although you said I put your books on the night-table and never touched them. You know how it is, here where I am: not something that can be explained to anyone who isn't here—they used to talk about secrets going to the grave, but the funny thing is there are no secrets here at all. If there was something you wanted to know, you should have known, if it doesn't let you lie quiet, then you can *have knowledge of it*, from here. Yes, you gave me that much credit, you said I was a true Kafka in 'strength. . .eloquence, endurance, a certain way of doing things on a grand scale' and I've not been content just to rot. In that way, I'm still the man I was, the go-getter. Restless. Restless. Taking whatever opportunity I can. There isn't anything, now, you can regard as hidden from me. Whether you say I left it unread on the night-table or whether you weren't man enough, even at the age of thirty-six, to show me a letter that was supposed to be for me.

I write to you after we are both dead. Whereas you don't stir. There won't be any response from you, I know that. You began that letter by saying you were afraid of me—and then you were afraid to let me read it. And now you've escaped altogether. Because without the Kafka will-power you can't reach out from nothing and nowhere. I was going to call it a desert, but where's the sand, where're the camels, where's the sun—I'm still *mensch* enough to crack a joke—you see? Oh excuse me, I forgot—you didn't like my jokes, my fooling around with kids. My poor boy, unfortunately you had no life in you, in all those books and diaries and letters (the ones you posted, to strangers, to women) you said it a hundred times before you put the words in my mouth, in your literary way, in that letter: you yourself were 'unfit for life'. So death comes, how would you say, quite naturally to you. It's not like that for a man of vigour like I was, I can tell you, and so here I am writing, talking. . .I don't know if there is a word for what this is. Anyway, it's *Hermann Kafka*. I've outlived you here, same as in Prague.

That is what you really accuse me of, you know, for sixty or so pages (I notice the length of that letter varies a bit from language to language, of course it's been translated into everything—I don't know what—Hottentot and Icelandic, Chinese, although you wrote it 'for me' in German). I *outlived* you, not for seven years, as an old sick man, after you died, but while you were young and alive. Clear as daylight, from the examples you give of being afraid of me, from the time you were a little boy: you were not afraid, you were envious. At first, when I took you swimming and you say you felt yourself a nothing, puny and weak beside my big, strong, naked body in the change-house—all right, you also say you were proud of such a father, a father with a fine physique. . . And may I remind you that father was taking the trouble and time, the few hours he could get away from the business, to try and make something of that *nebich*, develop his muscles, put some flesh on those poor little bones so he would grow up sturdy? But even before your barmitzvah the normal pride every boy has in his father changed to jealousy, with you. You couldn't be like me, so you decided I wasn't good enough for you: coarse, loud-mouthed, ate 'like a pig' (your very words), cut my fingernails at table, cleaned my ears with a toothpick. Oh yes, you can't hide anything from me, now, I've read it all, all the thousands and thousands of words you've used to shame your own family, your own father, before the whole world. And with your gift for words you turn everything inside-out and prove, like a circus magician, it's love, the piece of dirty paper's a beautiful silk flag, you *loved your father too much*, and so—what? *You* tell me. You couldn't be like him? You wanted to be like *him*? The *ghasa*, the shouter, the gobbler? Yes, my son, these 'insignificant details' you write down and quickly dismiss—these details hurt. Eternally. After all, you've become immortal through writing, as you insist you did, only about me, 'everything was about you, father'; a hundred years after your birth, the Czech Jew, son of Hermann and Julie Kafka, is supposed to be one of the greatest writers who ever lived. Your work will be read as long as there are people to read it. That's what they say everywhere, even the Germans who burned your sisters and my grandchildren in incinerators. Some say you were also some kind of prophet (God knows what you were thinking, shut away in your room while the rest of the family was having a game of cards in the evening); after you died, some countries built camps where the things you made up for that story *In The Penal Colony* were practised, and ever since then there have been countries in different parts of the world where the devil's work that came into your mind is still carried out—I don't want to think about it.

You were not blessed to bring any happiness to this world with your genius, my son. Not at home, either. Well, we had to accept what God gave. Do you ever stop to think whether it wasn't a sorrow for me (never mind—for once—how you felt) that your two brothers, who might have grown up to bring your mother and me joy, died as babies? And you sitting there at meals always with a pale, miserable, glum face, not a word to say for yourself, picking at your food. . .You haven't forgotten that I used to hold up the newspaper so as not to have to see that. You bear a grudge. You've told everybody. But you don't think about what there was in a father's heart From the beginning. I had to hide it behind a newspaper—anything. For your sake.

Because you were never like any other child. You admit it: however we had tried to bring you up, you say you would have become a 'weakly, timid, hesitant person'. What small boy doesn't enjoy a bit of a rough-house with his father? But writing at thirty-six years old, you can only remember being frightened when I chased you, in fun, round the table, and your mother, joining in, would snatch you up out of my way while you

shrieked. For God's sake, what's so terrible about that? I should
have such memories of my childhood! I know you never liked to
hear about it, it bored you, you don't spare me the written
information that it 'wore grooves in your brain', but when *I* was
seven years old I had to push my father's barrow from village to
village, with open sores on my legs in winter. Nobody gave me
delicacies to mess about on my plate; we were glad when we got
potatoes. You make a show of me, mimicking how I used to say
these things. But wasn't I right when I told you and your
sisters—provided for by me, living like fighting-cocks because I
stood in the business twelve hours a day—what did you know of
such things? What did anyone know, what I suffered as a child?
And then it's a sin if I wanted to give my own son a little pleasure
I never had.

And that other business you *schlepped* up out of the past—the
night I'm supposed to have shut you out on the *pavlatche*.
Because of you the whole world knows the Czech word for the
kind of balcony we had in Prague! Yes, the whole world knows
that story, too. I am famous, too. You made me famous as the
father who frightened his child once and for all: for life. Thank
you very much. I want to tell you that I don't even remember
that incident. I'm not saying it didn't happen, although you
always had an imagination such as nobody ever had before or
since, eh? But it could only have been the last resort your mother
and I turned to—you know that your mother spoilt you,
over-protected they would call it, now. You couldn't possibly
remember how naughty you were at night, what a little tyrant
you were, how you thought of every excuse to keep us sleepless.
It was all right for you, you could nap during the day, a small
child. But I had my business, I had to earn the living, I needed
some rest. Pieces of bread, a particular toy you fancied, make
wee-wee, another blanket on, a blanket taken off, drinks of
water—there was no end to your tricks and whining. I suppose I
couldn't stand it any longer. I feared to do you some harm. (You
admit I never beat you, only scared you a little by taking off my
braces in preparation to use them on you.) So I put you out of
harm's way. That night. Just for a few minutes. It couldn't have
been more than a minute. As if your mother would have let you
catch cold! God forbid! And you've held it against me all your

life. I'm sorry, I have to say it again, that old expression of mine that irritated you so much: I wish I had your worries.

Everything that went wrong for you is my fault. You write it down for sixty pages or so and at the same time you say to me 'I believe you are entirely blameless in the matter of our estrangement.' I was a 'true Kafka', you took after your mother's, the Löwy side etc.—all you inherited from me, according to you, were your bad traits, without having the benefit of my vitality. I was 'too strong' for you. You could not help it; I could not help it. So? All you wanted was *for me to admit that*, and we could have lived in peace. You were judge, you were jury, you were accused; you sentenced yourself, first. 'At my desk, that is my place. My head in my hands—that is my attitude.' (And that's what your poor mother and I had to look at, that was our pride and joy, our only surviving son!) But I was accused, too; you were judge, you were jury in my case, too. Right? By what right? Fancy goods—you despised the family business that fed us all, that paid for your education. What concern was it of yours, the way I treated the shop assistants? You only took an interest so you could judge, judge. It was a mistake to have let you study law. You did nothing with your qualification, your expensive education that I slaved and ruined my health for. Nothing but sentence me.—Now what did I want to say? Oh yes. Look what you wanted me to admit, under the great writer's beautiful words. If something goes wrong, somebody must be to blame, eh? We were not straw dolls, pulled about from above on strings. One of *us* must be to blame. And don't tell me you think it could be you. The stronger is always to blame, isn't that so? I'm not a deep thinker like you, only a dealer in retail fancy goods, but isn't that a law of life? 'The effect you had on me was the effect you could not help having.' You think I'll believe you're paying me a compliment, forgiving me, when you hand me the worst insult any father could receive? If it's what I am that's to blame, then I'm to blame, to the last drop of my heart's blood and whatever this is that's survived my body, for what *I am*, for being alive and begetting a son! You! Is that it? Because of you *I* should never have lived at all!

You always had a fine genius (never mind your literary one) for working me up. And you knew it was bad for my heart-

condition. Now, what does it matter. . .but, as God's my witness, you aggravate me. . .you make me. . .
Well.
All I know is that I am to blame for ever. You've seen to that.
It's written, and not alone by you. There are plenty of people
writing books about Kafka, Franz Kafka. I'm even blamed for the
name I handed down, our family name. *Kavka* is Czech for
jackdaw, so that's maybe the reason for your animal obsession.
Dafke! Insect, ape, dog, mouse, stag, what didn't you imagine
yourself. They say the beetle story is a great masterpiece, thanks
to me—I'm the one who treated you like an inferior species, gave
you the inspiration. . . You wake up as a bug, you give a lecture
as an ape. Do any of these wonderful scholars think what this
meant to me, having a son who didn't have enough self-respect
to feel himself a man?
You have such a craze for animals, but may I remind you,
when you were staying with Ottla at Zürau you wouldn't even
undress in front of a cat she'd brought in to get rid of the
mice. . .
Yet you imagined a dragon coming into your room. It said (an
educated dragon, *noch*): 'Drawn hitherto by your longing. . .I
offer myself to you.' Your longing, Franz: ugh, for monsters,
for perversion. You describe a person (yourself, of course) in
some crazy fantasy of living with a horse. Just listen to you,
'. . .for a year I lived together with a horse in such ways as, say,
a man would live with a girl whom he respects, but by whom he
is rejected.' You even gave the horse a girl's name, Eleanor. I ask
you, is that the kind of story made up by a normal young man? Is
it decent that people should read such things, long after you are
gone? But it's published, everything is published.
And worst of all, what about the animal in the synagogue.
Some sort of rat, weasel, a marten you call it. You tell how it ran
all over during prayers, running along the lattice of the women's
section and even climbing down to the curtain in front of the Ark
of the Covenant. A *schande*, an animal running about during
divine service. Even if it's only a story—only you would imagine
it. No respect.
You go on for several pages (in that secret letter) about my use
of vulgar Yiddish expressions, about my 'insignificant scrap of

Judaism', which was 'purely social' and so meant we couldn't 'find each other in Judaism' if in nothing else. This, from you! When you were a youngster and I had to drag you to the Yom Kippur services once a year you were sitting there making up stories about unclean animals approaching the Ark, the most holy object of the Jewish faith. Once you were grown up, you went exactly once to the Altneu synagogue. The people who write books about you say it must have been to please me. I'd be surprised. When you suddenly discovered you were a Jew, after all, of course your Judaism was highly intellectual, nothing in common with the Jewish customs I was taught to observe in my father's *shtetl*, pushing the barrow at the age of seven. Your Judaism was learnt at the Yiddish Theatre. That's a *nice* crowd! Those dirty-living travelling players you took up with at the Savoy Café. Your friend the actor Jizchak Löwy. No relation to your mother's family, thank God. I wouldn't let such a man even meet her. You had the disrespect to bring him into your parents' home, and I saw it was my duty to speak to him in such a way that he wouldn't ever dare to come back again. (Hah! I used to look down from the window and watch him, hanging around in the cold, outside the building, waiting for you.) And the Tschissik woman, that *nafke*, one of his actresses—I've found out you thought you were in love with her, a married woman (if you can call the way those people live a marriage). Apart from Fräulein Bauer you never fancied anything but a low type of woman. I say it again as I did then: if you lie down with dogs, you get up with fleas. You lost your temper (yes, you, this time), you flew into a rage at your father when he told you that. And when I reminded you of my heart-condition, you put yourself in the right again, as usual, you said (I remember like it was yesterday) 'I make great efforts to restrain myself.' But now I've read your diaries, the dead don't need to creep into your bedroom and read them behind your back (which you accused your mother and me of doing), I've read what you wrote afterwards, that you sensed in me, your father, 'as always at such moments of extremity, the existence of a wisdom which I can no more than scent'. So you *knew*, while you were defying me, you knew I was right!

The fact is that you were antisemitic, Franz. You were never interested in what was happening to your own people. The hooligans' attacks on Jews in the streets, on houses and shops, that took place while you were growing up—I don't see a word about them in your diaries, your notebooks. You were only *imagining* Jews. Imagining them tortured in places like your *Penal Colony*, maybe. I don't want to think about what that means.

Right, towards the end you studied Hebrew, you and your sister Ottla had some wild dream about going to Palestine. You, hardly able to breathe by then, digging potatoes on a kibbutz! The latest book about you says you were in revolt against the 'shopkeeper mentality' of your father's class of Jew; but it was the shopkeeper father, the buttons and buckles, braid, ribbons, ornamental combs, press-studs, hooks-and-eyes, boot laces, photo frames, shoe horns, novelties and notions that earned the bread for you to dream by. You were antisemitic, Franz; if such a thing is possible as for a Jew to cut himself in half. (For you, I suppose, anything is possible.) You told Ottla that to marry that goy Josef Davis was better than marrying ten Jews. When your great friend Brod wrote a book called 'The Jewesses' you wrote there were too many of them in it. You saw them like lizards. (Animals again, low animals.) 'However happy we are to watch a single lizard on a footpath in Italy, we would be horrified to see hundreds of them crawling over each other in a pickle jar.' From where did you get such ideas? Not from your home, that I know.

And look how Jewish you are, in spite of the way you despised us—Jews, your Jewish family! You answer questions with questions. I've discovered that's your style, your famous literary style: your Jewishness. Did you or did you not write the following story, playlet, wha'd'you-call-it, your friend Brod kept every scribble and you knew he wouldn't burn even a scrap. 'Once at a spiritualist seance a new spirit announced its presence, and the following conversation with it took place. The spirit: Excuse me. The spokesman: Who are you? The spirit: Excuse me. The spokesman: What do you want? The spirit: To go away. The spokesman: But you've only just come. The spirit: It's a mistake. The spokesman: No, it isn't a mistake. You've come and you'll stay. The spirit: I've just begun to feel ill. The spokesman: Badly? The spirit: Badly? The spokesman: Physically? The spirit: Physically? The spokesman: You answer with

questions. That will not do. We have ways of punishing you, so I advise you to answer, for then we shall soon dismiss you. The spirit: Soon? The spokesman: Soon. The spirit: In one minute? The spokesman: Don't go on in this miserable way. . .'
Questions without answers. Riddles. You wrote 'It is always only in contradiction that I can live. But this doubtless applies to everyone; for living, one dies, dying, one lives.' Speak for yourself! So who did you think you were when that whim took you—their prophet, Jesus Christ? What did you *want*? The *goyishe* heavenly hereafter? What did you mean when a lost man, far from his native country, says to someone he meets 'I am in your hands' and the other says, 'No. You are free and that is why you are lost'? What's the sense in writing about a woman 'I lie in wait for her ın order not to meet her'? There's only one of your riddles I think I understand, and then only because for forty-two years, God help me, I had to deal with you myself. 'A cage went in search of a bird.' That's you. The cage, not the bird. I don't know why. Maybe it will come to me. As I say, if a person wants to, he can know everything, here.

All that talk about going away. You called your home (more riddles) 'My prison—my fortress'. You grumbled—in print, everything ended up in print, my son—that your room was only a passage, a thoroughfare between the livingroom and your parents' bedroom. You complained you had to write in pencil because we took away your ink to stop you writing. It was for your own good, your health—already you were a grown man, a qualified lawyer, but you know you couldn't look after yourself. Scribbling away half the night, you'd have been too tired to work properly in the mornings, you'd have lost your position at the Assicurazioni Generali (or was it by then the Arbeiter-Unfall-Versicherungs-Anstalt für das Königreich Böhmen, my memory doesn't get any better, here). And I wasn't made of money. I couldn't go on supporting everybody for ever.

You've published every petty disagreement in the family. It was a terrible thing, according to you, we didn't want you to go out in bad weather, your poor mother wanted you to wrap up. You with your delicate health, always sickly—you didn't inherit my constitution, it was only a lifetime of hard work, the business, the family worries that got me, in the end! You recorded that you couldn't go for a walk without your parents making a fuss, but at twenty-eight you were still living at home. Going away. My poor boy. You could hardly get yourself to the next room. You shut yourself up when people came to visit. Always crawling off to bed, sleeping in the day (oh yes, you couldn't sleep at night, not like anybody else), sleeping your life away. You invented *Amerika* instead of having the guts to emigrate, get up off the bed, pack up and go there, make a new life! Even that girl you jilted twice managed it. Did you know Felice is still alive somewhere, there now, in America? She's an old, old woman with great-grandchildren. They didn't get her into the death camps those highly-educated people say you knew about before they happened. America you never went to, Spain you dreamt about. . .your Uncle Alfred was going to find you jobs there, in Madeira, the Azores. . .God knows where else. Grandson of a ritual slaughterer, a *schochet*, that was why you couldn't bear to eat meat, they say, and that made you weak and undecided. So that was my fault, too, because my poor father had to earn a living. When your mother was away from the flat, you'd have starved yourself to death if it hadn't been for me. And what was the result? You resented so much what I provided for you, you went and had your stomach pumped out! Like someone who's been poisoned! And you didn't forget to write it down, either: 'My feeling is that disgusting things will come out.'

Whatever I did for you was *dreck*. You felt 'despised, condemned, beaten down' by me. But you despised *me*; the only difference, I wasn't so easy to beat down, eh? How many times did you try to leave home, and you couldn't go? It's all there in your diaries, in the books they write about you. What about that other masterpiece of yours, *The Judgment*. A father and son quarrelling, and then the son goes and drowns himself, saying 'Dear parents, I have always loved you, all the same.' The wonderful discovery about that story, you might like to hear, it proves Hermann Kafka most likely didn't want his son to grow up and be a man, any more than his son wanted to manage without his parents' protection. The *meshuggener* who wrote that, may he get rich on it! I wouldn't wish it on him to try living with you, that's all, the way we had to. When your hunchback friend secretly showed your mother a complaining letter of yours, to get you out of your duty of going to the asbestos factory to help your own sister's husband, Brod kept back one thing you wrote. But now it's all published, all, all, all the terrible things you thought about your own flesh and blood. 'I hate them all': father, mother, sisters.

You couldn't do without us—without me. You only moved away from us when you were nearly thirty-two, a time when every *man* has a wife and children already, a home of his own.

You were always dependent on someone. Your friend Brod, poor devil. If it hadn't been for the little hunchback, who would know of your existence today? Between the incinerators that finished your sisters and the fire you wanted to burn up your manuscripts, nothing would be left. The kind of men you invented, the Gestapo, confiscated whatever papers of yours there were in Berlin, and no trace of them has ever been found, even by the great Kafka experts who stick their noses into everything. You said you loved Max Brod more than yourself. I can see that. You liked the idea he had of you, that you knew wasn't yourself (you see, sometimes I'm not so *grob*, uneducated, knowing nothing but fancy goods, maybe I got from you some 'insights'). Certainly, I wouldn't recognize my own son the way Brod described you: 'the aura Kafka gave out of extraordinary strength, something I've never encountered elsewhere, even in meetings with great and famous men. . .the infallible solidity of his insights never tolerated a single lacuna, nor did he ever speak an insignificant word. . . He was life-affirming, ironically tolerant towards the idiocies of the world, and therefore full of sad humour.'

I must say, your mother who put up with your faddiness when she came back from a day standing in the business, your sisters who acted in your plays to please you, your father who worked his heart out for his family—we never got the benefit of your tolerance. Your sisters (except Ottla, the one you admit you were a bad influence on, encouraging her to leave the shop and work on a farm like a peasant, to starve herself with you on rabbit-food, to marry that goy) were giggling idiots, so far as you were concerned. Your mother never felt the comfort of her son's strength. You never gave us anything to laugh at, sad or otherwise. And you hardly spoke to me at all, even an insignificant word. Whose fault was it you were that person you describe 'strolling about on the island in the pool, where there are neither books nor bridges, hearing the music, but not being heard.' You wouldn't cross a road, never mind a bridge, to pass the time of day, to be pleasant to other people, you shut yourself in your room and stuffed your ears with Oropax against the music of life, yes, the sounds of cooking, people coming and going (what were we supposed to do, pass through closed doors?), even the singing of the pet canaries annoyed you, laughter, the occasional family tiff, the bed squeaking where normal married people made love.

What I've just said may surprise. That last bit, I mean. But since I died in 1931 I know the world has changed a lot. People, even fathers and sons, are talking about things that shouldn't be talked about. People aren't ashamed to read anything, even private diaries, even letters. There's no shame, anywhere. With that, too, you were ahead of your time, Franz. You were not ashamed to write in your diary, which your friend Brod would publish—you must have known he would publish everything, make a living out of us—things that have led one of the famous Kafka scholars to *study* the noises in our family flat in Prague. Writing about me: 'It would have been out of character for Hermann Kafka to restrain any noises he felt like making during coupling; it would have been out of character for Kafka, who was ultra-sensitive to noise and had grown up with these noises, to mention the suffering they caused him.'

You left behind you for everyone to read that the sight of your parents' pyjamas and nightdress on the bed disgusted you. Let me also speak freely like everyone else. You were made in that bed. That disgusts me: your disgust over a place that should have been holy to you, a place to hold in the highest respect. Yet you are the one who complained about my coarseness when I suggested you ought to find yourself a woman—buy one, hire one—rather than try to prove yourself a man at last, at thirty-six, by marrying some Prague Jewish tart who shook her tits in a thin blouse. Yes, I'm speaking of that Julie Wohryzek, the shoemaker's daughter, your second fiancée. You even had the insolence to throw the remark in my face, in that letter you didn't send, but I've read it anyway, I've read everything now, although you said I put *In The Penal Colony* on the bedside table and never mentioned it again.

I have to talk about another matter we didn't discuss, father and son, while we were both alive—all right, it was my fault, maybe you're right, as I've said, times were different. . . Women. I must bring this up because—my poor boy—marriage was 'the greatest terror' of your life. You write that. You say your attempts to explain why you couldn't marry—on these depends the 'success' of the whole letter you didn't send. According to you, marrying, founding a family was 'the utmost a human being can succeed in doing at all'. Yet you couldn't marry. How is any ordinary human being to understand that? You wrote more than a quarter of a million words to Felice Bauer, but you couldn't be a husband to her. You put your parents through the farce of travelling all the way to Berlin for an engagement party (there's the photograph you had taken, the happy couple, in the books they write about you, by the way). The engagement was broken, was on again, off again. Can you wonder? Anyone who goes into a bookshop or library can read what you wrote to your fiancée when your sister Elli gave birth to our first grand-daughter. You felt nothing but nastiness, envy against your brother-in-law because 'I'll never have a child.' No, not with the Bauer girl, not in a decent marriage, like anybody else's son; but I've found out you had a child, Brod says so, by a woman, Grete Bloch, who was supposed to be the Bauer girl's best friend, who even acted as matchmaker between you! What do you say to that? Maybe it's news to you. I don't know. (That's how irresponsible you were.) They say she went away. Perhaps she never told you.

As for the next one you tried to marry, the one you make such a song and dance over because of my remark about Prague Jewesses and the blouse etc.—for once you came to your senses, and you called off the wedding only two days before it was supposed to take place. Not that I could have influenced you. Since when did you take into consideration what your parents thought? When you told me you wanted to marry the shoe-maker's daughter—naturally I was upset. At least the Bauer girl came from a nice family. What I said about the blouse just came out, I'm human, after all. But I was frank with you, man to man. You weren't a youngster anymore. A man doesn't have to marry a nothing who will go with anybody.

I saw what that marriage was about, my poor son. You wanted a woman. Nobody understood that better than I did, believe me, I was normal man enough, eh! There were places in Prague where one could get a woman. (I suppose whatever's happened, there still are, always will be.) I tried to help you; I offered to go along with you myself. I said it in front of your mother, who—yes, as you write you were so shocked to see, was in agreement with me. We wanted so much to help you, even your own mother would go so far as that.

But in that letter you didn't think I'd ever see, you accuse me of humiliating you and I don't know what else. You wanted to marry a tart, but you were insulted at the idea of buying one?

Writing that letter only a few days after you yourself called off your second try at getting married, aged thirty-six, you find that your father, as a man-of-the-world, not only showed 'contempt' for you on that occasion, but that when he had spoken to you as a broad-minded father when you were a youngster, he had given you information that set off the whole ridiculous business of your never being able to marry, ever. Already, twenty years before the Julie Wohryzek row, with 'a few frank words' (as you put it) your father made you incapable of taking a wife and pushed you down 'into the filth as if it were my destiny'. You remember some walk with your mother and me on the Josefsplatz when you showed curiosity about, well, men's feelings and women, and I was open and honest with you and told you I could give you advice about where to go so that these things could be done quite safely, without bringing home any disease. You were sixteen years old, physically a man, not a child, eh? Wasn't it time to talk about such things?

Shall I tell you what *I* remember? Once you picked a quarrel with your mother and me because we hadn't educated you sexually—your words. Now you complain because I tried to guide you in these matters. I did—I didn't. Make up your mind. Have it your own way. Whatever I did, you believed it was *because of what I did* that you couldn't bring yourself to marry. When you thought you wanted the Bauer girl, didn't I give in, to

please you? Although you were in no financial position to
marry, although I had to give your two married sisters financial
help, although I had worries enough, a sick man, you'd caused
me enough trouble by persuading me to invest in a *mechulah*
asbestos factory? Didn't I give in? And when the girl came to
Prague to meet your parents and sisters, you wrote, 'My family
likes her almost more than I'd like it to.' So it went as far as that:
you couldn't like anything we liked, was that why you couldn't
marry her?

A long time ago, a long way. . .ah, it all moves away, it's
getting faint. . . But I haven't finished. Wait.

You say you wrote your letter because you wanted to explain
why you couldn't marry. I'm writing this letter because you
tried to write it for me. *You would take even that away from
your father.* You answered your own letter, before I could. You
made what you imagine as my reply part of the letter you wrote
me. To save me the trouble. . . Brilliant, like they say. With
your great gifts as a famous writer, you express it all better than I
could. You are there, quickly, with an answer, before I can be.
You take the words out of my mouth: while you are accusing
yourself, in my name, of being 'too clever, obsequious, parasitic
and insincere' in blaming your life on me, you are—yet again,
one last time!—finally being too clever, obsequious, parasitic
and insincere in the trick of stealing your father's chance to
defend himself. A genius. What is left to say about you if—how
well you know yourself, my boy, it's terrible—you call yourself
the kind of vermin that doesn't only sting, but at the same time
sucks blood to keep itself alive? And even that isn't the end of the
twisting, the cheating. You then confess that this whole 'correc-
tion', 'rejoinder', as you, an expensively educated man, call it,
'does not originate' in your father but in you yourself, Franz
Kafka. So you see, here's the proof, something *I* know you, with
all your brains, can't know *for me*: you say you always wrote
about me, it was all about me, your father; but it was all about
you. The beetle. The bug that lay on its back waving its legs in
the air and couldn't get up to go and see America or the Great
Wall of China. You, you, self, self. And in your letter, after you
have defended me against yourself, when you finally make the
confession—right again, in the right again, always—you take

the last word, in proof of your saintliness I could know nothing about, never understand, a businessman, a shopkeeper. That is your 'truth' about us you hoped might be able to 'make our living and our dying easier'.

The way you ended up, Franz. The last woman you found yourself. It wasn't our wish, God knows. Living with that Eastern Jewess, and in sin. We sent you money; that was all we could do. If we'd come to see you, if we'd swallowed our pride, meeting that woman, our presence would only have made you worse. It's there in everything you've written, everything they write about you: everything connected with us made you depressed and ill. We knew she was giving you the wrong food, cooking like a gypsy on a spirit stove. She kept you in an unheated hovel in Berlin. . .may God forgive me (Brod has told the world), I had to turn my back on her at your funeral.

Franz. . . When you received copies of your book *In The Penal Colony* from Kurt Wolff Verlag that time. . . You gave me one and I said 'Put it on the night-table.' You say I never mentioned it again. Well, don't you understand—I'm not a literary man. I'm telling you now. I read a little bit, a page or two at a time. If you had seen that book, there was a pencil mark every two, three pages, so I would know next time where I left off. It wasn't like the books I knew—I hadn't much time for reading, working like a slave since I was a small boy, I wasn't like you, I couldn't shut myself up in a room with books, when I was young. I would have starved. But you know that. Can't you understand that I was—yes—not too proud—ashamed to let you know I didn't find it easy to understand your kind of writing, it was all strange to me.

Hah! I know I'm no intellectual, but I knew how to live!

Just a moment. . .give me time. . .there's a fading. . . Yes— can you imagine how we felt when Ottla told us you had tuberculosis? Oh how could you bring it over your heart to remind me I once said, in a temper, to a useless assistant coughing all over the shop (you should have had to deal with those lazy *goyim*), he ought to die, the sick dog. Did I know you would get tuberculosis, too? It wasn't our fault your lungs rotted. I tried to expand your chest when you were little, teaching you to swim; you should never have moved out of your own home, the care of your parents, to that rat-hole in the Schönbornpalais. And the hovel in Berlin. . . We had some good times, didn't we? Franz? When we had beer and sausages after the swimming lessons? At least you remembered the beer and sausages, when you were dying.

One more thing. It chokes me, I have to say it. I know you'll never answer. You once wrote 'Speech is possible only where one wants to lie.' You were too *ultra-sensitive* to speak to us, Franz. You kept silence, with the truth: those playing a game of cards, turning in bed on the other side of the wall—it was the sound of live people you didn't like. Your revenge, that you were too cowardly to take in life, you've taken here. We can't lie peacefully in our graves; dug up, unwrapped from our shrouds by your fame. To desecrate your parents' grave as well as their bed, aren't you ashamed? Aren't you ashamed—now? Well, what's the use of quarrelling. We lie together in the same grave—you, your mother and I. We've ended up as we always should have been, united. Rest in peace, my son. I wish you had let me.

Your father,
Hermann Kafka

Crimes of Conscience

Apparently they noticed each other at the same moment, coming down the steps of the Supreme Court on the third day of the trial. By then casual spectators who come for a look at the accused—to see for themselves who will risk prison walls round their bodies for ideas in their heads—have satisfied curiosity; only those who have some special interest attend day after day. He could have been a journalist; or an aide to the representative of one of the Western powers who 'observe' political trials in countries problematic for foreign policy and subject to human rights lobbying back in Western Europe and America. He wore a corduroy suit of unfamiliar cut. But when he spoke it was clear he was, like her, someone at home—he had the accent, and the casual, colloquial turn of phrase. 'What a session! I don't know. . . After two hours of that. . .feel like I'm caught in a roll of sticky tape. . .unreal. . .'

There was no mistaking her. She was a young woman whose cultivated gentleness of expression and shabby homespun style of dress, in the context in which she was encountered, suggested not transcendental meditation centre or environmental concern group or design studio, but a sign of identification with the humanity of those who had nothing and risked themselves. Her only adornment, a necklace of minute ostrich-shell discs stacked along a thread, moved tight at the base of her throat tendons as she smiled and agreed. 'Lawyers work like that. . .I've noticed. The first few days, it's a matter of people trying each to confuse the other side.'

Later in the week, they had coffee together during the court's lunch adjournment. He expressed some naïve impressions of the trial, but as if fully aware of gullibility. Why did the State call witnesses who came right out and said the regime oppressed their spirits and frustrated their normal ambitions? Surely that kind of testimony favoured the Defence, when the issue was a crime of conscience? She shook fine hair, ripply as a mohair rug. 'Just wait. Just wait. That's to establish credibility. To prove their involvement with the accused, their intimate knowledge of what the accused said and did, to *inculpate* the accused in what the Defence's going to deny. Don't you see?'

'Now I see.' He smiled at himself. 'When I was here before, I didn't take much interest in political things. . .activist politics, I suppose you'd call it? It's only since I've been back from overseas. . .'

She asked conversationally what was expected of her: how long had he been away?

'Nearly five years. Advertising, then computers. . .' The dying-out of the sentence suggested the lack of interest in which these careers had petered. 'Two years ago I just felt I wanted to come back. I couldn't give myself a real reason. I've been doing the same sort of work here—actually, I ran a course at the business school of a university, this year—and I'm slowly beginning to find out *why* I wanted to. To come back. It seems it's something to do with things like *this*.'

She had a face that showed her mind following another's; eyebrows and mouth expressed quiet understanding.

'I imagine all this sounds rather feeble to you. I don't suppose you're someone who stands on the sidelines.'

Her thin, knobbly little hands were like tools laid upon the formica counter of the coffee bar. In a moment of absence from their capability, they fiddled with the sugar sachets while she answered. 'What makes you think that.'

'You seem to know so much. As if you'd been through it yourself. . . Or maybe. . .you're a law student?'

'Me? Good lord, no.' After one or two swallows of coffee, she offered a friendly response. 'I work for a correspondence college.'

'Teacher.'

Smiling again: 'Teaching people I never see.'

'That doesn't fit too well. You look the kind of person who's more involved.'

For the first time, polite interest changed, warmed. 'That's what you missed, in London? Not being involved. . .?'

At that meeting he gave her a name, and she told him hers.

The name was Derek Felterman. It was his real name. He *had* spent five years in London; he *had* worked in an advertising company and then studied computer science at an appropriate institution, and it was in London that he was recruited by someone from the Embassy who wasn't a diplomat but a representative of the internal security section of State security in his native country. Nobody knows how secret police recognize likely candidates; it is as mysterious as sexing chickens. But if the definitive characteristic sought is there to be recognized, the recruiting agent will see it, no matter how deeply the individual may hide his likely candidacy from himself.

He was not employed to infiltrate refugee circles plotting abroad. It was decided that he would come home 'clean', and begin work in the political backwater of a coastal town, on a university campus. Then he was sent north to the mining and industrial centre of the country, told to get himself an ordinary commercial job without campus connections, and, as a new face, seek contacts wherever the information his employers wanted was likely to be let slip—left-wing cultural gatherings, poster-waving protest groups, the public gallery at political trials. His employers trusted him to know how to ingratiate himself; that was one of the qualities he had been fancied for, as a woman might fancy him for some other characteristic over which he had no volition—the way one corner of his mouth curled when he smiled, or the brown gloss of his eyes.

He, in his turn, had quickly recognized her—first as a type, and then, the third day, when he went away from the court for verification of her in police files, as the girl who had gone secretly to visit a woman friend who was under House Arrest, and subsequently had served a three-month jail sentence for refusing to testify in a case brought against the woman for breaking her isolation ban. Aly, she had called herself. Alison Jane Ross.

There was no direct connection to be found between Alison Jane Ross's interest in the present trial and the individuals on trial; but from the point of view of his avocation this did not exclude her possible involvement with a master organization or back-up group involved in continuing action of the subversive kind the charges named.

Felterman literally moved in to friendship with her, carrying a heavy case of books and a portable grill. He had asked if she would come to see a play with him on Saturday night. Alas, she was moving house that Saturday; perhaps he'd like to come and help, instead? The suggestion was added, tongue-in-cheek at her own presumption. He was there on time. Her family of friends, introduced by diminutives of their names, provided a combined service of old combi, springless station-wagon, take-away food and affectionate energy to fuel and accomplish the move from a flat to a tiny house with an ancient palm tree filling a square of garden, grating its dried fronds in the wind with the sound of a giant insect rubbing its legs together. To the night-song of that creature they made love for the first time a month later. Although all the Robs, Jimbos and Ricks, as well as the Jojos, Bets and Lils, kissed and hugged their friend Aly, there seemed to be no lover about who had therefore been supplanted. On the particular, delicate path of intimacy along which she drew him or that he laid out before her, there was room only for the two of them. At the beginning of ease between them, even before they were lovers, she had come of herself to the stage of mentioning that experience of going to prison, but she talked of it always in banal surface terms—how the blankets smelled of disinfectant and the Chief Wardress's cat used to do the inspection round with its mistress. Now she did not ask him about other women, although he was moved, occasionally, in some involuntary warm welling-up complementary to that other tide—of sexual pleasure spent—to confess by the indirection of an anecdote, past affairs, women who had had their time and place. When the right moment came naturally to her, she told without shame, resentment or vanity that she had just spent a year 'on her own' as something she felt she needed after living for three years with someone who, in the end, went back to his wife. Lately there had been one or two brief affairs—'Sometimes—don't you find—an old friend suddenly becomes something else. . .just for a little while, as if a face is turned to another angle. . ? And next day, it's the same old one again. Nothing's changed.'

'Friends are the most important thing for you, aren't they? I mean, everybody has friends, but you. . . You'd really do *anything*. For your friends. Wouldn't you?'

There seemed to come from her reaction rather than his words a reference to the three months she had spent in prison. She lifted the curly pelmet of hair from her forehead and the freckles faded against a flush colouring beneath: 'And they for me.'

'It's not just a matter of friendship, either—of course, I see that. Comrades—a band of brothers. . .'

She saw him as a child staring through a window at others playing. She leant over and took up his hand, kissed him with the kind of caress they had not exchanged before, on each eyelid.

Nevertheless her friends were a little neglected in favour of him. He would have liked to have been taken into the group more closely, but it is normal for two people involved in a passionate love affair to draw apart from others for a while. It would have looked unnatural to press to behave otherwise. It was also understood between them that Felterman didn't have much more than acquaintances to neglect; five years abroad and then two in the coastal town accounted for that. He revived for her pleasures she had left behind as a schoolgirl: took her water-skiing and climbing. They went to see indigenous people's theatre together, part of a course in the politics of culture she was giving him not by correspondence, without being aware of what she was doing and without giving it any such pompous name. She was not to be persuaded to go to a discothèque, but one of the valuable contacts he did have with her group of friends of different races and colours was an assumption that he would be with her at their parties, where she out-danced him, having been taught by blacks how to use her body to music. She was wild and nearly lovely, in this transformation, from where he drank and watched her and her associates at play. Every now and then she would come back to him: an offering, along with the food and drink she carried. As months went by, he was beginning to distinguish certain patterns in her friendships; these were extended beyond his life with her into proscribed places and among people restricted by law from contact, like the woman for whom she had gone to prison. Slowly she gained the confidence to introduce him to risk, never discussing but evidently always sensitively trying to gauge how much he really wanted to find out if 'why he wanted to come back' had to do with 'things like this'.

It was more and more difficult to leave her, even for one night, going out late, alone under the dry, chill agitation of the old palm tree, rustling through its files. But although he knew his place had been made for him to live in the cottage with her, he had to go back to his flat that was hardly more than an office, now, unoccupied except for the chair and dusty table at which he sat down to write his reports: he could hardly write them in the house he shared with her.

She spoke often of her time in prison. She herself was the one to find openings for the subject. But even now, when they lay in one another's arms, out of reach, undiscoverable to any investigation, out of scrutiny, she did not seem able to tell of the experience what there really was in her being, necessary to be told: why she risked, for whom and what she was committed. She seemed to be waiting passionately to be given the words, the key. From him.

It was a password he did not have. It was a code that was not supplied him.

And then one night it came to him; he found a code of his own; that night he had to speak. 'I've been spying on you.'

Her face drew into a moment of concentration akin to the animal world, where a threatened creature can turn into a ball of spikes or take on a fearsome aspect of blown-up muscle and defensive garishness.

The moment left her face instantly as it had taken her. He had turned away before it as a man does with a gun in his back.

She shuffled across the bed on her haunches and took his head in her hands, holding him.

Sins of the Third Age

Each came from a different country and they met in yet another, during a war. After the war, they lived in a fourth country, and married there, and had children who grew up with a national patrimony and a flag. The official title of the war was the Second World War, but Peter and Mania called it 'our war' apparently in distinction from the wars that followed. It was also a designation of territory in which their life together had begun. Under the left cuff of the freshly-laundered shirt he put on every day he had a number branded on his wrist; her hands, the nails professionally manicured and painted once a week with Dusty Rose No. 1, retained no mark of the grubbing—frost-cracked and bleeding—for frozen turnips, that had once kept her alive. Neither had any family left except that of their own procreation; and, of course, each other. They had each other. They had always had each other, in their definitive lives—a childhood that one has not grown out of but been exploded from in the cross-fire of armies explodes, at the same time, the theory of childhood as the basis to which the adult personality always refers itself. Destruction of places, habitations, is destruction of the touchstone they held. There was no church, schoolhouse or tree left standing to bring Peter or Mania back on a pilgrimage. There was no face in which to trace a young face remembered from the height of a child. Unfurnished, unpeopled by the past, there was their life together.

It was a well-made life. It did not happen; was carefully constructed. Right from the start, when they had no money and a new language to learn in that fourth country they had chosen as their home, they determined never to lose control of their lives as they had had no choice but to do in their war. They were enthusiastic, energetic, industrious, modestly ambitious, and this was part of their loving. They worked with and for each other, improving their grasp of the language while they talked and caressed over washing dishes or cooking together, murmuring soothing lies while confessing to each other—voices blurred by the pillows, between love-making and sleep—difficulties and loneliness encountered in their jobs.

She was employed as an interpreter at a conference centre. He lugged a range of medical supplies round the offices of city doctors and dentists, and, according to plan, studied electronics at night school in preparation for the technological expansion that could be foreseen. When the children were born, the young mother and father staggered their hours of employment so that she would not have to give up work. They were saving to buy an apartment of their own but they had too much loss behind them to forgo the only certainty of immediate pleasures and they also kept aside every week a sum for entertainment.

As the years went by, they could afford seasonal subscriptions to the opera and concerts. They bought something better than an apartment—a small house with a basement room they rented to a student. Peter became an assistant sales manager in a multinational company; Mania had opportunities to travel, now and then, with a team of translators sent to international conferences. Their children took guitar lessons, learnt to ski, and won state scholarships to universities, where they demonstrated against wars in Asia, Latin America, the Middle East and Africa they did not have to experience themselves. These same children came of age to vote against the government of their parents' adopted country, which the children said was authoritarian, neo-colonialist in its treatment of 'guest workers' from poorer countries, and in danger of turning fascist. Their parents were anti-authoritarian, anti-colonialist, anti-fascist—with their past, how could they not be? But if a socialist government came to power taxes would be raised, and so they voted for the sitting government. Doesn't everyone over forty know that it is not the real exploiters, the powerful and the rich, but the middle class, the modest planners, the savers for a comfortable and

independent retirement who suffer under measures meant to
spread wealth and extend justice?

There were arguments around the evening meal, to which
those children no longer living at home often turned up, with
their lovers, hungry and angry.

'You would never have been born if it hadn't been for the
decent welfare and health services provided for the past twenty
years by this government.' Peter's standard statement was
intended to be the last word.

It roused outcry against self-interest, smugness, selling-out.
Once, it touched off flippancy. The darling, blonde, only daughter was present. She peered from the privacy of her tresses,
cuddling her breasts delightedly between arms crossed over her
T-shirt. 'So you lied about how babies are made, after all,
Mama!' Mania supported Peter. 'It's true—we couldn't have
afforded to bring you up. Certainly you wouldn't have been able
to go to university.'

Even at the stage when one's children turn against one, at least
they always had each other.

Mania's work as an interpreter had taken her to places as remote
from their plans as Abidjan (Ivory Coast, WHO conference on
water-borne diseases), Atlanta, Georgia (international congress
of librarians) and, since the '70s, OPEC gatherings in new cities
she described in long letters to Peter as air-conditioned shopping
malls set down in the desert. But she also had been sent many
times to Rome and Milan, and Peter had joined her by way of an
excursion flight whenever her period of duty was contiguous
with a long weekend or his yearly holiday leave. Then they
would hire a small car and drive, each time through a different
region of Italy. They felt the usual enthusiasm of Northerners
for Tuscany and the South; it was only when, from Milan one
year, they took a meandering route via the Turin road to Genoa
through the maritime alps that this tourist pleasure, accepted as
something to be put away with holiday clothes for next time,
changed to the possibility of permanent attachment to a fifth
country.

At first it was one of those visions engendered, like the

beginning of a love affair, by the odd charm of an afternoon in the square of a small Piedmontese town. They had never heard of it; come upon it by hazard. They sat on the square into which mole-runs of streets debouched provincial Italians busy with their own lives. Nobody touted or offered services as a guide. Shopkeepers sent shutters flying as they opened for business after the siesta. Small children, pigeon-toed in boots, ate cakes as they were walked home from school. Old women wearing black formed groups of the Fates on corners, and slowly climbed the steps of the church, each leg lifted and placed like a stake. At five o'clock, when Peter and Mania were sitting between tubs of red geraniums eating ice-cream, the figure of a blackamoor in doublet and gold turban swung out stiffly under a black-and-gold palanquin at the top of the church tower, and struck the hour with his pagan hand. Nobody hawked postcards of him; at six, when Peter and Mania had not moved, but moved on from ice-cream to Campari and soda, they saw local inhabitants checking their watches against his punctual reappearance. There was a kind of cake honouring him, the travellers discovered later; round, covered with the bitter-sweet black chocolate Mania liked best, the confections were called 'The Moor's Balls', and these were what good children were rewarded with.

Peter and Mania found a *pensione* whose view was of chestnut woods and a horizon looped by peaks lustred with last winter's snow, distant in time as well as space. They shone pink in the twilight. Peter spoke. 'Wherever you lived, round about here, you'd be able to see the mountains. From the smallest shack.' Mania had acquired Italian, in the course of qualifying for advancement in her job. She got talking to the proprietor of the *pensione* and listened to his lament that land values were dropping—the country people were dying out, the young moved away to Turin and Milan. When Peter and Mania returned the following year to the town, to the square with *il moro* in his tower, to the same *pensione*, the proprietor took them to visit his brother-in-law in a little farmhouse with an iron gallery hung with grapes; they drank home-made wine on yellow plastic chairs among giant cucurbits dangling from a vine and orange mushrooms set out to dry.

That same year Mania was again in Milan, and when she had a

free weekend took a train and bus to the town; just to sit among the local people on the square and let the moor mark the passing of time (she would be retiring on pension in a few years), just to spend one evening on the balcony of the now familiar room at the *pensione*. Middle age made it difficult for her to see without glasses anything close by. She was becoming more and more far-sighted; but here her gaze was freed even as high and far as the snow from the past that would soon weld with the snow of winter ahead. In his usual long account of family misfortunes, the proprietor came to the necessity to sell the brother-in-law's property; that night Mania sat up in the *pensione* room until two, calculating the budgets and savings, over the years, she had by heart. When she got back home to Peter, she had only to write the figures down for him, and how they were arrived at. He went over them again, alone; they discussed at length what margin in their calculations should be allowed for the effects of inflation upon a fixed income. In his late fifties he had grown gaunt as she had padded out. Dressed, his were the flat belly and narrow waist of a boy, but naked he looked closer to the other end of life, and he was getting deaf. His deepened eyes and lengthened nose faced her with likenesses she would never recognize because no photographs had survived. But she knew, now, what he was thinking; and he saw, and smiled: he was thinking that there was not one habitation, however small, from which you wouldn't have the horizon of alps.

They raised a mortgage on their house and bought the farmhouse in Italy. It was not a dream, a crazy idea, but part of a perfectly practical preparation for retirement. The Italian property was a bargain, and when they were ready to sell their house they could count on making sufficient profit both to pay off the mortgage and finance the move abroad. Living was cheap in that safe, unfashionable part of Italy, far from political kidnappings and smart international expatriates. Their pensions (fully transferable under exchange control regulations, they had ascertained) would go much further than at home. They would grow some of their own food and make their own wine. He would smoke trout. In the meantime, they had a free holiday house for the years of waiting—and anticipation. Once they had dared buy the farmhouse they knew that, from the afternoon they had first sat in the square of *il moro*, this had become the place in the world they had been planning to deserve, to enjoy, all their life together. The preparation continued with Detto, the *pensione* proprietor, and his wife looking after farmhouse and garden in return for the produce they grew for themselves, and Peter and Mania spending every holiday painting, repairing and renovating the premises. By the time Peter's retirement was due, Mania had even retraced, in fresh colours, the mildewed painted garlands under the eaves, with their peasant design of flowers and fruit.

Peter's retirement came eighteen months before Mania's. They had planned accordingly, all along: he would move first, to Italy, settle in with the household goods, while she sat on in interpreters' glass booths hearing—each time nearer the final time—the disputes and deliberations of the world that had filled her ears since the noise of bombs ended, long ago in the country where she and Peter began. She saved money in every way she could. She worked through that summer. He was chopping wood, he said over the telephone, for winter storage: he had found there was a little cultural circle in the town, and had boldly joined in order to improve his Italian. She was sent to Washington and wrote that she thanked god every day it was the last time; the heat was primeval, she wouldn't have been surprised to see crocodiles slothful on the banks of the Potomac—O for the sky lifted to the alps! He wrote that the cultural circle was putting on a Goldoni play, and—he wasn't proud—he was a stage-hand along with kids of fifteen! It is always easier to give way to emotion in a letter than face-to-face—the recipient doesn't have to dissimulate in response. She wrote telling him how she had always admired him for his lack of pretension, his willingness to learn and adapt.

She knew he would know she was saying she loved him for these things, that were still with them although she was thick-ankled and his pliant muscles had shrunk away against his bones.

After Washington it was Sydney, and then she went back to autumn in the room she was occupying in her daughter's basement apartment, now that the city house had been sold. She scraped off the sweet-smelling mat of rotting wet leaves that stuck to the heels of her shoes: this time next year, she would be living in Italy. In old sweaters, she and Peter would walk into town and drink hot coffee and wait for the moor to strike twelve.

That evening she was about to phone the *pensione* and leave a message for Peter to say she had returned (they didn't yet have a phone in the farmhouse) when he walked into the apartment. Mother and daughter, like two blonde sheepdogs, almost knocked him over in their excitement. How much better than a phone-call! Husband and wife were getting a bit too middle-aged, now, to mark every reunion with love-making, but in bed, when she began to settle in for a long talk in the dark, he took her gross breasts, through which he used to be able to feel her ribs, and manipulated the nipples deliberately as a combination lock calculated to rouse both him and her. After the love-making he fell asleep, and she lay against his back; she hoped their daughter hadn't heard anything.

In the morning the daughter went to work and over a long breakfast they were engrossed in practical matters concerning the farmhouse in Italy and residence there—taxes, permits, house and medical insurance. The roof repairs would have to be done sooner or later and would cost more than anticipated—'A good thing I decided to work this summer.' However, Detto had made the suggestion Peter might do the repairs himself. Detto offered to help—through his foresight, Peter had bought cheaply and stored away the necessary materials. 'Leave it until next year when I'll be there to help, too—so long as it won't leak on you this winter?' 'Heavy plastic sheeting, Detto says, and the snow will pack down. . .I'll be all right.' And while she washed her hair Peter went off into the city to enquire about a method of insulating walls he couldn't find any information on, in Italy—at least not in the region of the moor's sovereignty.

Mania was using the hair-dryer when she heard him return. She called out a greeting but could not catch his reply because of the tempest blowing about her head. Presently he came into the bedroom with a handful of brochures and stood, in the doorway. He signalled to her to switch off; she smiled and did so, ready to listen to advice he had gleaned about damp rot. What he said was 'I want to tell you why I came.'

She was smiling again and at once had an instinct of embarrassment at that smile and its implication: to be here when I came back.

He walked into the room as if she had summoned him; Mania, sitting there with her tinted blonde hair dragged up in rollers, the dryer still in her hand.

'I've met somebody.'

Mania said nothing. She looked at him, waiting for him to go on speaking. He did not, and her gaze wavered and dropped; she saw her own big bosom, rising and falling with faster and faster breaths. The dryer began to wobble in her hand. She put it on the bed.

'In the play. I told you they were putting on a Goldoni play.'

Her brain was neatly stocked with thousands of words in five languages but she could think of nothing she wanted to say; nothing she wanted to ask. She slowly nodded: you told me about the play.

He was waiting for *her* to speak. They were two new people, just introduced with the words *I've met somebody*, and they didn't know what subject they had in common.

He struggled for recognition. 'What do you want to do.' He made it a conclusion, not a question.

'I? *I* do?'

She had pushed up one of the metal spokes that held the rollers in place and he saw the red indentation it left on her pink forehead.

He insisted quietly. 'All the things are there. . .furniture, everything. The property. The new material for the roof.'

'You want to go away.'

'It's not possible. The person—she has to look after her grandmother. And she's got a small child.'

Mania was breathing fast with her mouth open, as she knew she did, now that she was fat, when they climbed a hill together. She also knew that when she was a child tears had followed deep, sharp breaths. Before that happened, she had to speak quickly. 'What do you want me to do?'

'It's so difficult. Because everything's been arranged. . .so long. All sold up, here.'

Their life had come to a stop, the way the hair-dryer had been switched off; here in a room in her daughter's life she would stay. 'I could bring things back.'

He was looking at the quarter-inch of grey that made a stripe below the blonde in hair bound over the rollers. 'I don't take her to the farmhouse.'

Mania had a vision of him, as she knew him, domestically naked about the bedroom; his thin thighs—and for the first time, a young Italian woman with black hair and a crucifix.

'Where does she come from?'

'Come from? You mean where does she live. . .in the town. Right in town.'

Oh yes. Near the square—the moor struck again and again—all those little streets that lead to the square, one of those streets off the square.

Suddenly, Mania forgot everything else; remembered. Her face swelled drunk with shame. 'Why did you do that. . .last night. Why? Why?'

He stood there and watched her sobbing.

She did not tell the daughter. Discussions about the farmhouse, the property in Italy, continued like the workings of a business under appointed executors after the principals have died. Some crates of books were at the shippers; so was Mania's sewing machine—one could not stop the process now. Damp rot could not be left to creep up the walls of the house, whatever happened—there are already some brown spots appearing on your frieze, Peter remarked—and he took back with him the necessary chemicals for injection into the brick.

His letters and hers were almost the same as before—an exchange of his news about the farmhouse and garden for hers about the grown-up children and her work. They continued to sign themselves 'your Peter' and 'your Mania' because this must have become a formula for a commitment that had long been expressed in ways other than possession and meant nothing in itself. She postponed any decision, any thought of a decision about what she would do when her retirement came. A year was a long time, the one friend in whom she confided kept telling her; a lot can happen in a year. She was advised according to female lore to let the affair wear itself out. But just before the year was up she came to a decision she did not confess. She wrote to Peter telling him she would come to Italy as planned, if he did not object, and he could continue seeing ('being with' she phrased it) the person he had found. She would not reproach or interfere. He wrote back and rather hurtfully did not mention the person, as if this were so private and precious a matter he did not want her to approach that part of his life even with tolerant words. He phrased his consent in the form of the remark that he was satisfied he had got everything more or less organized: she could count on finding the house and garden in fair order.

Mania knew she was sufficiently self-disciplined—held herself, now, in a particular sense like that of a military bearing or a sailor's sea-legs—to keep her word about reproaches or interference. Once she was living with him in the farmhouse she realized that this intention had to be extended to include glances, pauses of a particular weight, even aspects of personal equanimity—if a headache inclined her to be quieter than usual, she had best be careful the mood did not look like something else. Peter did not make love to her ever again and she didn't expect it. That time—that was the last time.

She presumed he had a place to meet the person. Perhaps Detto, simple good soul, and a man himself, of course, who had become such an understanding friend to the foreign couple, had put Peter in the way of finding somewhere, just as he had put them in the way of finding the farmhouse to which the remote exaltation of the alps was linked as domestically as a pet kept in the yard. Peter must have found some place, if the person had the grandmother and a child living with her. . .but pious old women in black, children with fat little calves laced into boots—these thoughts were out of bounds for a woman standing ground where Mania was. She did not allow herself, either, to look for signs (what would they be? all had black hair and wore crucifixes) among the young women who carried shopping-bags, flowering magnificent vegetables, across the square of the moor.

Peter went with her on shopping trips into the town. A pleasant, unvarying round. The post office for stamps, and the bank where a young teller sleek as the film stars of their youth counted out millionaire stacks of lire that paid for a little fruit from the old man they always patronized in the market, and bread from the woman with prematurely grey hair and shiny cheekbones who served alongside her floury father or husband. It was autumn, yes; sometimes they did go on foot, wearing their old sweaters. They drank coffee at an outside table if the sun was shining, and got up to trudge back at the convenient signal of *il moro* striking his baton twelve times. But Peter did not go out alone, and for the first few weeks after her arrival she thought this was some quaint respect or dutiful homage: when she had settled in and he knew she did not feel herself a new arrival in her status as resident, he would take up again—what he had found.

He seemed reluctant, indeed, to go anywhere. Detto came by to invite him to go mushrooming, or hunting boars in the mountains, something Peter had talked about doing (why not?) all the years of anticipation; he yawned, in his slippers, looking out at the soft mist that wrapped house and alps in a single silence, and watched the old man disappear into it alone. One of their retirement plans had been to do some langlauf skiing, you didn't have to be young for that, and there was a bus to a small ski resort only an hour away. The snow came; she suggested a day trip. He smiled and blew through his lips, dropping his book in his lap at the interruption. She felt like a child nagging to be taken to the swings. They stayed at home with the TV he kept flickering, along with the fire.

It was true that he had got everything more or less organized, on the property. When she asked him what he planned to do next—plant new vines, build the little smoke-house they'd talked of, to smoke the excellent local trout—he joked with her, apparently: 'I'm retired, aren't I?' And when spring came he did nothing, he still watched TV most of the day. 'It improves my Italian.' She busied herself making curtains and chair-covers. She would wrap up for a walk and when she came home, expect he might have taken the opportunity, gone out. Even before she entered the house, she would see through the window the harsh barred light that flowed on the black-and-white television screen, a tide constantly rising and falling back over the glass. He was always there.

She found minute white violets in the woods. She went up to

him that day, sitting in his chair, and held the fragile bouquet under his nose, cold and sweet. He revived; met her eyes; he seemed to have come to in a place as remote as the peaks where the snow never melts.

She made coffee and he raked up the fire. They were sitting cosily drinking, she was stirring her cup and she said, 'I shouldn't have come.'

He looked up from the newspaper as if she had passed a remark about the weather.

It was an effort to speak again. 'You can go out, you know.'

He said from behind the paper, 'I gave up that person.'

She felt herself being drawn into a desolation she had never known. She got up quietly, tactfully, and went into the kitchen as she might to some task there, but whatever she did, that day, the sense of being bereft would not leave her. She did not think of Peter. Only that Peter, in spite of what he had just told her, could do nothing for her; nothing could be done for her, despite the coming about of the prediction of female lore. She carried on with what she had planned: finished the curtains and fitted the chair-covers, and a day came when she was released by what had seized her and she hadn't understood, and she went to Detto's wife to learn, as promised, how to fry pumpkin flowers in batter. A stray dog adopted Peter and her, and joyously accompanied her walks. It was no use trying to get Peter to come; he stayed at the farmhouse while a contractor repaired the roof, and listened to Detto's stories while Detto planted the new vines and tended the garden. They did go into town to do the household shopping together, though, and sometimes in the summer evenings would sit in the square until the moor swung out to strike nine. One evening the woman from the baker's shop passed, carrying two ice-cream cones. 'That was the person,' Peter said. She didn't have black hair or wear a crucifix, she was the tall one with the shiny sad cheekbones and prematurely grey hair cut page-boy style. They had been into the baker's shop together—Peter and Mania—day after day, and taken bread from her hands, and there had never been a sign of what had been found, and lost again.

Blinder

Rose lives in the backyard. She has lived there from the time when she washed the napkins of the children in the house, who are now university students. Her husband had disappeared before she took the job. Her lover, Ephraim, who works for Cerberus Security Guards, has lived with her in the yard for as long as anyone in the house can remember. He used to be night watchman at a parking garage, and the children, leaving for school in the morning after Rose had cooked breakfast for them, would meet 'Rose's husband' in his khaki drill uniform, wheeling his bicycle through the gateway as he came off shift. His earlobes were loops that must once have been filled by ornamental plugs, his smile was sweetened by splayed front teeth about which, being what he was, who he was, he was quite unselfconscious.

That is what they remember, the day they hear that he is dead. The news comes by word-of-mouth, as all news seems to in the backyards of the suburb; who is in jail, caught without a pass, and must be bailed out, who has been told to leave a job and backyard at the end of the month, who has heard of the birth of a child, fathered on annual leave, away in the country. There is a howling and keening in the laundry and the lady of the house thinks Rose is off on a blinder again. In her forties Rose began to have what the family and their friends call a drinking problem. Nothing, in the end, has been done about it. The lady of the house thought it might be menopausal, and had Rose examined by her own doctor. He found she had high blood pressure and treated her for that, telling her employer the drinking absolutely must be stopped, it exacerbated hypertension. The lady of the house made enquiries, heard of a Methodist Church that ran a non-racial Alcoholics Anonymous as part of its community programme, and delivered Rose by car to the weekly meetings in a church hall. Rose calls the AA euphemistically 'my club' and is no longer sloshed and juggling dishes by the family's dinner-hour every night, but she still goes off every two months or so on a week's blinder. There is nothing to be done about it; the lady of the house—the family, the grown children for whom Rose is the innocence of childhood—can't throw her out on the street. She has nowhere to go. If dismissed, what kind of reference can be given her? One can't perjure oneself on the most important of the three requirements of prospective employers: honesty, industry, sobriety.

Over the years, Ephraim has been drawn into discussions about Rose's drinking. Of course, if anyone is able to help her, it should be he, her lover. Though to talk of those two as lovers . . . The men always must have a woman, the women always seem to find a man; if it's not one, then another will do. The lady of the house is the authority who has gone out to the yard from time to time to speak to Ephraim. The man of the house has no time or tact for domestic matters.

Ephraim, what are we going to do about Rose?

I know, madam.

Can't you get her to stop? Can't you see to it that she doesn't keep any of the stuff in the room?

(It is a small room; with two large people living there, Rose and Ephraim, there can't be much space left to hide brandy and beer bottles.)

But she goes round the corner.

(Of course. Shebeens in every lane.)

So what can we do, Ephraim? Can't you talk to her?

What I can do? I talk. Myself, I'm not drinking. The madam ever see me I'm drunk?

I know, Ephraim.

And now Ephraim is dead, they say, and Rose is weeping and gasping in the laundry. The lady of the house does not know whether Rose was in the laundry when one of Ephraim's brothers (as Rose says, meaning his fellow workers) from Cerberus Security Guards came with the news, or whether the laundry, that dank place of greasy slivers of soap, wire coat hangers and cobwebs, was her place to run to, as everyone has a place in which the package of misery is to be unpacked alone, after it is delivered. Rose sits on an upturned bucket and the water from her eyes and nose makes papier mâché heads, in her fist, out of the Floral Bouquet paper handkerchiefs she helps herself to (after such a long service, one can't call it stealing) in the lady of the house's bathroom. Ephraim has been dead a week, although the news comes only now. He went home last week on leave to his village near Umzimkulu. The bus in which he was travelling overturned and he was among those killed. His bicycle, a chain and padlock on the back wheel, is there where he stored it safely against his return, propped beside the washing machine with its murky submarine eye.

It is a delicate matter to know how to deal with Rose. The ordinarily humane thing to do—tell her not to come back into the house to prepare dinner, take off a few days, recover from the shock—is not the humane thing to do, for her. Under that bed of hers on its brick stilts there quickly will be a crate of bottles supplied by willing 'friends'; it is quite natural that someone with her history will turn to drink. So the lady of the house makes a pot of tea and gently calls Rose to their only common ground, the kitchen, and sits with her a while, drinking tea with her on this rare occasion, just as she will go to visit a friend she hasn't seen for years, if he is dying, or will put in a duty appearance at a wedding in some branch of kin from which she has distanced herself in social status, tastes and interests.

Flesh and tears seem to fuse naturally on Rose's face; it is a sight that causes the face itself to be seen afresh, dissolved of so long a familiarity, here in the kitchen, drunk and sober, cooking a leg of lamb as only she can, or grovelling awfully, little plaited horns of dull hair sticking out under the respectability of her maid's cap fallen askew as she so far forgets herself, in embarrassing alcoholic remorse, to try to kiss the hand of the lady of the house. That face—Rose's face—has changed, the lady of the house notices, just as she daily examines the ageing of her own. The fat smooth brown cheeks have resting upon them beneath the eyes two hollowed stains, the colour of a banana skin gone bad. The drinking has stored its poison there, its fatigue and useless repentance. The body is what the sea recently has been discovered to be: an entity into which no abuse can be thrown away, only cast up again.

Rose doesn't ask, what's for dinner?—not tonight. She is scrubbing potatoes, she has taken the T-bone steaks out of the refrigerator, as if this provides a ritual in place of mourning. It is best to leave her to it, the calm of her daily task. The grown children, when they arrive at different intervals later in the afternoon or evening, go one by one back to childhood to put their arms around Rose, this once, again, in the kitchen, and there are tears again from her. They talk about Ephraim, coming home to the backyard early in the morning, just as they were leaving for school, and she actually laughs, a spluttery sob, saying: I used to fry for him some bread and eggs in the fat left from your bacon! —A collusion between the children and the servant over something the lady of the house didn't know, or pretended never to have known. The grown children also recall for Rose how one or other of them, riding a motorcycle or driving a car, passed him only the other day, where he singled himself out, waving and calling a greeting from the uniformed corps in the Cerberus Security Guards transport vehicle. The daughter of the house recently happened to enter the head-quarters of a mining corporation, where he was on duty in the glassy foyer with his shabby wolf of a guard dog slumped beside him. She had said, poor thing, put out a hand to stroke it, and Ephraim had expertly jerked the dog away to a safe distance, laughing, while it came to life in a snarl. He's very good with those dogs, Rose says, that dog won't let anyone come near him, *any*one. . .

But it is over. Ephraim has been buried already; it's all over. She has heard about his death only after he has been buried because she is not the one to be informed officially. He has—had, always had—a wife and children there where he came from, where he was going back to, when he was killed. Oh yes. Rose knows about that. The lady of the house, the family, know about that; it was the usual thing, a young man comes to work in a city, he spends his whole life there away from his home because he has to earn money to send home, and so—the family in the house privately reasoned—his home really is the backyard where his town woman lives? As a socio-political concept the life is a paradigm (the grown child who is studying social science knows) of the break-up of families as a result of the migratory labour system. And that system (the one studying political science knows) ensures that blacks function as units of labour instead of living as men, with the right to bring their families to live in town with them.

But Ephraim deluded himself, apparently, that this backyard where he was so much at home was not his home, and Rose, apparently, accepted his delusion. This was not the first time he had gone home to his wife and children of course. Sometimes the family in the house hadn't noticed his absence at all, until he came back. Rose would be cooking up a strange mess, in the kitchen: Ephraim had brought a chunk of some slaughtered beast for her; she nibbled his gift of sugar-cane, spitting out the fibre. Poor old Rose. No wonder she took to drink (yes, the lady of the house had thought of that, privately) made a convenience of by a man who lived on her and sent his earnings to a wife and children. Now the man dies and Rose is nothing. Nobody. The wife buries him, the wife mourns him. Her children get the bicycle; one of his brothers from Cerberus Security Guards comes to take it from the laundry and bandage it in brown paper and string, foraged from the kitchen, for transport by rail to Umzimkulu.

When the bus flung Ephraim out and he rolled down and died in the brilliant sugar-cane field, he was going home because there was trouble over the land. What land? His father's land, his brothers' land, his land. Rose gives a garbled version anyone from that house, where at least two newspapers a day are read, can interpret: the long-service employee of Cerberus Security Guards was to be spokesman for his family in a dispute over ancestral land granted them by their local chief. Boundary lines have been drawn by government surveyors, on one side there has been a new flag run up, new uniforms put on, speeches made—the portion of the local chief's territory that falls on that side is no longer part of South Africa. The portion that remains on the other side now belongs to the South African government and will be sold to white farmers—Ephraim's father's land, his brothers' land, his land. They are to get some compensation—

money, that disappears in school fees and food, not land, that lasts forever.

The lady of the house never does get to hear what happened, now that Ephraim is dead. Rose doesn't say; isn't asked; probably is never told. She appears to get over Ephraim's death very quickly, as these people do, after the first burst of emotion—perhaps it would be better to assume she has to take it philosophically. People whose lives are not easy, poor people, to whom things happen but who don't have the resources to make things happen, don't have the means, either, to extricate themselves from what has happened. Of the remedies of a change of scene, a different job, another man, only the possibility of another man is open to her, and she's no beauty any longer, Rose, even by tolerant black standards. That other remedy—drink—one couldn't say she turns to that, either. Since Ephraim has disappeared from the backyard she drinks neither more nor less. The lady of the house, refurbishing it, thinks of offering an old club armchair to Rose. She asks if there is place in her room, and Rose says, Oh yes! Plenty place.

There is the space that was occupied by Ephraim, his thick spread of legs in khaki drill, his back in braces, his Primus stove and big chromium-fronted radio. Rose spends the whole afternoon cleaning the upholstery with carbon tetrachloride, before getting one of the grown children to help her move the chair across the yard. The lady of the house smiles; there was never any attempt to clean the chair while this was part of the duty of cleaning the house.

On Saturdays, occasionally, all members of the family are home for lunch, as they never are on other days. There is white wine this Saturday, as a treat. Rose has baked a fish dish with a covering of mashed potato corrugated by strokes of a fork and browned crisp along the ridges—it is delicious, the kind of food promoted to luxury class by the everyday norm of cafeterias and fast-food counters. In the middle of the meal, Rose appears in the diningroom. The clump of feet that has preceded her gives away that there is someone behind her, out of sight in the passage. The dark hollows under Rose's eyes are wrinkled up with excitement, she shows off: Look who I've got to see you! Look who is here!

The lady of the house is taking good, indulgent, suspicious stock of her, she knows her so well she can tell at once whether or not she's been at the bottle. No—the lady of the house signals with her eyes to the others—Rose is not drunk. Everyone stops eating. Rose is cajoling, high, in her own language, and gesturing back into the passage, her heavy lifted arm showing a shaking jowl of flesh through the tear in her overall—Rose can never be persuaded to mend anything, like the drinking, there is nothing to be done. . . She loses patience—making a quick, conniving face for the eyes of the family—and goes back into the passage to fetch whoever it is. Heads at table return to plates, hands go out for bread or salt. Wine goes to a mouth. Rose shushes and pushes into the room a little group captured and corralled, bringing with them—a draught from another place and time suddenly blowing through the door—odours that have never been in the house before. Hair ruffles along the small dog's back; one of the grown children quickly and secretly puts a hand on its collar. Smell of wood-smoke, of blankets and clothes stored on mud floors between mud walls that live with the seasons, shedding dust and exuding damp that makes things hatch and sprout; smell of condensed milk, of ashes, of rags saved, of wadded newspapers salvaged, of burning paraffin, of thatch, fowl droppings, leaching red soap, of warm skin and fur, cold earth: the family round the table pause over their meal, its flavour and savour are blown away, the utensils they've been eating with remain in their hands, the presence of a strangeness is out of all proportion to the sight of the black country woman and her children, one close beside her, one on her back. The woman never takes her eyes off Rose, who has set her down there. The baby under the blanket closed over her breast with a giant safety-pin cannot be seen except for a green wool bonnet. Only the small child looks round and round the room; the faces, the table, dishes, glasses, flowers, wine bottle; and seems not to breathe. The dog rumbles and its collar is jerked.

Rose is leaning towards the woman, smiling, hands on the sides of her stomach, and encourages her in their language. She displays her to the assembly caught at table. You know who this is, madam? You don't know? She's from Umzimkulu. It's

Ephraim's wife. (She swoops up the small child, stiff in her hands.) Ephraim's children. Youngest and second youngest. Look—the baby; it's a little girl. —And she giggles, for the woman who won't respond, can't respond to what is being said about her.

The lady of the house has got up from her chair. She's waiting for Rose to stop jabbering so that she can greet the woman. She goes over to her and puts out her hand, but the woman draws her own palms together and claps them faintly, swaying politely on her feet, which are wearing a pair of men's shoes below thick beaded anklets. So the lady of the house puts a hand on the woman's back, on the blanket that holds the lump of baby, and says to Rose, Tell her I'm very glad to meet her.

As if they were children again, the young people at the table recite the ragged mumble of a greeting, smiling, the males half-rising. The man of the house draws his eyebrows together and nods absently.

She's here about the pension, Rose says, they say she can get a pension from Cerberus Security Guards.

She laughs at the daring, or simpleton trust?—she doesn't know. But the heads around the table know about such things. The children have grown up so clever.

The lady of the house has always been spokesman and diplomat: Did she get anything?

Not yet, they didn't give. . . But they'll write a letter, maybe next month, Rose says, and—this time the performance is surely for the benefit of the country woman instead of the family— leans across to the fruit bowl on a side table and twists off a bunch of grapes which she then pokes at the belly of the small child, who is too immobilized by force of impressions to grasp it. Rose encourages him, coyly, in their language, setting him down on his feet.

Rose, says the lady of the house, Give them something to eat, mmh? There's cold meat. . .or if you want to take eggs. . .

Rose says, thank you, mam—procedurally, as if the kitchen were not hers to dispense from, anyway.

The woman has been got in, now there is the manoeuvre of getting her out; she stands as if she would stand for ever, with her baby on her back and her child holding a bunch of grapes that he is afraid to look at, while nobody knows whether to go on eating or wait till Rose takes her away.

The lady of the house is used to making things easy for others: Tell her—thank her for coming to see us.

Rose says something in their language and, after a pause, the woman suddenly begins to speak, turned to Rose but obviously addressing the faces at table through her, through the medium, the mediator of that beer-bloated body, that face ennobled with the bottle's mimesis of the lines and shadings of worldly wisdom. Rose follows with agreeing movements of lips and head, reverberating hum of punctuation. She says: She thanks you. She says goodbye.

Hardly has Rose removed her little troupe when she is back again. Perhaps she remembers the family is eating lunch, has come to ask if they'll want coffee? But no. With exaggerated self-effacement, not looking at anyone else, she asks whether she can talk to the madam a moment?

Now?

Yes, please, now.

The lady of the house follows her into the passage.

Can you borrow me ten rands, please madam.

(This will be an advance on her monthly wages.)

Right away?

Please, mam.

So, interrupting her family meal, the lady of the house goes upstairs and fetches two five rand notes from her purse. She sees Rose, as she comes back down the stairs, waiting in the passage like one of the strangers whose knock at the front door Rose herself will answer but whom she does not let into the living-rooms and keeps standing while she goes to call the lady of the house.

Two fives all right? The lady of the house holds out the notes.

Thank you, thanks very much; Rose pushes the money into her overall pocket, that is ripped away at one corner.

For the bus, Rose says, by way of apology for the urgency. Because she's going back there, now, to that place, Umzimkulu.

Rags and Bones

A woman named Beryl Fels recently picked up an old tin chest in a junk shop. It appeared to contain, as a bonus, some odds and ends of velvet and brocade. When she got it home to her flat she saw that under the material was a different find—letters.

She telephoned friends and had something more amusing to exchange than news of business trips and children's colds. 'What do you do with other people's letters?' 'Take them back'—but that was a stupid answer. Back where? The old man who ran the shop wouldn't know to whom they belonged; these rag-and-bone men wouldn't tell a buyer, ever, where they found the things they scavenged from house sales, pawnshops, and people more in need of money than possessions whose associations they either did not know or no longer cared about.

'Read them. Oh, of course, read them.' The antiquarian dealer and bookseller was at once in character; he was good fun, this permanently young man of forty-five, homosexual and bibliophile. He and Beryl Fels went to the theatre and avant-garde films together, a plausible if inauthentic couple.

'Burn them, I suppose. What else could one do?'—the lying rectitude of a most devious woman, who eavesdropped on her adolescent children's telephone conversations.

'What did you want a tin chest for?'—this from someone who had no leisure to spend Saturday mornings pottering about among bric-à-brac and making trips across town to some special shop where one could buy a particular cheese or discover a good inexpensive wine not easy to get.

Beryl Fels had thought the chest would be the thing to hold

spare keys, fuse-wire, picture hooks. Living without a man, she was efficient as any male about household maintenance, no trouble at all to her, although her hands were creamed and manicured, as perfectly useless-looking as any man with an ideal of femininity could have wished for. She had been looking out for something that would clear from her lovely yellow-wood desk (another Saturday-morning find) a miscellany that didn't belong there.

Some of the letters were banded together, and probably all had been, once. All were addressed to the same name, a woman's, and to a box number in one town, or *poste restante* in other towns and even, she saw, in other countries. She had not thought of the chest as a receptacle for letters. But, of course, if one were to have so many letters to keep! She counted: 307 letters and 9 postcards. And telegrams, many telegrams, some stuffed into their original orange window-envelopes. There is something queer about preserving telegrams. She held them: at once urgent and old, they don't keep. She read one; telegrams are hardly private, the words counted out by a post office clerk under the public eye. It was terse and unsigned, a date, a time, a railway station platform number, a cryptic addition whose message was not very difficult to guess. *Yes yes yes.* A lover's affirmation. What can 307 letters be but love letters? And it seemed that probably the person they belonged to had not put them in the chest—some were wadded as if they had lain pushed behind heavy objects. Someone had found them, perhaps, and tossed them into the tin chest that the woman to whom they had been written didn't own. Beryl Fels saw, as she tipped them all out, that they had been thrown in carelessly in reverse order, the top of the pile was at the bottom of the chest, and there was the very sheet of paper (the old foolscap size) with the instruction that would have met the eye of anyone on opening the drawer or lifting the lid of the place where the letters originally would have been kept. *These letters and documents are to be preserved unread until twenty years after the date of my death, and then are to be presented to an appropriate library or archives.* The signature was the name on the envelopes. The postmarks—the letters were not in chronological order anymore, so one would have to go through the lot to see how long the affair had

lasted—were from the 1940s (which explained why the tele-
gram she'd read gave a railway station platform number rather
than a flight number). If the woman had died, then the em-
bargo was lapsed. If she were still alive, she certainly would
have destroyed her letters rather than let them out of her
hands.

Beryl Fels began to read while she drank her coffee late on
Sunday morning. She did not get out of her dressing-gown or
make her bed or tend her balcony herb garden to the sound of
Mozart or punk rock (she was interested in everything that was a
craze or passion in other people's lives), as she usually did on
Sundays. She had had two invitations to lunch at the homes of
couples, one hetero- the other homosexual, options she had left
open to herself if a preferable third—she was a free agent—did
not turn up, but she did not go out and ate no lunch. At times,
while she read, her heart made itself heard in her ears like a
sound from someone moving about in the flat. The tendons
behind her knees were tense and her long-nailed forefinger
stroked the wings of her nose, which felt warm and greasy. The
woman to whom the letters were written was not merely some
Emma Bovary; the man who wrote them was her confidant and
critic as well as her lover. He wrote most passionately when he
had just had the experience of hearing her praised by people who
did not know he knew her. He wanted terribly to make love to
her, he said, when he saw her up there on the platform giving a
lecture, with her glasses hiding her eyes from everybody. He felt
himself swelling when he saw her name in print. Whole long
letters analysed the behaviour of people who would, he felt, do
this rather than that, express themselves in these words and
gestures rather than those, were 'there' or 'simply *not there*'. It
became clear these were characters in a novel or play: she was a
writer.

And he—he seemed to have been a scientist of some sort,
engaged in research. It was difficult, without having access to her
letters to him, to discover what exactly it was he hoped to
achieve, what it was that he was climbing towards over the years
the letters covered. There was the impression that the specialized

nature of his work was something his mistress did not have the type of intellect or education to follow, despite her brilliance, attested to in every letter, and her success, which was as strong an erotic stimulus as whatever beauty she might have had ('. . .against that field of female cabbages your face was stamped out like a fern'—he strained to be literary, too). But that she was ambitious for him, that she jealously bristled when others received promotions, awards, honours he was in the running for, was plain from the passages in his letters calming her with his more cynical, stoic view of talents and rewards in his field. To her he unburdened himself scatologically of all the malice he felt— *he* and *she* felt—towards those who advanced themselves by means he certainly wouldn't stoop to. She also consoled; he found endearing—and did not deny, since no doubt he knew his worth—her assurances that, whatever small kudos others might pick up on the way, he would get one of the Nobel Prizes one day.

At some stage he did receive some signal honour for his work; as a lover he took what evidently must have been her stern triumphant pride as a new and particularly voluptuous kind of caress between them; and at the same time he was concealing from himself, in order to enjoy the triumph unalloyed, the knowledge that she was not fitted to judge the scale of such achievements or the significance of such honours. This last came out in certain small embarrassed phrases, and half-sentences scored over but not made illegible (as if he couldn't bear to have secrets from her, not even those he was concealing for both of them). The stranger, reading, took up the pathetic cunning of these phrases and half-remarks, whereas between the distinguished man writing them and the distinguished woman to whom they were addressed the grit of doubt would be enveloped in emotion and mutual self-esteem as the lubrication of the eye coats tiny foreign bodies and prevents them from irritating the eyeball.

The distinguished woman schemed to attend the ceremony at which her lover was to be honoured; letters covering the wrangling of a whole month between them first persuaded, finally implored her to give up the idea. 'Even if you could approach Fraser through Ebenstein, how can he not smell a rat?

A bedroom rat, quite frankly, my love. Only members of the Society and their wives will be present. The press, you say! They don't come to things like this. It's not exactly a world-shaking event. They get a handout, perhaps, with the list of awards, afterwards. And since when have you been known as a journalist? Why on earth should you suddenly express great interest in the proceedings of the Society? You'd be recognized at once by someone who's seen your photograph on your books, for God's sake! Someone would start sniffing around for a connection, the reason for your being there. And how could we *not* look at each other? You know it's impossible. You're not just anybody, even if you sometimes want to be.' And in answer to what must have been resentful disappointment: 'There are some things we can't have. As you often say, we have so much; more than other people can even dream of, I'm superstitious to spell it out, not only 'us', our great joy in each other's bodies and friendship, but success and real achievement—certainly you, my darling, I am well aware, quite objectively, you are one of the great names coming. . . If we don't suffer the attrition of farmyard domesticity, then we can't have the sort of public display of participation in each other's achievements married couples have—and most of the time it's all they do have. Why should you want to sit like some faculty wife (like mine, whose husband doesn't want to sleep with her and can't talk to her anymore) wearing an appropriate smile for the occasion, as she does a hat. . . ?'

Again, she must have wanted to dedicate a book to him. He tormentedly regretted he must forgo this. 'No matter how you juggle initials or code-names known only to us, you give away our private world. You acknowledge its existence, to others. Let's keep it as we've managed to do for nearly five years. Separately, we are both people in the public eye; it's the price or the reward, God knows, of what we both happen to be. Let the media scrabble and speculate over that. I know the book is mine; and it is my posterity.'

At five in the afternoon Beryl Fels read the last letter. It was not one of the momentous ones—reflected no crisis—nor was it the type of note, strangled terse with erotic excitement, that immediately preceded planned meetings. He was writing while eating a sandwich at his desk; he was thinking about his damned lecture for the Hong Kong conference; he'd read only five pages (this must refer to some piece of her work she had given him) but could not wait to tell her how moving in a new way and at the same time witty. . .hence the scribble. . .

Beryl Fels stood up. Belches kept rising from her empty stomach. Outlines in the room jumped. Thirteen cigarette stubs—she counted dully—in the ashtray. The dazedness came from the change of focus for her eyes: there were her other 'finds' around her, to establish the equilibrium of her own existence. She gazed at her beautiful yellow-wood desk, subdued in its presence as if, entering into the past of other lives, she had dislodged the order of her own and retrogressed to the shallow-breathing stillness of being caught out—brought back to the angles and polished surfaces of the headmistress's study from blurred fearful pleasures in an overgrown corner of a garden. She put her hands to her nose, the child sniffing the secret odour on the fingers.

Running a bath, making her neglected bed, and choosing one of her silk shirts to wear with trousers provided the routine that accomplished the shift: from the experience of reading the letters to an interpretation of her possession of them appropriate to her well-arranged life. Like the other finds—the desk perfectly at home between balcony door and old Cape lyre-backed chair —this one found its place. It became one of her interests and diversions as a lively personality. A pity the day was Sunday; she could have telephoned the public library to ask if they had any of the woman's books. She could have gone down at once herself, to read up about her. Perhaps the identity of the man was known to people more widely read than she was. If not, the letters might be even more important—a discovery, even a literary sensation, as well as a find. She telephoned her antiquarian friend again and again, but of course he would always be at some party on a Sunday evening; he was asked everywhere. Having overcome an unusual (for her) reluctance to talk to anybody—it just showed how one needs to get out and among people, how quickly solitude takes hold—Beryl Fels impatiently awaited Monday morning.

In the week that followed, she asked the antiquarian friend and the chief librarians at the public library and a university library (both acquaintances) about the woman writer. None of these had heard of her. Each was cautious to say so; each uneasy, in case this pat ignorance should prove to be a professional lapse, the name that of some esoteric but important writers' writer he should have known. But library catalogues revealed not a single book by anyone of the name was on the shelves. Several titles had been at one time catalogued as in the store, the morgue stacks from which books no longer in general demand were taken out for borrowers on special request, but these must have been disposed of in one of the job lots that libraries sell off, now and then.

Determinedly, so good at tracking down things she wanted, Beryl Fels got someone to introduce her to a professor in the science faculty at the most prestigious university. She did not show him her find but jotted down for him all the facts gleaned from the letters that could lead to an identification of the other personality who made up the pair of distinguished lovers. There was no one, no one at all fitting the given period, field of activity (quickly established as geophysics), and country of origin whose work was sufficiently original or important for his name to be remembered. There was certainly no one, in the list of Nobel Prize winners for science, who could have been or could be him—should he still be alive.

The antiquarian dealer said she should keep the letters anyway. 'Beryl darling, for our grandchildren—' He was conducting one of the unruly lunches expected at his table, and timed the laugh, pausing—with a kick-up-the-heels wriggle—not a second too long. 'Even letters written by ordinary people become saleable if you wait fifty years or so. Like old seaside postcards. Laundry lists. Don't I know? How else could I afford to give you all such a good meal? People will collect anything.'

Terminal

'Even the cat buries its dirt; I carry mine around with me.' She thought of saying it aloud many times in the weeks after she came home from the hospital. She did not know if he would decide to laugh—whether they would go so far as to laugh. The only time the existence of such a contraption had ever been mentioned by them before the illness happened was a few years ago, when—exchanging sheets of newspaper as they usually did, lovely weekend mornings in bed—she had been reading some article about unemployment and teen-age prostitutes, and had remarked to him, my God, the job the welfare people found for this girl was in a factory that makes those rubber bag things for people who have to have their stomachs cut out—no wonder she went on the streets, poor little wretch. . .

She remembered that morning, that newspaper, clearly. More and more of their conversation kept coming back. They had drifted to talk about the dreariness of industrialization; how early Marxists had ascribed this to alienation, which would disappear when the means of production were owned by the workers, but the factories of the Soviet Union and China were surely just as dreary as those of the West? And she remembered she had reminded him (they had visited Peking together) that at least the Chinese factory workers had ten-minute breaks for compulsory calisthenics twice a day—and he had said, would you swop that for a tea-break and a fag?

The rubber thing that went past on the assembly belt before the sixteen-year-old future prostitute was remote from the two of them, laughing in bed on a Sunday morning, as the life of any factory worker.

Now the contraption was attached to her own body. It issued from her, from the small wound hidden under her clothing. She had moved from their shared bedroom and he understood without a word. She had been taught at the hospital how to deal with the thing, it was horribly private in a way natural functions were not, since natural functions were—had been—experienced by them both. She was alone with her dirt.

The doctors said the thing would be taken away in time. Six weeks, the first one predicted, not more than three months was what the second one told her. They should have co-ordinated their fairy story. They said that (after six weeks or three months) everything would be reconnected inside her. The wound that was kept open would be sewn up. She would be whole again, repaired, everything would work. She would go back to her teaching at the music school. She could go back there now—why not?—if she wanted to, so long as she didn't tire herself. But she didn't want to, carrying that thing with her. She had to listen to more stories—from encouraging friends—about how wonderfully other people managed, lived perfectly normal lives. Even a member of the British royal family, it was said. She shut them up with the fairy story, saying, but for me it's only for six weeks (or three months), I don't have to manage. He bought her two beautiful caftans, choosing them himself, and so perfectly right for her, just her colours, her style—in her pleasure she forgot (which she knew later was exactly what he hoped) she would be wearing them to cover that thing. She put on one or the other when the friends came to visit, and her outfit was admired, they said she must be malingering, she looked so marvellous. He confirmed to them that she was making good progress.

They had talked, once, early on. They had talked before that, in their lives, in the skein of their mingled lives—but how impersonal it was, really, then! A childish pact, blood-brotherhood; on a par with that endlessly rhetorical question, d'you love me, will you always love me: if either of us were to be incurably ill, neither would let the other suffer, would they? But when it happens—well, it never happens. Not in that silly, dramatic, clear-cut abstraction. Who can say what is 'incurable'?

Who can be sure what suffering is terminal, not worth prolong-
ing in order to survive it? This one had a breast off twenty years
ago, and is still going to the races every week. That one lost his
prostates, can be seen knocking back gin-and-tonics at any
cocktail party, with his third wife.

But just before she went into hospital for the exploratory
operation she found the time and place to reaffirm. 'If it turns
out to be bad, if it gets very bad. . .at any time, you promise
you'll help me out of it. I would do it for you.' He couldn't speak.
She was lying with him in the dark; he nodded so hard the pact
was driven into her shoulder by his chin. The bone hurt her.
Then he made love to her, entering her body in covenant.

After the operation she found the tube leading out of her, the
contraption. They did not talk again; only of cheerful things,
only of getting better. The thing—the wound it issued from,
that, unlike any other wound, couldn't be allowed to close, was
like a contingent love affair concealed in his life or hers whose
weight would tear their integument if admitted. They smiled at
each other at once, every time their eyes met. It couldn't be
borne, after all. There had to be a fairy story. It was told over and
over, every day, in every plan they made for next week or next
month or next year, never blinking an eyelid; in every assumption of continuing daily life neither believed. There were no
words that were not lies. *Did the groceries come. There's been
another hi-jack. Are you all right in that chair. They say the
election's set for Spring. We need new wine-glasses. I should
write letters. Order coffee and matches. Another crisis in the
Middle East. Draw the curtains, the sun's in your eyes. I must
have my hair done, Thursday.* If she took his hand now, it was
only in the lie of immortality. The flesh, therefore, was not real
for them, anymore.

There was only one thing left that could not, by its very
nature, have become a lie. There was only one place where love
could survive: life was betrayed, but the covenant was not with
life.

He drove her to the hairdresser that Thursday afternoon and
when he came to fetch her he told her she looked pretty. She
thanked him awkwardly as a girl with her first compliment.
Beneath it she was overcome—the first strong emotion except

fear and disgust, for many months—by an overwhelming trust in him. That night, alone in the room that was now her bedroom she counted out the hoarded pills and, before she washed them down with plain water, set under the paperweight of her cigarette lighter her note for him. 'Keep your promise. Don't have me revived.'

Ever since she was a child she had understood it as a deep sleep, that's all. Ever since she saw the first bird, lying under a hedge, whose eyes hadn't opened when it was poked with a twig. But one can only be aware of a sleep as one awakens from it, and so one will never be aware of that deep sleep— She had no fear of death but now she had the terror of feeling herself waking from it, herself coming back from what was not death at all, then, could not be. Her eyelids were rosy blinds through which light glowed. She opened them on the glossy walls of a hospital room. There was a hand in hers; his.

A Correspondence Course

Pat Haberman has been alone with Harriet since she divorced Harriet's father. Harriet was five then; too young to be tainted by Haberman's money-grubbing and country-club life—leave that to the children of his second marriage. The maintenance provided for Harriet was always inadequate, but Pat and little Harriet didn't want anything from him, Pat could and did earn their keep, and by the time Harriet was twenty she had her degree and was working on a literacy programme for blacks sponsored by a liberal foundation. Both women do jobs that are more than a way of earning a modest living—Pat (saved, thank god) refers as to a criminal record to the businessmen's dinners, drunken golf-club dances, gymkhanas she left behind with Haberman, and is secretary to the Dean of the Medical School—a fixture there.

Harriet is studying for her Master's by correspondence and has already published a contribution to a symposium on *Literacy and the Media*. She wears German print wrap-around skirts decorated with braid by Xhosa women in a Soweto self-help project, sandals thonged between the toes, and last year cut her shawl of pale brown hair into a permed Afro, so that when she lies soaking in her bath—her mother is amused to see—the hair on her head and her soft pubic hair match.

She is a quiet girl who, her mother is sure, smokes a bit of pot at parties, like all young people today. 'And who are we to talk?' Pat Haberman goes through two packs a day—as she says: just ordinary, lung-destroying tobacco. Once she had a three-year affair with a lawyer who has since left the country, but Harriet was too young at the time to have been aware, and Pat has not decided whether or not to tell her. She is sometimes on the point of doing so: this becomes tempting when she notices that the girl is interested in a new boy. Harriet is probably not as promiscuous as it is customary for her generation to be, but she goes away on paired-off weekend trips and holidays with an often-changing group of friends—the young males leave for military service on the border, or they disappear, fleeing military service. This one or that has skipped; the laconic phrase contains, for all this generation of white South Africans in the know, dumped by their elders with the deadly task of defending a life they haven't chosen for themselves, the singular heritage of their whiteness. Pat and Harriet, mother and daughter, often wonder whether they should not emigrate, too. Harriet has been brought up to realize her life of choices and decent comfort is not shared by the people in whose blackness it is embedded: once protected by them, now threatened. They are all round her; she is not of them. And since she has been adult she has had her place—even if silent—in the ritualistic discussion of what can be done about this by people who have no aptitude for politics but who won't live like Haberman (Harriet, too, thinks of the man who is her father as he was named long ago in the divorce order of Haberman v. Haberman), making money from the blacks and going off to gamble among beauty queens and fellow super-market kings at the casinos which represent progress in poor, neighbouring black 'states'.

She keeps in touch with her friends who have skipped to Canada or Australia; for a year, now, she has even been writing to a political prisoner at home in South Africa. There his letter was, among circulars from film clubs, bills, and aerogrammes with 'And when are you coming over?' scribbled on the back. *Pretoria Central Prison*—this one rubber-stamped, with the prison censor's signature superimposed. Inside was a closely-handwritten sheet of lined paper neatly torn from an exercise book. *Dear Harriet Haberman.* But her eyes dropped to the signature before reading any further. *Roland Carter.* Slowly skimming the letter as her feet felt their own way down the stone path, she went into the garden where Pat was on her knees among boxes of marigold seedlings.

' "Roland Carter" mean anything to you?'

Her mother's nose was running with the effort of bending and digging; she smeared at it with the back of her earth-caked hand. Harriet repeated: 'Roland—Carter.'

Pat sniffed. 'Of course. He got nine years. The journalist from East London.'

'What did he do? He's written to me. . .'

'Give me my hanky out of my pocket. . . Furthering the aims of the African National Congress, something like that. Smuggled in false identity papers. Or was he one of the pamphlet bomb people? No, that was Cape Town. Can't you remember? —Let's see?'

'Was he the one who said in court he had no regrets?'

'That's him—but what does he write to you about?'

Her mother scrambled up, levering herself from the ground by one firmly-planted palm. The two women stood there in their tiny garden, singled out. 'My god! What a nice letter! Harriet?' She drew back and looked at her daughter, a streak of honest mud on the face of one who recognizes the mark of grace on another. They read on. The mother murmured aloud. ' "Your article transported me for more than a whole day. . .I have agreed with you and argued with you. . .some of your conclusions are, forgive me, indefensible. . .so much on my mind that I've decided to take up. . .if you feel you can reply, could you possibly do so next month, as I'm allowed only one letter a month and I'm taking a chance and electing one from you. . ." '

Harriet seemed to read more slowly, or wished to test for herself the business of bringing to life, in her own comprehension, these quotations from Piaget (?) and these shy touches of wit (directed against the writer himself) and sarcasm (directed against the prison warder who would censor the letter). Written in a cell. Sitting on a prison bed. Or did prisoners—white ones, at least—have a table? A window with bars and steel netting (she had seen those, driving past prisons). A heavy door with a warder's spy-hole behind the back bent, writing. 'D'you remember what he looked like?'

Her mother was very confiding. 'Funny enough—I do. You know what a newspaper addict I am. I can see the photograph that was in the papers often during the trial, and then when he was given that ghastly sentence. Nine years. . . A neat, strong—a *sceptical* face. Short nose. A successful face—you know what I mean? He didn't look fanatic. And no beard. Big dark eyes and a brush-cut. More like an athlete. . .one of those pictures of swimmers, after winning a race. Perhaps it *was* taken when he'd been swimming; a photograph dug up somewhere, probably from his family. I wonder how he managed to get hold of your article? Well, I suppose that sort of academic journal could have been in the prison library. But how did he have our address?'

Harriet showed the envelope, forwarded from the journal.

'Well. . .it's really rather nice to think something you wrote has given a breath of life to someone like this in prison, darling? I told you, you expressed yourself very well—'

The girl smiled. 'I've never even read Piaget.'

Her mother had not touched the letter, only read it over Harriet's shoulder. She held muddy hands away from her sides. 'You're going to write to him?' Piaget was dismissed: 'What does that matter.'

Harriet was waving the letter slowly, as if drying the ink on it. 'I suppose I must.'

'Poor young man. You forget they're in there. Read about the sensation in the papers, and then the years go by.' Pat Haberman looked at her hands, at the plastic boxes of marigolds, her nostrils moving at the rind-bitter, weedy scent of them; she recalled what she had been interrupted at, and got back on her knees.

'How could one refuse?' She flattered the Dean goadingly with this assumption of shared courage of one's convictions. She and the Dean often talk in lowered voices between themselves, although no one can hear them in his inner office where he dictates letters, of the problems of their grown-up children as well as the equally confidential problems of personality clashes among the Medical School staff. There was—no doubt, although she wasn't going to bring it up with Harriet—the likelihood that your name would go into some file. They certainly keep a record of anyone who associates him- or herself in any way with a political prisoner. Even if he wrote to one out of the blue. Even if one had never so much as met him before.

There were often appropriate turns in conversation among friends or at friends' houses where she met new people, for her to remark on how wonderfully Roland Carter, already four years inside and five to go, kept his spirit unbroken, his mind lively, could still make jokes—her daughter Harriet exchanged letters with him. This remark would immediately 'place' her and her daughter in respect, for people who had not met them before. Sometimes she added what a pity it was that more people who talked liberalism didn't make the effort to write to political prisoners, show them they still were regarded by some as part of the community. Did people realize that in South Africa common criminals, thieves and forgers, were better treated than prisoners of conscience? Roly Carter (after the first few letters he had begun to sign himself simply 'Roly') would get no remission of sentence for good behaviour.

She read Roland Carter's letters—or rather Harriet read them aloud to her—but of course she didn't read those Harriet wrote back. Not that there could be anything particularly personal in them—Harriet had never met the fellow, he was married anyway (Pat had gone to a newspaper library, where a friend of hers worked, and looked up the file of cuttings on his trial), and her letters, like his, would be read by the prison censor. But Harriet was a grown woman, Pat had always respected her child's privacy; in fact taught her, very young, one never ever read anyone else's letters, even if they were left lying about. Harriet typed her letters to Roland Carter in Pretoria Prison; maybe she sensibly wanted to show the prison authorities that all was open to inspection—no ambiguities concealed by illegible handwriting, her law-abiding motive in the correspondence as clear as the type. Pat supposed the letters she heard being composed—Harriet typed slowly, there were long pauses—were much like the letters that came from prison: two young people with shared interests exchanging views on education in Africa. There could be political implications in the subject, heaven knows, but he seemed to assume—and get away with his assumption—that the names of educationalists would belong to too specialized a field for these to be included on the list of Leftist thinkers likely to be familiar to a prison censor.

While the two women were spending a Sunday morning

writing their Christmas cards, Pat remarked she supposed prisoners would be allowed to receive cards?

Harriet rarely initiated anything, a stillness in her undisturbed by, quiescently agreeable to her mother's suggestions. 'We can try.'

Christmas; another year of prison, beginning behind those walls. She read through the messages printed in the cards she had bought. *Peace and joy on Christmas Day   Good wishes for the festive season and may the New Year bring every happiness*   She leaned back in her chair.

Her mother was working efficiently: cards, address book, sheets of stamps. 'Are you short? Here, take one of these.'

Harriet wrote, without reading the message, her name below it on a card that showed an otter surfacing amid ripples sold to benefit some wild-life protection society. Pat signed too; Harriet must surely have mentioned in one of the letters that she had a mother?

She remembered to buy Piaget in paperback for what she still thought of as a stocking stuffer, although it was more than ten years since Harriet had been young enough to have a stocking.

Pat Haberman likes to work in the garden for an hour when she comes home from work in the afternoons. When the evening newspaper flops through the slot in the gate onto the grass she looks at the headlines while guiding the jet of the hose with her other hand. She feels at this time of day and in this (she knows) frail set of circumstances—the soothing hiss of the water, the nearness of sunset bird-calls and the distance of the traffic breaking beyond the reef of the quiet suburb—a balance. She ventures out to earn her living every day, but no longer is one of those truly out there, driven by adrenalin and sex hormones, surging along, black skins, white skins, inhaling toxic ambitions, the stresses of solving, of becoming—and what? The five-thirty to six-thirty hour is an illusion of peace in middle age just as the innocence of Cape thrush calls and the freshness of leaves spattered by water from the municipal supply is an illusion of undestroyed nature. Yet while she holds the nozzle of the hose against the snaking energy of piped water's pressure, and reads that a diplomat has been kidnapped, that oil has again been ransomed in the holy money war between the arabs and the West, even that leaders of the black workers' walk-out at a steel foundry in this same city are being detained by the police, there is this interlude of feeling herself regarding from a base of the calm and eternal what is feverish and constantly whirling away. Later she will read the paper with the background knowledgeability, the watchfulness, the sense of continuity with statements and struggles of black and white, that reasserts involvement and rescues her from that strange pleasant lapse, dangerous white suburban amnesia.

Harriet is out there; she is not deafened by the music in the discothèques, she is not afraid of becoming addicted to drugs. The crack with which the white personality splits and threatens to dribble its endowment like a drying pomegranate is a long way off for her, and perhaps there won't be time enough left for it ever to happen. When she comes home she is on the telephone, or putting in some work on her thesis, or washing her hair preparatory to going out again, in the manner of young girls.

On an evening like any other, the headline Pat saw at once was not the boldest banner; that had to do with a leap in the price of gold. The particular headline was across a double column on the side of the front page; she read it as she picked up in her wet hand the paper from the grass she had just watered. Three long-term political prisoners had escaped from maximum security in Pretoria Prison. The second name was that of Roland Carter. They had all been locked in their cells as usual at 4 p.m. The warder on night patrol had been fooled by dummy bundles placed in their beds. Their disappearance was discovered only at 7 a.m.; it was possible they had a ten- or twelve-hour start on the countrywide search, border post and airport checks now set up to catch them.

Washing her hair: it was over the basin in the bathroom that Pat found Harriet. The girl looked up to her mother's face wide with the sensation of what she had to tell. In a whisper, shoulders hunched: 'He's out.' Pat drew a slithering breath of glee and hugged the paper. 'He's escaped.'

While Harriet read the report her mother was giggling, shaking her clasped hands, unable to keep still. 'Isn't it great?

Good for them! Marvellous! It shows you, with enough courage, people never give up.' She speculated over the spitting steak in the pan, between stove and kitchen nook where they ate— 'How many hours to Swaziland? But to the Botswana border, they could be there in five. Supposing they broke out by midnight, they could have been across before the dummies had even been discovered.' Harriet was sent to fetch the A.A. map out of the glove-box in Pat's car. *Here's to Roly*—Pat clinked her glass against Harriet's, the girl who had kept his spirits up, faithfully written to him for more than a year. The bottle of wine Pat had opened stood next to the map, and various convenient borders were traced from the central point of Pretoria. The men might be on a plane to Europe by now. From Maputo in Mozambique; from Gaborone in Botswana. If they were making for Europe via Zambia, they probably hadn't arrived in Lusaka yet. The radio was clicked on for the news at nine; there was no news: still at large—free. Free!

'What will they do to him if they catch him?'

The girl's question sounded unfair. 'Oh what has he to lose? I suppose some sort of deprivation, solitary confinement. He had nearly four years in there still ahead of him anyway.'

The girl depended on her mother, so well-informed about the strategies of prisoners on the run and their pursuers. 'The police wouldn't shoot them?'

Her mother bunched her mouth, frowning, shaking her head in total reassurance of the absurdity of the idea as she had done when withholding from the child something unpleasant she surely didn't need to know. The thought, *only if they were to resist capture*, was transformed: 'They'd go back where they were, that's all. . .'

Pat appeared at seven in the morning, when the first newscast of the day was broadcast, gliding into her daughter's room with the transistor nursed beside her ear. The curtains were still drawn. Harriet opened her eyes and lay on her back, obedient but not awake. Pat raised her eyebrows high and held up her free hand to stay any distraction when the radio voice referred to the jail-breakers. On the second day a warder was taken into custody on a charge of aiding and abetting. 'Naturally—without help from inside how could they have got out of maximum security?

And there must have been brilliant contingency planning—'
'What's that?'
'People outside ready, for weeks or even months, maybe, to act at a given signal exactly as decided upon. Cars, a hideout, money—maybe they've even split up, for safety—'
Harriet slowly came to, out of that deep, helpless morning sleep of the young, who are never tired at night. 'Not his family.'
'No-o! Good lord, no. He wouldn't dare get in touch with *them*.'
'Who?'
'I don't know—associates; it'll be all set up. People they can trust. Maybe from abroad. Somebody could have been brought into the country specially. . . ?'
After a week, the three escapers were still at large. At first the radio repeated the same news: that they were believed to be heading for a neighbouring country. Then no mention of them was made at all. The newspapers rephrased the little information the police had released; the authorities in the traditional neighbouring countries of political refuge denied the men had entered their territories. The warder appeared in court, was charged and remanded. There were rumours that one or other of the three had been seen in Gaborone, Lusaka or Maputo. 'Refugee circles' and exiled political organizations in London were 'jubilant' but would make no statement until the men were safely out of Africa. 'One of them's the young man Harriet used to write to, Roland Carter, you know.'
The Dean had heard about that correspondence often enough. 'I shouldn't be too eager to spread that piece of information, if I were you, Pat. The next thing, you'll have the police coming round.'
She tugged smilingly at her ear-ring; at his lily-liveredness. 'They've read all the letters. She's got nothing to hide. They're welcome.'
But the police didn't come; and still the men were not captured. Pat and Harriet Haberman did not know enough about Roland Carter to keep talking of him at every meal they shared. Pat had asked Harriet whether there was ever any kind of inkling, anything at all in the letters that suggested he

might. . . ? Nothing explicit, of course, but one of those oblique chance remarks one sometimes lets slip, could let slip, even in a letter that was going to be read by a prison censor? But Harriet said there was nothing she could think of; nothing. 'You read the letters, Mum.'

It was so. Yet, pulling up the petunias and marigolds she grew for summer and digging over the earth in preparation for daffodils and freesias, she heard or mouthed phrases from the letters. People of the same generation understand things differently from the way they are understood by one of another generation. Turns of phrase. Vocabulary—words change meanings (take the adjective 'gay'. . .). The phrases presented themselves to her from somewhere. As she dug and then forked and raked, hearing a sizzling in her ears, closer than the bird-calls, from the dizzying effort, sometimes she had the feeling that *he* was thinking of her rather than she of him—although he didn't know her, it was not to her he had written. She most likely never had been mentioned; if he had not been allowed to receive the Christmas card that time, he might not know she existed. Somewhere: out there in the distant traffic, the traffic of the world, their prisoner—hers and Harriet's—*he* existed as another being who was no longer a prisoner. He suffered, perhaps. He hid. He was hungry; and hunted. Literally: they used dogs with faithful names like *Wagter, †Boetie, who attacked on command. He prowled in those swamps of the cities, the Hillbrow bars where everybody was immigrant and an unrecognized stranger, the drinking places of blacks in urine-smelling lanes where nameless whites could buy pot, or he yanked again and again at the handle of a fruit machine, bullying luck, one among the crowds in their uniform of humorous T-shirts in a casino across the border, his danger ticking for him, a parcel-bomb left in a gold plastic bag of exactly the type their women carried. The grip on the commonplace and eternal she took with this earth that she handled, lost its meaning. It was only dirt her hands were coated in, as a black servant's hands are coated with white gloves when he waits at table in certain pretentious houses (Haberman's). Somewhere out there beyond her garden a suburban burglar

* Watchman   † Brother

alarm went Wagnerian and there was the flying wail of ambulances and police cars. The bulbs she had saved from last year were going to be buried in this cloying, suffocating earth and would live again; but when a human being is at last shut in it she will never break out.

She had begun to check the doors and windows before switching off her bedroom light at night. She held breath, moving in Harriet's room, but the girl did not ever know she was there. She bolted the gate, which they never bothered to do, and since she was sure to be awake first in the mornings, could unbolt it again before her daughter got up. Once Harriet complained her room was stuffy; she had found her window shut. Yes, her mother thought she'd heard something—that old tom cat who used to jump in and had once pissed against Harriet's dressing-gown— so she had got up in the night to close it. They laughed a little at the reminder of the dreadful cat.

'With the window shut, the smell still comes back.'

'I'm sorry, darling. I'll shampoo that bit of carpet again.'

If Harriet noticed that all doors and windows were locked now, she said nothing. One early morning when Pat went across the lawn in pyjamas to slide back the bolt the morning paper was not on the grass—must have fallen backwards through the slot. She opened the gate. The paper was there outside, on the pavement; as she bent for it her eyes were on a level with a bundle that had been left half-concealed (if you were to have been upright, chances were you would have missed it) by the jasmine that incorporated in its thicket an old wire fence between the garden and a lane that divided their cottage from the next property. Placed, not left. The unisex clothing in a tramp's bundle was Harriet's jeans, the too-big pair she hardly wore, the Mykonos fisherman's sweater from her trip, the men's thick socks young girls had a fad to wear with clogs. In just this way she had put out milk for the fairies (or stray cats?) when she was a little girl. She had believed in the Easter bunny when on Easter morning she found chocolate eggs hidden like this. . . The paper Pat held carried a report from reliable sources that the Russians had planned and executed the prison-break and the three political prisoners were believed to be already in Moscow.

Whether Harriet had taken the offering back in again herself, or whether one of the white tramps or black out-of-works who frequented the lane had had a windfall, the bundle was not there two days later. Pat said nothing. Just as long ago, she didn't want to make the child feel foolish.

On the evening a man appeared at the open kitchen door, Harriet did not know who it was but Pat Haberman recognized him instantly. Hiccups of fear loosed inside her. They were uncontrollable but her body stood there and barred what was beyond the limit, more than could be expected or asked. He saw she knew him; drew down a smile in acknowledgement of the claim he represented, and said, You are alone?

And at that, Harriet stood up calmly as if she had heard her name called; and went to close the door behind him.

Liquid flashes like the sweeps of heat that had gone through her blood at fifty took Pat to her bedroom. She locked that door, wanted to beat upon it, whimper. She went and sat on her bed, hands clamped together between her thighs. The walls that closed her in were observing her. She tried not to hear the voices that came through them; even a subdued laugh. She stood up and paced out the room with the hesitancy of anguish. To do something with her hands she filled a tooth-glass at the wash-hand basin and, a prisoner tending his one sprig of green, gave water to the pot of African violets for what she had done, done to her darling girl, *done for.*

Something Out There

Stanley Dobrow, using the Canonball Sure-
shot, one of three cameras he was given for his barmitzvah,
photographed it. He did. *I promise you*, he said—as children
adjure integrity by pledging to the future something that has
already happened. His friends Hilton and Sharon also saw it:
Stanley jacked himself from the pool, ran through the house
leaving wet footprints all the way up the new stair carpet, and
fetched the Canonball Sureshot.

The thrashing together of two tree-tops—that was all that
came out.

When other people claimed to have seen it—or another one
like it: there were reports from other suburbs, quite far away—
and someone's beautiful Persian tabby and someone else's
fourteen-year-old dachshund were found mauled and dead,
Stanley's father believed him and phoned a newspaper to report
his son's witness. *Predator At Large In Plush Suburbs* was the
headline tried out by a university graduate newly hired as a
sub-editor; the chief sub thought 'predator' an upstage word for
a mass-circulation Sunday paper and substituted 'wild animal',
adding a question mark at the end of the line. The report claimed
a thirteen-year-old schoolboy had been the first to see the
creature, and had attempted to photograph it. Stanley's name,
which had lost a syllable when his great-grandfather Leib
Dobrowsky landed from Lithuania in 1920, was misspelt as
'Dobrov'. His mother carefully corrected this in the cuttings she
sent to her mother-in-law, a cousin abroad, and to the collateral
family who had given the camera. People telephoned: I believe
your Stan was in the paper! *What* was it he saw?

A vet said the teeth-marks on the dead pets, Mrs Sheena McLeod's 'Natasha' and the Bezuidenhout family's beloved 'Fritzie', were consistent with the type of bite given by a wild cat. Less than a hundred years ago, *viverra civetta* must have been a common species in the koppies around the city; nature sometimes came back, forgot time and survived eight-lane freeways, returning to ancestral haunts. He recalled the suicidal swim of two elephants who struck out making for ancient mating grounds across Lake Kariba, beneath which 5,000 square kilometres of their old ruminants' pathways were drowned in a man-made sea. A former pet-shop owner wrote to *Readers' Views* with the opinion that the animal almost certainly was a vervet monkey, an escaped pet. Those who had seen it insisted it was a larger species, though most likely of the ape family. Stanley Dobrow and his two friends described the face reflected between trees, beside them on the surface of the swimming pool: dark face with 'far-back' eyes—whether what broke the image was Stanley's scramble from the water or the advance of the caterpillar device that crawled about the pool sucking up dirt, they never agreed.

Whatever it was, it made a nice change from the usual sort of news, these days. Nothing but strikes, exchanges of insults between factions of what used to be a power to be relied upon, disputes over boundaries that had been supposed to divide peace and prosperity between all, rioting students, farmers dissatisfied with low prices, consumers paying more for bread and mealie-meal, more insults—these coming in the form of boycotts and censures from abroad, beyond the fished-out territorial waters. It was said the local fishing industry was ruined by poaching Russians (same old bad news).

Now this event that was causing excitement over in the Johannesburg suburbs: that was the kind of item there used to be—before the papers started calling blacks 'Mr' and publishing the terrible things Communists taught them to say about the white man. Those good old stories of giant pumpkins and—Mrs Naas Klopper remembered it so well—when she was a little child, that lion that lived with a little fox terrier in its cage at the

Jo'burg zoo; this monkey or whatever it was gave you something to wonder about again, talk about; it had something to do with your own life, it could happen to you (imagine! what a scare, to see a thing like that, some creature jumping out in your own yard), not like all that other stuff, that happened somewhere else, somewhere you'd never seen and never would, the United Nations there in New York, or the blacks' places—Soweto.

Mrs Naas Klopper (she always called herself, although her name was Hester) read in *Die Transvaaler* about the creature in the Johannesburg suburbs while waiting for the rice to boil in time for lunch. She sat in the split-level lounge of what she was always quietly aware of as her 'lovely home' Naas had built according to her artistic ideas when first he began to make money out of his agency for the sale of farmland and agricultural plots, fifteen years ago. Set on several acres outside a satellite country town where Klopper's Eiendoms Beperk flourished, the house had all the features of prosperous suburban houses in Johannesburg or Pretoria. The rice was boiling in an all-electric kitchen with eye-level microwave oven and cabinet deep-freezer. The bedrooms were *en suite*, with pot-plants in the respectively pink and green bathrooms. The livingroom in which she sat on a nylon velvet-covered sofa had pastel plastic Venetian blinds as well as net curtains and matching nylon velvet drapes, and the twelve chairs in the dining area were covered with needlepoint worked in a design of shepherdesses and courtiers by Mrs Naas Klopper herself; the dried-flower-and-shell pictures were also her work, she had crocheted the tasselled slings by which plants were suspended above the cane furniture on the glassed sun-porch, and it was on a trip to the Victoria Falls, when Rhodesia was still Rhodesia, that she had bought the hammered copper plaques. The TV set was behind a carved console door. Stools set around the mini bar again bore the original touch—they were covered not exactly with modish zebra skin, but with the skins of Impala which Naas himself had shot. Outside, there was a palette-shaped swimming pool like the one in which Stanley and friends, forty kilometres away in Johannesburg, had seen the face.

Yet although the lovely home was every brick as good as any

modern lovely home in the city, it had something of the enclosing gloom of the farmhouse in which Naas had spent his childhood. He never brought that childhood to the light of reminiscence or reflection because he had put all behind him; he was on the other side of the divide history had opened between the farmer and the trader, the past when the Boers were a rural people and the *uitlanders* ran commerce, and the present, when the Afrikaners governed an industrialized state and had become entrepreneurs, stockbrokers, beer millionaires—all the synonyms for traders. When he began to plan the walls to house his wife's artistic ideas, a conception of dimness, long gaunt passages by which he had been contained at his Ma's place, and his Ouma's, loomed its proportions around the ideas. He met Mrs Naas now in the dark bare passage that led to the kitchen, on her way to drain the rice. They never used the front door, except for visitors; it seemed there were visitors: Ag, Hester, can you quickly make some coffee or tea?

—I'm just getting lunch! It's all ready.—

There was something unnatural, assumed, about him that she had long associated with him 'doing business'. He did not have time to doff the manner for her, as a man will throw down his hat as he comes into the kitchen from his car in the yard. —All right. Who is it, then?—

—Some people about the Kleynhans place. They're in the car, so long. A young couple. Unlock the front door.—

—Why'd you say tea?—

—They speak English.—

A good businessman thinks of everything; his wife smiled. And a good home-maker is always prepared. Her arched step in high-heeled shoes went to slide the bolt on the Spanish-style hand-carved door; while her husband flushed the lavatory and went out again through the kitchen, she took down her cake tins filled with rusks and home-made glazed biscuits to suit all tastes, English and other. The kettle was on and the cups set out on a cross-stitched traycloth before she sensed a press of bodies through the front entrance. She kept no servant in the house— had the gardener's wife in to clean three times a week, and the washwoman worked outside in the laundry—and could always feel at once, even if no sound were made, when the pine aerosol-fresh space in her lovely home was displaced by any body other than her own.

Naas's voice, speaking English the way we Afrikaners do (she thought of it), making it a softer, kinder language than it is, was the one she could make out, coming from the lounge. When he paused, perhaps they were merely smiling in the gap; were shy.

A young man got up to take the tray from her the moment she appeared; yes, silent, clumsy, polite—nicely brought-up. The introductions were a bit confused, Naas didn't seem sure he had the name right, and she, Mrs Naas, had to say in *her* English, comfortable and friendly—turning to the young woman: —What was your name, again?— And the young man answered for his wife. —She's Anna.—

Mrs Naas laughed. —Yes, Anna, that's a good Afrikaans name, too, you know. But the other name?—

—I'm Charles Rosser.— He was looking anxiously for a place to set down the tray. Mrs Naas guided him to one of her coffee tables, moving a vase of flowers.

—Now is it with milk and sugar, Mrs Rosser? I've got lemon here, too, our own lemons from the garden.—

The young woman didn't expect to be waited on: really well-brought-up people. She was already there, standing to help serve the men; tall, my, and how thin! You could see her hip-bones through her crinkly cotton skirt, one of those Indian skirts all the girls go around in nowadays. She wore glasses. A long thin nose spoilt her face, otherwise quite nice-looking, nothing on it but a bit of blue on the eyelids, and the forehead tugged tight by flat blonde hair twisted into a knob.

—It's tiring work all right, looking for accommodation.— (Naas knew all the estate agent's words, in English, he hardly ever was caught out saying 'house' when a more professional term existed.)—Thirsty work.—

The young man checked the long draught he was taking from his cup. He smiled to Mrs Naas. —This is very welcome.—

—Oh only a pleasure. I know when I go to town to shop—I can tell you, I come home and I'm finished! That's why we built out here, you know; I said to my husband, it's going to be nothing but more cars, cars, and more motor-bikes—

—And she's talking of fifteen years ago! Now it's a madhouse,

Friday and Saturday, all the Bantu buses coming into town from the location, the papers and beer cans thrown every-where—(Naas offered rusks and biscuits again)—that's why you're wise to look for somewhere a bit out—not far out, mind you, the wife needs to be able to come in to go to the supermarket and that, you don't want to feel *cut off*—

—I must say, I never feel cut off!—his wife enjoyed support-ing him.—I've got my peace and quiet, and there's always something to do with my hands.—

Naas spoke as if he had not already told her:—We're going to look over the Kleynhans place.—

—Oh, I thought you've come from there!—

—We going now-now. I just thought, why pass by the house, let's at least have a cup of tea. . .—

—Is there anybody there?—

—Just the boy who looks after the garden and so on.—

When they spoke English together it seemed to them to come out like the dialogue from a television series. And the young couple sat mute, as the Klopper grandchildren did before the console when they came to spend a night.

—Can I fill up?— Standing beside her with his cup the young man reminded her not of Dawie who had Naas's brown eyes, didn't take after her side of the family at all, but of Herman, her sister Miemie's son. The same glistening, young blond beard, so manly it seemed growing like a plant while you looked at it. The short pink nose. Even the lips, pink and sun-cracked as a kid's.

—Come on! Have some more biscuits—please help your-self. . . And Mrs Rosser?—*please*—there's another whole tin in the kitchen. . . I forget there's no children in the house any-more, I bake too much every time.—

She was shy, that girl; at last a smile out of her.

—Thanks, I'll have a rusk.—

—Well I'm glad you enjoy my rusks, an old, old family recipe. —Oh you'll like the Kleynhans place. I always liked it, didn't I, Naas—I often say to my husband, that's the kind of place we ought to have. I've got a lovely home here, of course I wouldn't really change it, but it's so big, now, too big for two people. A lot of work; I do it all myself, I don't want anyone in my place, I don't want all that business of having to lock up my sugar and

123

tea—no, I'll rather do everything myself. I can't stand to feel one of them there at my back all the time.—

—But there's nothing to be afraid of in this area.— Naas did not look at her but corrected her drift at a touch of the invisible signals of long familiarity.

—Oh no, this's a safe place to live. I'm alone all day, only the dog in the yard, and she's so old now—did she even wake up and come round the front when you came?—ag, poor old Ounooi! It's safe here, not like the *other* side of the town, near the location. You can't even keep your garden hose there, even the fence around your house—they'll come and take everything. But this side. . .no one will worry you.—

Perhaps the young man was not quite reassured.—How far away would the nearest neighbours be?—

—No, not far. There's Reynecke about three or four kilometres, the other side of the koppie—there's a nice little koppie, a bit of real veld, you know, on the southern border of the property.—

—And the other sides? Facing the house?— The young man looked over to his wife, whose feet were together under her long skirt, cup neatly balanced on her lap, and eyes on cup, inattentive; then he smiled to Mr and Mrs Naas. —We don't want to live in the country and at the same time be disturbed by neighbours' noise.—

Naas laughed and put a hand on each knee, thrusting his head forward amiably; over the years he had developed gestures that marked each stage in the conclusion of a land deal, as each clause goes to comprise a contract.

—You won't hear nothing but the birds.—

On a Thursday afternoon Doctors Milton Caro, pathologist, Grahame Fraser-Smith, maxillo-facial surgeon, Arthur Methus, gynaecologist, and Dolf van Gelder, orthopaedic surgeon, had an encounter on Houghton Golf Course. Doctors Caro, Fraser-Smith, Methus and van Gelder are all distinguished specialists in their fields, with degrees from universities abroad as well as at home, and they are not available to the sick at all hours and on all days, like any general practitioner. In fact, since so many of the younger medical specialists have emigrated to take up appointments in safer countries—America, Canada, Australia—patients sometimes have the embarrassment of having recovered spontaneously before arriving for appointments that have to be booked a minimum of three months ahead. Others may have died; in which case, the ruling by the Medical Association that appointments not kept will be charged for, is waived.

The doctors do not consult on Thursday afternoons. The foursome, long-standing members of the Houghton Club, has an almost equally long-standing arrangement to tee off at 2 p.m. (Caro and van Gelder also take long walks together, carrying stout sticks, on Sunday mornings. Van Gelder would like to make jogging a punishable offence, like drunken driving. He sees too many cases of attributable Achilles tendonitis, of chondromalacia patellae caused by repetitive gliding of the patella over the femur, and, of course, of chronic strain of the ligaments, particularly in flat-footed patients.) On this particular afternoon Fraser-Smith and van Gelder were a strong partnership, and Methus was letting Caro down rather badly. It is this phenomenon of an erratic handicap that provides the pleasure mutually generated by the company. The style of their communication is banter; without error, there would be nothing to banter about. This Thursday the supreme opportunity arose because it was not Methus, in his ham-handed phase, who sent a ball way off into a grove of trees, but Fraser-Smith, who on the previous hole had scored an eagle. Van Gelder groaned, Fraser-Smith cursed himself in an amazement that heightened Caro's and Methus's mock glee. And then Caro, who had marked where the ball fell into shade, went good-naturedly with Fraser-Smith, who was short-sighted, over to the trees. Fraser-Smith, still cursing amiably, moved into the grove where Caro directed.

—Which side of the bush? Here? I'll never find the sodding thing.— At Guy's Hospital thirty years before he had picked up the panache of British cuss-words he never allowed himself to forget.

Caro, despite the Mayo Clinic and distinguished participation at international congresses on forensic medicine, called back in the gruff, slow homeliness of a Jewish country storekeeper's son whose early schooling was in Afrikaans. —Ag, man, d'you want me to come and bleddy well hit it for you? It must be just on the left there, man!—

Exactly where the two men were gazing, someone—something that must have been crouching—rose, a shape broken by the shapes of trees; there was an instant when they, it, were aware of one another. And then whoever or whatever it was was gone, in a soft crashing confusion among branches and bushes. Caro shouted—ridiculously, he was the first to admit—Hey! Hey!

—Well (they were embellishing their story at the clubhouse) I thought he'd pinched old Grahame's ball, and I wanted to say thanks very much, because Methus and I, we were playing like a pair of clowns, we needed some monkey-business to help us out. . .—

Fraser-Smith was sure the creature had gone up a tree, although when the foursome went to look where he thought it had climbed, there was nothing. Methus said if it hadn't been for all the newspaper tales they'd been reading, none of them would have got the mad idea it was anything but a man—one of the black out-of-works, the *dronkies* who have their drinking sessions in there; wasn't it true they were a problem for the groundsmen, no fence seemed to keep them and their litter out? There were the usual empty beer cans under the tree where Fraser-Smith said he. . . —Anyway, the papers talked about a monkey, and we all saw—this was something big. . .a black, that's all, and he got a scare. . .you know how you can't make out a black face in shadow, among leaves.—

Caro spoke aside: —A black having a crap, exactly. . .—

But van Gelder was certain. No one had seen, in the moment the being had looked at the foursome, and the foursome had looked at it, a face, distinct garments, limbs. Van Gelder had observed the gait, and in gait van Gelder read bones. —It was not a monkey. It was not a man. That was a baboon.—

The couple didn't have much to say for themselves, that day while Naas Klopper was showing them over the Kleynhans place. In his experience this was a bad sign. Clients who took an instant liking to a property always thought they were being shrewd by concealing their keenness to buy under voluble fault-picking calculated to bring down the price. They would pounce on disadvantages in every feature of aspect and construction. This meant the deed of sale was as good as signed. Those who said nothing were the ones who had taken an instant dislike to a property, or—as if they could read his mind, because, hell man, he was an old hand at the game, he never let slip a thing—uncannily understood at once that it was a bad buy. When people trailed around in silence behind him he filled that silence entirely by himself, every step and second of it, slapping with the flat of a hand the pump of whose specifications, volume of water per hour etcetera he spared no detail, opening stuck cupboard doors and scratching a white-ridged thumb-nail down painted walls to the accompaniment of patter about storage space and spotless condition; and all the time he was wanting just to turn round and herd right out the front door people who were wasting his time.

But this girl didn't have the averted face of the wives who had made up their minds they wouldn't let their husbands buy. Naas knows what interests the ladies. They don't notice if guttering is rotted or electrical wiring is old and unsafe. What they care about is fitted kitchen units and whether the new suite will look right in what will be the lounge. When he pointed out the glassed-in stoep that would make a nice room for sewing and that, or a kiddies' playroom (but I don't suppose you've got any youngsters? —not yet, ay) she stood looking over it obediently through her big round glasses as if taking instructions. And the lounge, a bit original (two small rooms of the old farmhouse from the '20s knocked into one) with half the ceiling patterned pressed lead and the other 'modernized' with pine strips and an ox-wagon wheel adapted as a chandelier—she smiled, showing beautiful teeth, and nodded slowly all round the room, turning on her heel.

Same thing outside, with the husband. He was interested in the outhouses, of course. Nice double shed, could garage two cars—full of junk, naturally, when a place's been empty, only a boy in charge—Kleynhans's old boy, and his hundred-and-one hangers-on, wife, children, whatnot. . . —But we'll get that all cleaned up for you, no problem.— Naas shouted for the boy, but the outhouse where he'd been allowed to live was closed, an old padlock on the door. —He's gone off somewhere. Never here whenever I come, that's how he looks after the place. Well—I wanted to show you the room but I suppose it doesn't matter, the usual boy's room. . .p'raps you won't want to have anybody, like Mrs Klopper, you'll rather do for yourselves? Specially as you from overseas, ay. . .—

The young husband asked how big the room was, and whether, since the shed was open, there was no other closed storage room.

—Oh, like I said, just the usual boy's room, not *very* small, no. But you can easy brick in the shed if you want, I can send you good boys for building, it won't cost a lot. And there's those houses for pigs, at one time Kleynhans was keeping pigs. Clean them up—no problem. But man, I'm sure if you been doing a bit of farming in England you good with your hands, ay? You used to repairs and that? Of course. And here it doesn't cost much to get someone in to help. . . . You know (he cocked his head coyly) you and your wife, you don't sound like the English from England usually speak. . . ? You sound more like the English here.—

The wife looked at the husband and this time she was the one to answer at once, for him. —Well, no. Because, you see—we're really Australian. Australians speak English quite a lot like South Africans.—

The husband added—We've been *living* in England, that's all.—

—Well, I thought so. I thought, well, if they English, it's from some part where I never heard the people speak!— Naas felt, in a blush of confidence, he was getting on well with this couple. —Australian, that's good. A good country. A lot like ours. Only without our problems, ay—(Naas allowed himself to pause and shake his head, exclaim, although it was a rule never to talk politics with clients.) —There's a lot of exchange between sheep farmers in Australia and here in South Africa. Last year I think it was, my brother-in-law had some Australian farmers come to see him at his place in the Karoo—that's our best sheep country.

He even ordered a ram from them. Six thousand Australian dollars! A lot of money, ay? Oh but what an animal. You should see—bee-yeu-tiful.—

In the house, neither husband nor wife remarked that the porcelain lid of the lavatory cistern was broken, and Naas generously drew their attention to it himself. —I'll get you a new one cheap. Jewish chappies I know who run plumbing supplies, they'll always do me a favour. Anything you want in that line, you just tell me.—

In the garden, finally (Naas never let clients linger in a garden before entering a house on a property that had been empty a long time—a neglected garden puts people off), he sensed a heightened interest alerting the young couple. They walked round the walls of the house, shading their eyes to look at the view from all sides, while Naas tried to prop up a fallen arch of the wire pergola left from the days when Mrs Kleynhans was still alive. To tell the truth the view wasn't much. Apart from the koppie behind the house, just bare veld with black, burned patches, now, before the rains. Old Kleynhans liked to live isolated on this dreary bit of land, the last years he hadn't even let out the hundred acres of his plot to the Portuguese vegetable farmers, as he used to. As for the garden—nothing left, the blacks had broken the fruit trees for firewood, a plaster Snow White had fallen into the dry fishpond. It was difficult to find some feature of interest or beauty to comment on as he stood beside the couple after their round of the house, looking across the veld. He pointed. —Those things over there, way over there. That's the cooling towers of the power station.— They followed his arm politely.

Of course, he should have suspected something. Unlikely that you could at last get rid of the Kleynhans place so easily. When they were back in town in Klopper's Eiendoms Beperk and Juffrou Jansens had brought the necessary documents into his office, it turned out that they wanted to rent the place for six months, with the option of purchase. They didn't want to buy outright. He knew it must be because they didn't have the money, but they wouldn't admit that. The husband brushed aside suggestions that a bond could be arranged on a very small deposit, Naas Klopper was an expert in these matters.

—You see, my wife is expecting a child, we want to be in the

country for a while. But we're not sure if we're going to
settle. . .—

Naas became warmly fatherly. —But if you starting a family,
that's the time to settle! You can run chickens there, man, start
up the pigs again. Or hire out the land for someone else to work.
In six months' time, who knows what's going to happen to land
prices? Now it's rock-bottom, man. I'll get you a ninety-per-
cent bond.—

The girl looked impatient; it must have been embarrassment.

—She—my wife—she's had several miscarriages. A lot depends on that. . .if this time there's a child, we can make up our
minds whether we want to farm here or not. If something goes
wrong again. . .she might want to go back.—

—To Australia.— The girl spoke without looking at the men.

The Kleynhans place had been on Klopper's Eiendoms Beperk's books for nearly three years. And it seemed true what the
husband said, they had money. They paid six months' rent in
advance. So there was nothing to lose, so far as Mathilda Beukes,
née Kleynhans, who had inherited the place, was concerned.
Naas took their cheque. They didn't even want the place cleaned
up before they moved in; energetic youngsters, they'd do it
themselves. He gave them one last piece of advice, along with the
keys. —Don't keep on Kleynhans's old boy, he'll come to you
with a long story, but I've told him before, he'll have to get off
the place when someone moves in. He's no good.—

The couple agreed at once. In fact, the husband made their first
and only request. —Would you see to it, then, that he leaves by
the end of the week? We want him to be gone before we arrive.—

—No-o-o problem. And listen, if you want a boy, I can get
you one. My garden boy knows he can't send me *skelms*.— The
young wife had been stroking, again and again, with one finger,
the silver-furred petal of a protea in an arrangement of dried
Cape flowers Naas had had on his desk almost as long as the
Kleynhans place had been on his books. —You love flowers, ay?
I can see it! Here—take these with you. Please; have it. Mrs
Klopper makes the arrangements herself.—

A baboon; unlikely.

Although the medical profession tacitly disapproves of gratuitous publicity among its members (as if an orthopaedic surgeon of the eminence of Dolf van Gelder needs to attract patients!) and Dr van Gelder refused an interview with a fat Sunday paper, the paper put together its story anyway. The journalist went to the head of the Department of Anthropology at the Medical School, and snipped out of a long disquisition recorded there on tape a popular account, translated into mass-circulation vocabulary, of the differences in the skeletal conformation and articulation in man, ape and baboon. The old girls yellowing along with the cuttings in the newspaper group's research library dug up one of those charts that show the evolutionary phases of anthropoid to hominid, with man an identikit compilation of his past and present. As there was no photograph of whatever the doctors had seen, the paper made do with the chart, blacking out the human genitalia, but leaving the anthropoids'. It was, after all, a family paper. WILL YOU KNOW HIM WHEN YOU MEET HIM? Families read that the ape-like creature which was 'terrorizing' the Northern Suburbs was not, in the expert opinion of the Professor of Anthropology, likely to be a baboon, whatever conclusions his respected colleague, orthopaedic surgeon and osteologist Dr Dolf van Gelder, had drawn from the bone conformation indicated by its stance or gait.

The Johannesburg zoo stated once again that no member of the ape family was missing, including any specimen of the genus *anthropopithecus*, which is most likely to be mistaken for man. There are regular checks of all inmates and of security precautions. The SPCA warned the public that whether a baboon or not, a member of the ape family is a danger to cats and dogs, and people should keep their pets indoors at night.

Since the paper was not a daily, a whole week had to go by before the result of the strange stirring in the fecund mud of association that causes people to write to newspapers about secret preoccupations set off by the subject of an article, could be read by them in print. 'Only Man Is Vile' (Rondebosch) wrote that since a coronary attack some years ago he had been advised to keep a pet to lessen cardiac anxiety. His marmoset, a Golden Lion Tamarin from South America, had the run of the house 'including two cats and a Schipperke' and was like a mother to them. He could only urge other cardiac sufferers to ignore warnings about the dangers of pets. 'Had Enough' (Roosevelt Park) invited the ape, baboon, monkey etc. to come and kill her neighbour's dog, who barked all night and was responsible for her daughter's *anorexia nervosa*. Howard C. Butterfield III had 'enjoyed your lovely country' until he and his wife were mugged only ten yards from the Moulin Rouge Hotel in Hillbrow, Johannesburg. He'd like to avail himself of the hospitality of 'your fine paper' to tell the black man who slapped his wife before snatching her purse that he had broken her dental bridgework, causing pain and inconvenience on what was to have been the holiday of a lifetime, and that he was no better than any uncivilized ape at large.

Mrs Naas Klopper made a detour on her way to visit her sister Miemie in Pretoria. She had her own car, of course, a ladies' car Naas provided for her, smaller than his Mercedes, a pretty green Toyota. She hadn't seen the Kleynhans place for, oh, four or five years—before the old man died. A shock. It *was* a mess; she felt sorry for that young couple. . .really.

She and her sister dressed up for each other, showing off new clothes as they had done when they were girls; the clean soles of her new ankle-strap shoes gritted against the stony drive as she planted the high heels well apart, for balance, and leaned into the back of the car to take out her house-warming present.

The girl appeared in the garden, from the backyard. She must have heard the approach of a car.

Mrs Naas Klopper was coming towards her through weeds, insteps arched like proud fists under an intricacy of narrow yellow straps, the *bombé* of breasts flashing gold chains on blue polka dots that crowded together to form a border at the hem of the dress. The girl's recognition of the face, seen only once before, was oddly strengthened, like a touched-up photograph, by make-up the original hadn't been wearing: teeth brightly circled by red lips, blinking blue eyes shuttered with matching lids. Carried before the bosom was a large round biscuit drum flashing tinny colours.

Mrs Naas saw that she'd interrupted the girl in the middle of some dirty task—of course, settling in. The dull hair was broken free of the knot, on one side. Hooked behind an ear, it stuck to the sweaty neck. The breasts (Mrs Naas couldn't help noticing; why don't these young girls wear bras these days) were squashed by a shrunken T-shirt and the feet were in split *takkies*. The only evidence of femininity to which Mrs Naas's grooming could respond (as owners of the same make of vehicle, one humble, one a luxury model, passing on the highway silently acknowledge one another with a flick of headlights) was the Indian dingley-dangleys the girl wore in her ears, answering the big fake pearls sitting on Mrs Naas's plump lobes.

—I'm not going to come in. I know how it is. . . This is just some of my buttermilk rusks you liked.—

The girl was looking at the tin, now in her hands, at the painted face of a smiling blonde child with a puppy and a bunch of roses, looking back at her. She said something, in her shy way, about Mrs Naas being generous.

—Ag, it's nothing. I was baking for myself, and I always take to my sister in Pretoria. You know, in our family we say, it's not the things you buy with money that counts, it's what you put your heart into when you make something. Even if it's only a rusk, ay? Is everything going all right?—

—Oh yes. We're fine, thank you.—

Mrs Naas tried to keep the weight on the balls of her feet; she could feel the spindle heels of her new shoes sinking into the weeds, that kind of green stain would never come off.—Moving in! Don't tell me! I say to Naas, whatever happens, we have to stay in this house until I die. A person can never move all the stuff we've collected.—

What a shy girl she was. Mrs Naas had always heard Australians were friendly, like Afrikaners. The girl hardly smiled, her thick eyebrows moved in some kind of inhibition or agitation. —We haven't got too much, luckily.—

—Has everything arrived now?—

—Oh. . .I think just about. Still a few packing cases to open.—

Mrs Naas was agreeing, shifting her heels unobtrusively.
—Unpacking is nothing, it's finding where to put things, ay. Ag,
but it's a nice roomy old house—

A black man came round from the yard, as the lady of the
house had, but he didn't come nearer, only stood a moment,
hammer in hand; wanting some further instructions from the
missus, probably, and then seeing she was with another white
person, knowing he mustn't interrupt.

—So at least you've got someone to help. That's good. I hope
you didn't take a boy off the streets, my dear? There some
terrible loafers coming to the back door for work, criminals—my!—you must be careful, you know.—

The girl looked very solemn, impressed. —No, we wouldn't
do that.—

—Did someone find him for you?—

—No—well, not someone here. Friends in town. He had
references.—She stopped a moment, and looked at Mrs Naas.
—So it's all right, I think. I'm sure. Thank you.—

She walked with Mrs Naas back to the car, hugging the biscuit
tin.

—Well, there's plenty to keep him busy in this garden.
Shame. . .the pergola was so pretty. But the grapes will climb
again, you'll see, if you get all the rubbish cleared away. But
don't *you* start digging and that. . .be careful of yourself. Have
you been feeling all right?—And Mrs Naas put her left hand,
with its diamond thrust up on a stalagmite of gold (her old
engagement ring remodelled since Naas's prosperity by a Jew
jeweller who gave him a good deal), on her own stomach,
rounded only by good eating.

The girl looked puzzled. Then she forgot, at last, that shyness
of hers and laughed, laughed and shook her head.

—No morning-sickness?—

—No, no. I'm fine. Not sick at all.—

Mrs Naas saw that the girl, expecting in a strange country,
must be comforted to have a talk with a motherly woman. Mrs
Naas's body, which had housed Dawie, Andries, Aletta and Klein
Dolfie, expanded against the tight clothes from which it would
never burgeon irresistibly again, as the girl's would soon.—I'll
tell you something. This's the best time of your life. The first

baby. That's something you'll never know again, never.—She drove off before the girl could see the tears that came to her eyes.

The girl went round back into the yard with her tall stalk, flat-footed in the old *takkies*.

The black man's gaze was fixed where she must reappear. He still held the hammer; uselessly.—Is it all right?—

—Of course it's all right.—

—What's she want?—

—Didn't want anything. She brought us a present—this.— Her palm came down over the grin of the child on the tin drum.

He looked at the tin, cautious to see it for what it was.

—Biscuits. *Rusks*. The *vrou* of the agent who let this place to us. Charles and I had to have tea with her the first day we were here.—

—That's what she came for?—

—*Yes*. That's all. Don't you give something—take food when new neighbours move in?— As she heard herself saying it, she remembered that whatever the custom was among blacks—and god knows, they were the most hospitable if the poorest of people—he hadn't lived anywhere that could be called 'at home' for years, and his 'neighbours' had been fellow refugees in camps and military training centres. She gave him her big, culpable smile to apologize for her bourgeois naïvety; it still surfaced from time to time, and it was best to admit so, openly. —Nothing to get worried about. I don't mean they're really neighbours. . .— She made an arc with her chin and long neck, from side to side, sweeping the isolation of the house and yard within the veld.

The black man implied no suggestion that the white couple did not know their job, no criticism of the choice of place. Hardly! It could not have been better situated.—Is she going to keep turning up, hey. . .What'll she think? I shouldn't have come into the garden.—

—No, no, Vusi. She won't think anything. It was okay she saw you. She just naturally assumes there'll be a black working away somewhere in the yard.—

—And Eddie?—

She placed the biscuit tin on the kennel, with its rusty chain to which no dog was attached.

—Okay, two blacks. After all, this is a farming plot, isn't it? There's building going on. Where is he?—

—He went into the house as soon as I came back and told him. . .—

She was levering, with her fingernails, under the lid of the tin. —Can you do this? My fingers aren't strong enough.—

The black man found the hammer in his hand, put it down and grasped the tin, his small brown nose wrinkling with effort. The lid flew off with a twang and went bowling down the yard, the girl laughing after it. It looped back towards the man and he leant gracefully and caught it up, laughing.

—What is this *boere* food, anyway?—

—Try it. They're good.—

They crunched rusks together in the sun, the black man's attention turning contemplatively, mind running ahead to what was not yet there, to the shed (big enough for two cars) before which the raw vigour of new bricks, cement and tools was dumped against the stagnation and decay of the yard.

The girl chewed energetically, wanting to free her mouth to speak. —We'll have to get used to the idea people may turn up, for some reason or another. We'll just have to be prepared. So long as they don't find us in the house. . .it'll be all right.—

The black man no longer saw what was constructed in his mind; he saw the rusty chain, he leant again with that same straight-backed, sideways movement with which he had caught the lid, and jingled the links. —Maybe we should get a dog, man. To warn.—

—That's an idea.— Then her face bunched unattractively, a yes-but. —What do we do with it afterwards?—

He smiled at her indulgently; at things she still didn't understand, even though she chose to be here, in this place, with Eddie and with him.

The white couple had known two black men would be coming but not exactly when or how. Charles must have believed they would come at night, that would be the likeliest because the safest; the first three nights in the house he dragged the mattress off her bed into the kitchen, and his into the 'lounge', on which the front door opened directly, so that he or she would hear the men wherever they sought entry. Charles had great difficulty in sleeping with one eye open; he could stay awake until very late, but once his head was on a pillow sleep buried him deep within the hot, curly beard. She dozed off where she was—meetings, cinemas, parties, even driving—after around half-past ten, but she could give her subconscious instructions, before going to bed, to wake her at any awaited signal of sound or movement. She set her inner alarm at hair-trigger, those three nights. An owl sent her swiftly to Charles; it might be a man imitating the call. She responded to a belch from the sink drain, skittering in the roof (mice?), even the faint thread of a cat's mew, that might have been in a dream, since she could not catch it again once it had awakened her.

But they came at two o'clock on the fourth afternoon. A small sagging van of the kind used by the petty entrepreneurs in firewood and junk commerce, *dagga*-running, livestock and human transport between black communities on either side of the borders with Swaziland, Lesotho or Botswana, backed down to the gate it had overshot. There were women and children with blankets covering their mouths against the dust, in the open rear. A young man jumped from the cab and dragged aside the sagging, silvery wire-and-scroll gate, with its plate 'Plot 185 Koppiesdrif'. Charles was out the front door and reversing the initiative at once: he it was who came to the man. His green eyes, at twenty-eight, already were narrowed by the plump fold of the lower lid that marks joviality—whether cruelly shrewd or good-natured—in middle age. The young black man was chewing gum. He did not interrupt the rhythms of his jaw:—Charles.—

The couple had not been told what the men would look like. The man identified himself by the procedure (questions and specific answers) Charles had been taught to expect. Charles asked whether they wouldn't drive round to the yard. The other understood at once; it was more natural for blacks to conduct any business with a white man at his back door. Charles himself was staging the arrival in keeping with the unremarkable deliveries of building material that already had been made to the new occupiers of the plot. He walked ahead of the van, business-like. In the yard another young man got out of the cab, and, with the first, from among the women swung down two zippered carry-alls and a crammed paper carrier. That was all.

The women and children, like sheep dazed by their last journey to the abattoir, moved only when the van drove off again, jolting them.

Charles and the girl had not been told the names or identity of the pair they expected. They exchanged only first names—Eddie was the one who had opened the gate, Vusi the one who had sat beside the unknown driver and got down in the yard. The girl introduced herself as 'Joy'. One of the men asked if there was something to eat. The white couple at once got in one another's way, suddenly unrehearsed now that the reality had begun, exchanging terse instructions in the kitchen, jostling one another to find sugar, a knife to slice tomatoes, a frying pan for the sausages which she forgot to prick. It seemed there was no special attitude, social formula of ease, created by a situation so far removed from the normal pattern of human concourse; so it was just the old, inappropriate one of stilted hospitality to unexpected guests that had to do, although these were not guests, the white couple were not hosts, and the arrival was according to plan. When sleeping arrangements came up, the men assumed the white couple were sleeping together and put their own things in the second bedroom. It was small and dark, unfurnished except for two new mattresses on the floor separated by an old trunk with a reading lamp standing on it, but there was no question of the other two favouring themselves with a better room; this one faced on the yard, no one would see blacks moving around at night in the bedroom of a white man's house.

The two zippered carry-alls, cheap copies of the hand luggage of jet-flight holiday-makers, held a change of jeans, a couple of shirts printed with bright leisure symbols of the Caribbean, a few books, and—in Eddie's—a mock-suède jacket with Indian fringes, Wild West style. As soon as they all knew each other well enough, he was teased about it, and had his quick riposte.— But I'm not going to be extinct.— The strong paper carrier was one of those imprinted with a pop star's face black kids shake for sale on the street corners of Johannesburg. What came out of it, the white couple saw, was as ordinary as the loaves of bread and cardboard litres of *mageu* such bags usually carry; a transistor-tape player, Vusi's spare pair of sneakers, a pink towel and a plastic briefcase emptied of papers. Charles was to provide everything they might need. He himself had been provided with a combi. He went to the appointed places, at appointed times, to pick up what was necessary.

The combi had housewifely curtains across the windows—a practical adornment popular with farming families, whose children may sleep away a journey. It was impossible to tell, when Charles drove off or came back, whether there was anything inside it. On one of his return trips, he drew up at the level crossing and found himself beside Naas Klopper and Mrs Naas in the Mercedes. A train shuttered past like a camera gone berserk, lens opening and closing, with each flying segment of rolling stock, on flashes of the veld behind it. The optical explosion invigorated Charles. He waved and grinned at the estate agent and his wife.

They had used all three Holiday Inns in the vicinity. They had even driven out to cheap motels, which were safer, since local people of their class would be unlikely to be encountered there, but the time spent on the road cut into the afternoons which were all they had together. Besides, he felt the beds were dirty—a superficial papering of laundered sheets overlaid the sordidness that was other people's sex. He told her he could not bear to bring her to such rooms.

She did not care where she was, so long as she was with him and there was a bed. She said so, which was probably a mistake; but she wanted, with him, no cunning female strategy of being desired more than desiring: —You are my first and last lover.— She was not hurt when he did not trade—at least—that there had not been anything like it before, for him, if he could not commit himself about what might come after. He was uneasy at the total, totted-up weight of precious privilege, finally, in his hands. He worried about security—her security. What would happen to her if her husband found out and divorced her? She didn't give this a thought; only worried, in her sense of responsibility for his career, what would happen if his wife found out and made a scandal.

His wife was away in Europe, the house was empty. A large house with a pan-handle drive, tunnelled through trees, the house itself in a lair of trees. But you are never alone in this country. They are always there; the houseboy, the gardenboy mowing the lawn. They see everything; you can only do, in the end, what it is all right for them to see and remember. Impossible to take this newly-beloved woman home where he longed to make love to her in his own bed. Even if by some pretext he managed to get rid of them, give them all a day off at once. They changed the sheets and brushed the carpets; a tender stain, a single hair of unfamiliar colour—impossible. So in the end even his room, his own bed, in a house where he paid for everything—nothing is your own, once you are married.

Ah, what recklessness the postponement of gratification produces, when it does not produce sublimation. (Could Freud have known that!) He had come back to the parking lot from the reception desk of a suburban hotel, his very legs and arms drawn together stiffly in shock; as he was about to enquire about bed and breakfast (they always asked for this, paid in advance, and disappeared at the end of an afternoon) he had seen a business acquaintance and a journalist to whom he was well known, coming straight towards him out of the hotel restaurant, loosening their ties against the high temperature. She drove off with him at once, but where to? There was nowhere. Yet never had they reached such painful tension of arousal, not touching or speaking as she drove. In the heat wave that afternoon she took a road to the old mine dumps. There, hidden from the freeway by Pharaonic pyramids of sand from which gold had been extracted by the cyanide process, she took off the wisp of nylon and lace between her legs, unzipped his beautiful Italian linen trousers, and, covering their bodies by the drop of her skirt, sat him into her. In their fine clothes, they were joined like two butterflies in the heat of a summer garden. When they slackened, had done, and he set himself to rights, he was appalled to see her, her lips

swollen, her cheekbones fiery, the hair in front of her ears ringlets of sweat. In a car! The car her husband had given her, only a month before, new, to please her, because he had become aware, without knowing why, he couldn't please her anymore. She, too, had nothing that was her own; her husband paid for everything that was hers. She said only one thing to him:
—When I was a little girl, I was always asking to be allowed to go and slide down the mine dumps. They promised to take me, they never did. I always think of that when I see mine dumps.—

But today she had thought of something else. He made up his mind he would have to take into his confidence a friend (himself suspected of running affairs from time to time) who had a cottage, at present untenanted, on one of his properties. There, among the deserted stables of an old riding school, mature lovers could let their urgencies of sex, confessional friendship and sweet clandestine companionship take their course in peace and dignity. The bed had been occupied only by people of their own kind. There was a refrigerator; ice and whisky. Sometimes she arrived with a rose and put it in a glass beside the bed. He couldn't remember when last he read a poem, since leaving school; or would again. She brought an old book with her maiden name on the fly-leaf and read Pablo Neruda to him. Afterwards they fell asleep, and then woke to make love once more before losing each other safely in the rush-hour traffic back to town. (After the encounter at the hotel, they had decided it was best to travel separately.)

They were secure in that cottage—for as long as they would need security. Sometimes he would find the opportunity to remark: We are not children. I know, she would agree. He could be reassured she accepted that love could only have its span and must end without tears. One late afternoon they were lying timelessly, although they had less than half-an-hour left (it was the way to deal with an association absolutely restricted to the hours between three and six), naked, quiet, her hand languidly comforting his lolling penis, when they heard a scratching at the ox-eye window above the bedhead. He sat up. Jumped up, standing on the bed. She rolled over onto her face. There was the sound of something, feet, a body, landing on earth, scuffling, slap of branches. A spray of the old bougainvillaea that climbed the roof snapped back against the window. The window was empty.

He gently freed her face from the pillow.—It's all right.—

She lay there looking at him. —She's hired someone to follow you.—

—Don't be silly.—

—I know it. Did you see? A white man?—

He began to dress.

—Don't go out, my darling. For god's sake! Wait for him to go away.—

He sat on the side of the bed, in shirt and trousers. They listened for the sound of a car leaving. They knew why they had not heard it arrive; they had been making love.

Still no sound of a car.

—He must have walked through the bushes, all the way from the road.—

Her lover was deeply silent and thoughtful; as if this that had happened to them were something to which there was a way out, a solution!

—Somehow climbed up the bougainvillaea.— She began to shiver.

—It could have been a cat, you know, gone wild. Trying to get in. There are always cats around stables.—

—Oh no, oh no.— She pulled the bed-clothes up to the level of her armpits, spoke with difficulty.—I heard him laugh. A horrible little coughing laugh. That's why I put my face in the pillow.— Her cheeks flattened, a desperate expressionlessness.

He stroked her hand, denying, denying that someone could have been laughing at them, that they could ever be something to laugh at.

After a safe interval she dressed and they went outside. The bougainvillaea would give foothold up to the small window, but was cruelly thorny. She began to be able to believe that what she had heard was some sort of suppressed exclamation of pain—and serve the bastard right. Then they searched the ground for shoe-prints but found nothing. The red earth crumbled with worm-shredded leaves would have packed down under the soles of shoes, but, as he pointed out to her, might not show the print of bare feet. Would some dirty Peeping Tom of a private

142

detective take off his shoes and tear his clothes in the cause of his disgusting profession? She a little behind him—but she wouldn't let him go alone—they walked in every direction away from the cottage, and through the deserted stables where there were obvious hiding places. But there was no one, one could feel there was no one, and on the paved paths over which rains had washed sand, no footprints but their own. On the way to their cars, they passed the granadilla vine they had remarked to one another on their way in, that had spread its glossy coat-of-mail over weakening shrubs and was baubled with unripe fruit. Now the ground was scattered with green eggs of granadillas, bitten into and then half-eaten or thrown away. He and she broke from one another, gathering them, examining them. Only a hungry fruit-eating animal would plunder so indiscriminately. He was the first to give spoken credence.—I didn't want to tell you, but I thought I heard something, too. Not a laugh, a sort of bark or cough.—

Suddenly she had him by the waist, her head against his chest, they were laughing and giddy together. —Poor monkey. Poor, poor old lonely monkey. Well, he's lucky; he can rest assured we won't tell anyone where to find him.—

When she was in her car, he lingered at her face, as always, turned to him through the window. There was curiosity mingled with tenderness in his.—You don't mind a monkey watching us making love?—

She looked back at him with the honesty that she industriously shored up against illusions of any kind, preparing herself for—some day—their last afternoon.—No, I don't mind. I don't mind at all.—

While Charles drove about the country fetching what was needed—sometimes away several days, covering long distances—Vusi and Eddie bricked up the fourth wall of the shed. The girl insisted on helping although she knew nothing about the type of work.—Just show me.— That was her humble yet obstinate plea. She learnt how to mix cement in a puddle of the right consistency. Her long skinny arms with the blue vein running down the inside of the elbows were stronger than they looked; she steadied timber for the door-frame. The only thing was, she didn't seem to want to cook. They would rather have had her cook better meals for them than help with what they could have managed for themselves. She seemed to expect everyone in the house to prepare his own meals when he might feel hungry. The white man, Charles, did so, or cooked with her; this must be some special arrangement decided between them, a black woman would always cook every night for her lover, indeed for all the men in the house. She went to town once a week, when the combi was available, to buy food, but the kind of thing she bought was not what they wanted, what they felt like eating for these few weeks when they were sure there would be food available. Yoghurt, cheese, brown rice, nuts and fruit—the fruit was nice (Vusi had not seen apricots for so long, he ate a whole bagful at a sitting) but the frozen pork sausages she brought for them (she and Charles were vegetarian) weren't real meat. Eddie didn't want to complain but Vusi insisted, talking in their room at night, it was their right.—That's what she's here for, isn't it, what they're both here for. We each do our job.—He asked her next day.—Joy, man, bring some meat from town, man, not sausages.—

Eddie was emboldened, frowned agreement, but giggling. —And some mealie-meal. Not always rice.—

—Oh Charles and I like mealie-pap too. But I thought you'd be insulted, you'd think I bought it specially for you.—

They all laughed with her, at her. As Vusi remarked once when the black men talked in the privacy of their own language, 'Joy' was a funny kind of cell-name for that girl, without flesh or flirtatiousness for any man to enjoy. Yet she was the one who came out bluntly with things that detached the four of them from their separate, unknown existences behind them and the separate existences that would be taken up ahead, and made a life of their own together, in this house and yard.

It took Charles, Vusi and Eddie to hang an articulated metal garage door in the entrance of the converted shed. It thundered smoothly down and was secured by a heavy padlock to a ring embedded in Joy's cement. There was the pleasure to be expected of any structure of brick and mortar successfully completed; a satisfaction in itself, no matter what mere stage of means to an end it might represent. They stood about, looking at it. Charles put his arm on the girl's shoulder, and she put out an arm on Vusi's.

Eddie raised and lowered the door again, for them.

—It reminds me of my grandfather's big old roll-top desk.—

Eddie looked up at the girl, from their handiwork.—Desk like that? I never saw one. What did your grandfather do?—

—He was a magistrate. Sent people to jail.— She smiled.

—Hell, Joy, man!— Either it was a marvel that the girl's progenitor should have been a magistrate, or a marvel that a magistrate should have had her for a granddaughter.

One thing she never forgot to bring from town was beer. All four drank a lot of beer; the bottom shelf of the refrigerator was neatly stocked with cans. Charles went and fetched some and they sat in the yard before the shining door, slowly drinking. Vusi picked up tidily the tagged metal rings that snapped off the cans when they were opened.

Until the garage door was in place the necessities Charles brought in the combi had had to be stored in the house. Over the weeks the bedroom empty except for two mattresses and a trunk with a lamp was slowly furnished behind drawn curtains and a locked door whose key was kept in a place known only to Vusi—though, as Charles said to Joy, what sense in that? If anyone came they would kick in any locked door.

At night Eddie and Vusi lay low on their mattresses in a perspective that enclosed them with boxes and packing cases like a skyline of children's piled blocks. Eddie slept quickly but Vusi, with his shaved head with the tiny, gristly ears placed at exactly the level of the cheekbones that stretched his face and formed the widest plane of the whole skull, lay longing to smoke. Yet the craving was just another appetite, some petty recurrence, assuaged a thousand times and easily to be so again with something bought across a corner shop counter. Around him in the dark, an horizon darker than the dark held the cold forms in which the old real, terrible needs of his life, his father's life and his father's father's life were now so strangely realized. He had sat at school farting the gases of an empty stomach, he had seen

fathers, uncles, brothers, come home without work from days-
long queues, he had watched, too young to understand, the tin
and board that had been the shack he was born in, carted away by
government demolishers. His bare feet had been shod in shoes
worn to the shape of a white child's feet. He had sniffed glue to
see a rosy future. He had taken a diploma by correspondence to
better himself. He had spoken nobody's name under interrogation. He had left a girl and baby without hope of being able to
show himself to them again. You could not eat the AKM assault
rifles that Charles had brought in golf-bags, you could not dig a
road or turn a lathe with the limpet mines, could not shoe and
clothe feet and body with the offensive and defensive hand-
grenades, could not use the AKM bayonets to compete with the
white man's education, or to thrust a way out of solitary
confinement in maximum security, and the wooden boxes that
held hundreds of rounds of ammunition would not make even a
squatter's shack for the girl and child. But all these hungers
found their shape, distorted, forged as no one could conceive
they ever should have to be, in the objects packed around him.
These were made not for life; for death. He and Eddie lay there
protected by it as they had never been by life.

During the day, he instructed Eddie in the correct use and
maintenance of their necessities. He was the more experienced;
he had been operational like this before. He checked detonators
and timing devices, and the state of the ammunition. Necessities
obtained the way these were were not always complete and in
good order. He and Charles discussed the mechanisms and
merits of various makes and classes of necessities; Charles had
done his South African army service and understood such
things.

Once the garage door like a grandfather's roll-top desk was
installed, they were able to move everything into the shed. They
did so at night, without talking and without light. There had
been rain, by then. A bullfrog that had waited a whole season
underground came up that night and accompanied the silent
activity with his retching bellow.

A chimpanzee, some insist.

Just a large monkey, say others.

It was seen again in the suburb of wooded gardens where Stanley Dobrow took the only photograph so far obtained. If you could call that image of clashed branches a likeness of anything.

Every household in the fine suburb had several black servants—trusted cooks who were allowed to invite their grandchildren to spend their holidays in the backyard, faithful gardeners from whom the family watch-dog was inseparable, a shifting population of pretty young housemaids whose long red nails and pertness not only asserted the indignity of being undiscovered or out-of-work fashion models but kept hoisted a cocky guerrilla pride against servitude to whites: there are many forms of resistance not recognized in orthodox revolutionary strategy. One of these girls said the beast slipped out of her room one night, just as she was crossing the yard from the kitchen. She had dropped her dinner, carried in one enamel dish covered with another to keep it hot. The cook, twenty-one years with the white family, told the lady of the house more likely it was one of the girl's boy-friends who had been to her room to 'check out' if there was another boy-friend there with her. Why hadn't she screamed?

The girl left without notice, anyway, first blazing out at the cook and the old gardener that if they didn't mind living 'like chickens in a *hok*', stuck away in a shit yard where anyone could come in over the wall and steal your things, murder you, while the whites had a burglar siren that went off if you breathed on their windows—if they were happy to yesbaas and yesmissus, with that horrible thing loose, baboons could bite off your whole hand—she wasn't. Couldn't they see the whites always ran away and hid and left us to be hurt?

And she didn't even have the respect not to bring up what had happened to the cook's brother, although the cook was still wearing the mourning band on the sleeve of the pastel-coloured overalls she spent her life in. He had been a watchman at a block of flats, sitting all night in the underground garage to guard the tenants' cars. He had an army surplus overcoat provided to keep him warm and a *knobkerrie* to defend himself with. But the thieves had a revolver and shot him in the stomach while the owners of the cars went on sleeping, stacked twelve storeys high over his dead body.

Other servants round about reported signs of something out there. It was common talk where they gathered, to hear from the Chinese runner what symbol had come up in their daily gamble on the numbers game, in a lane between two of 'their' houses—after ten or twenty years, living just across the yard from the big house, there develops such a thing as a deferred sense of property, just as there can be deferred pain felt in a part of the human body other than that of its source. Since no one actually saw whoever or whatever was watching them—timid or threatening?—rumour began to go round that it was what (to reduce any power of malediction it might possess) they called—not in their own language with its rich vocabulary recognizing the supernatural, but adopting the childish Afrikaans word—a spook.

An urban haunter, a factory or kitchen ghost. Powerless like themselves, long migrated from the remotest possibility of being a spirit of the ancestors just as they themselves, that kind of inner attention broken by the batter and scream of commuter trains, the jumping of mine drills and the harangue of pop music, were far from the possibility of any oracle making itself heard to them. A heavy drinker reminded how, two Christmases ago, on the koppie behind 'your' house (he indicated the Dobrow cook, Sophie) a man must have lost his footing coming over the rocks from the shebeen there, and was found dead on Boxing Day. They said that one came from Transkei. Someone like that had woken up now, without his body, and was trying to find his way back to the hostel where his worker's contract, thumb-print affixed, had long ago run out. That was all.

Eddie wanted Charles to hire a TV set.

—But Charlie, he just laughs, man, he doesn't do anything about it.— Eddie complained to him through remarks addressed to the others. And they laughed, too.

It was the time when what there was to be done was wait. Charles brought the Sunday papers. He had finished reading a leader that tried to find a moral lesson for both victim and perpetrator in one of the small massacres of an undeclared and unending war. His whole face, beard—like the head of a disgruntled lion resting on its paws—was slumped between two fists. —You want to watch cabinet ministers preaching lies? Homeland chiefs getting twenty-one-gun salutes? Better go and weed your mealies if you're bored, man.— A small patch of these, evidently planted by the man who had looked after the Kleynhans place while it was unoccupied, had begun to grow silky in the sun, since the rain, and Eddie monitored their progress as though he and Vusi, Charles and Joy would be harvesting the cobs months ahead.

The girl sat on the floor under the ox-wagon wheel chandelier with its pink shades like carnival hats askew, sucking a strand of her hair as she read. Vusi had the single armchair and Eddie and Charles the sofa, whose snot-green plaid Joy could not tolerate, even here, and kept covered with a length of African cotton patterned with indigo cowrie shells: every time she entered this room, a reminder that one really had one's sense of being (but could not, absolutely not, now) among beautiful, loved objects of familiar use. The four exchanged sheets of newspaper restlessly, searching for the world around them with which they had no connection. The Prime Minister had made another of his speeches of reconciliation; each except Charles read in silence the threats of which it was composed. Charles spoke through lips distorted by the pressure of his fists under his fleshy face, one of those grotesque mouths of ancient Mediterranean cultures from which sibylline utterances are supposed to well. *This government will not stand by and see the peace of mind of its peoples destroyed. It will not see the security of your homes, of your children asleep in their beds, threatened by those who lurk, outside law and order, ready to strike in the dark. It will not see the food snatched from your children's mouths by those who seek the economic destruction of our country through boycotts in the so-called United Nations and violence at home. I say to countries on our borders to whom we have been and shall continue to be good neighbours: we shall not hesitate to strike with all our might at those who harbour terrorists: . .*

When they heard this rhetoric on the radio, they were accustomed to smile as people will when they must realize that those being referred to as monsters are the human beings drinking a glass of water, cutting a hang-nail, writing a letter, in the same room; are themselves. Sometimes they would restore their sense of reality by derision (all of them) or one of them (Vusi or Charles) would reply to thin air with the other rhetoric, of rebellion; but the closer time drew them to act, the less need there was for platform language.

—Scared. Afraid.—

Vusi dropped single words, as if to see what rings of meaning others would feel ripple from them.

The girl looked up, not knowing if this was a question and if anyone was expected to answer it.

Eddie sniffed with a twist of the nose and cocked his head indifferently, parrying the words towards the public office, occupied by interchangeable faces, that had made the speech.

The moment passed, and with it perhaps some passing test Vusi had put them to—and himself. He had opened a hand on the extreme danger hidden in this boring, fly-buzzing Sunday 'livingroom'; in that instant they had all looked at it; and their silence said, calm: I know.

The allusion swerved away from themselves. Vusi was still speaking.—Can't give any other reason why he should have them in his power, so he's got to scare them into it. Scare. That's all they've got left. What else is in that speech? After three-hundred-and-fifty years. After how many governments? Spook people.—

It was a proposition that had comforted, spurred, lulled or inspired over many years.—So?— Charles's beard jutted.— That goes to show the power of fear, not the collapse of power.—

—Exactly. Otherwise we wouldn't need to be here.— Joy's reference to this house, their presence and purpose, sounded innocently vulgar: to be there was to have gone beyond discussion of why; to be freed of words.

Eddie gave hers a different, general application.—If whites could have been cured of being scared of blacks, that would have solved everything?— He was laughing at the old liberal theory.

Charles swallowed a rough crumb of impulse to tell Eddie he didn't need Eddie to give him a lesson on class and economics. —Hell, man. . . Just that there's no point in telling ourselves they're finished, they're running down.—

Joy heard in Charles's nervous asperity the fear of faltering he guarded against in others because it was in himself. There should be no love affairs between people doing this kind of—thing— (she still could not think of it as she wished to, as work to be done). She did not, now, want to be known by him as *she* knew *him*; there should be some conscious mental process available by which such knowledge would be withdrawn.

—Don't worry. If they're running down, it's because they know who's after them.— Eddie, talking big, seemed to become again the kid he must have been in street-gang rivalries that unknowingly rehearsed, for his generation of blacks, the awful adventure that was coming to them.

—They were finished when they took the first slave.— Knowledge of Vusi was barred somewhere between his murmured commonplaces and that face of his. He was not looking at any of them, now; but Joy had said once to Charles, in a lapse to referents of an esoteric culture she carefully avoided because these distanced him and her from Vusi and Eddie, that if Vusi were to be painted, the portrait would be one of those, like Velázquez' Philip IV, whose eyes would meet yours no matter from what angle the painting were to be seen.

Vusi and Eddie had not been on student tours to the Prado. Vusi's voice was matter-of-fact, hoarse. —It doesn't matter how many times we have to sit here like this. They can't stop us because we can't stop. Never. Every time, when I'm waiting, I know I'm coming nearer.—

Eddie crackled back a page to frame something. —Opening of Koeberg's going to be delayed by months and months, it says, ay Vusi?—

—Ja, I saw.—

Charles and Joy did not know if Vusi was one of those who had attacked the nuclear reactor installation at the Cape before it was ready to operate, earlier in the year. A classic mission; that was the phrase. A strategic target successfully hit; serious material damage, no deaths, no blood shed. This terrifying task produces its outstanding practitioners, like any other. They did not know if Eddie knew something about Vusi they didn't, had been told some night in the dark of the back room, while the two men lay there alone on their mattresses. Eddie's remark might indicate he did know; or that he was fascinatedly curious and thought Vusi might be coaxed, without realizing it, into saying something revealing. But Vusi didn't understand flattery.

Eddie gave up. —What's this committee of Cape Town whites who want it shut down?—

Charles took the paper from him.—Koeberg's only thirty kilometres from Cape Town. A bicycle ride, man. Imagine what could happen once it's producing. But d'you see the way the story's handled? They write about 'security' as if the place's a jeweller's shop that might be burgled, not a target we've already hit once.—

Joy read at an angle over his shoulder, an ugly strain on the tendons of her neck.—Nobody wants to go to jail.—

Charles gave the sweet smile of his most critical mood, for the benefit of Vusi and Eddie.—Ah well, but there are ways and ways, ay? A journalist learns to say what he wants without appearing to. But these fellows sit with the book of rules under their backsides. . .well, what'm I talking about—you need wits to outwit.—

—What makes you think they even want to?—

—Because it's their job! Let's leave convictions out of it!—

—No, she's right, man. If you work on these papers, you're just part of the system.— Eddie kept as souvenirs the catch-all terms from his Soweto days.

—To be fair—(for which ideal the girl hankered so seriously that she would not hesitate to contradict herself) there are some who want to. . . A few who've lost their jobs.—

—Someone reads this, what can he know afterwards?—A sheet went sailing from Vusi's hand to join those already spread about the floor. —You must call in an interpreter, like in court, to know what's going on.—

—Like in court? *Jwaleka tsekisong?*— Eddie went zestfully into an act. A long burst in Sesotho; then in English: *He can't remember a thing, My Lord.* Another lengthy Sesotho sentence, with the cadence, glares and head-shakings of vehement denial: *He says yes, My Lord.* A rigmarole of obvious agreement: *He says no, My Lord.* The pantomime of the bewildered, garrulous black witness, the white Afrikaner prosecutor fond of long English words and not much surer of their meaning than the witness or the bored black interpreter:

I put it to you that you claim convenable amnesia.

He says he doesn't know that Amnesia woman.

I put it to you it's inconceivable you don't remember whether you were present on the night of the crime.

He says he never made a child with that woman, My Lord.

Out of their amusement at his nonsense there was a rise of animation, change of key to talk of what or was not to be understood between the lines of reportage and guards of commentary; in this—the events of their world, which moved beneath the events of the world the newspapers reflected—the real intimacy latent in their strangeness to one another, their apparent ill-assortment, discovered itself. There was sudden happiness—yes, unlike any private happiness left behind, independent of circumstance, because all four had left behind, too, the 'normal' fears, repugnancies, prejudices, reservations that 'circumstance' as they had known it—what colour they were, what that colour had meant where they lived—had been for them. Nothing but a surge of intermittent current: but the knowledge that it would well up again made it possible to live with the irritations and inadequacies they chafed against one another now, waiting. Charles said it for them, grinning suddenly after an argument one day:—Getting in one another's hair, here—it's a form of freedom, ay?—

Apart from politics, there wasn't much to engage, in Charles's Sunday papers. One printed for blacks reported the usual slum murders perpetrated with unorthodox weapons to hand; a soccer club scandal, and deaths at a wedding after drinking tainted home brew. The whites' papers, of which Charles had brought several, and in two languages, had a financial crash, a millionaire's divorce settlement, a piece about that monkey no one could catch, which had stolen a maid's dinner.

Sunday torpor settled on the four. Charles slept with his beard-ringed mouth bubbling slightly, as Naas Klopper was sleeping ten kilometres away in his split-level lounge. Eddie wandered out to the yard, took off his shirt and sat on the back step in the sun, smoking, drinking a coke and listening to a reggae tape as any young labourer would spend his lunch-hour on the pavement outside whites' shops.

On a radio panel 'Talking of Nature' an SPCA official took the opportunity to condemn the cruelty of throwing out pet monkeys to fend for themselves when they outgrow the dimensions of a suitable domestic pet. Mariella Chapman heard him while preparing plums for jam according to the recipe given by her new mother-in-law over the weekend. Mariella and her husband had gone to visit his parents on the farm for the first time since their marriage five months ago, and had come home with a supermarket bag of fresh-picked plums and a leg of venison. Marais (his given name was his mother's maiden name) hung the leg before he went on duty early on Monday at John Vorster Square; he had to put up a hook in the kitchen window because their modern house didn't have a back stoep like the old house at home.

At police headquarters Sergeant Chapman (an English stoker in the 1880s jumped ship, married an Afrikaans girl and left the name scratched on a Boer family tree) took over the 7 a.m. shift of interrogation of one of the people held in detention there. It was a nice-enough-looking place to be stationed, right in town. The blue spandrel panels and glimpses of potted plants in the facade it presented to the passing city freeway could have been those of an apartment block; the cells in which these people were kept were within the core of the building.

It was tiring work, you need a lot of concentration, watching the faces of these politicals, never mind just getting something out of their mouths. He kept his hands off them. Unless, of course, expressly instructed by his superiors to do certain things necessary to make some of them talk. When they got out—particularly the white ones, with their clever lawyer friends and plenty money coming from the churches and the Communists overseas—they often brought court cases against the State, you could find yourself standing there accused of assault, they tried to blacken your name in front of your wife, your mother and dad, who knew only your kindness and caresses. He wanted promotion, but he didn't want that. He did his duty. He did what he was told. And if it ever came to court—oh boy, I'm telling you, *jong*—all was on the Major's instructions, he could swear on the bible to that.

No wonder most of them talked in the end. It was hard enough to do a number of shifts with them during the day or night, with breaks in between for a cup of coffee, something to eat, and best of all, a walk outside in the street; whereas most of them, like this tough nut he was handling with the Major now, were questioned by a roster of personnel twenty-four, thirty-six hours non-stop. And, as the Major had taught, even when these people were given coffee, a cigarette, allowed to sit down, they knew they were being watched and had to watch themselves all the time, for what they might let slip. It was one of the elementary lessons of this work that the gratification of a draw of smoke into the lungs might suddenly succeed in breaking the stoniest will and breaching trained revolutionary hostility towards and contempt for interrogators. (The Major was a very clever, highly-educated and well-read man—you had to have someone like that for the class of detainee that was coming in these days, they'd just run rings round someone who'd only got his matric.) The Major said it didn't even matter if you got to feel sorry for them—the Major knew about this, although you always hid it; 'a bond of sympathy' was the first real step on the way to extracting a confession. Well, Sergeant Chapman didn't have any such feelings today. Inside his uniform his body was filled with the sap of sun and fresh air; the sight of the sleepless, unshaven man standing there, dazed and smelly (they sweated even if they shivered, under interrogation) made him sick (the Major warned that occasional revulsion was natural, but unproductive).

Why couldn't these people live like any normal person? A man with this one's brains and university degrees, English-speaking and whatnot, could become a big shot in business instead of a trade unionist letting a bunch of blacks strike and get him in trouble. When you interrogated a detainee, you had to familiarize yourself with all the details supplied by informers for his file; this one had a well-off father, a doctor wife, twin babies, an affair with a pretty student (admittedly, he had met her through her research connected with unions) and his parents-in-law's cottage at one of the best places for fishing on the coast, for his holidays. What more does a white man want? With a black man, all right, he wants what he can't have, and that can make a man sit eating his heart out in jail half his life. But how good to walk, on Saturday, to the dam where you used to swim as a kid, to be greeted (these people who incite blacks against us should just have seen) by the farm boys at the kraal with laughter and pleasure at your acquisition of a wife; to go out with your father to shoot jackals at sunset. There's something wrong with all these people who become enemies of their own country: this private theory was really the only aspect of his work—for security reasons—he talked about to his girl, who, of course (he sometimes smiled to forget), was now his wife. Something wrong with them. They're enemies because they can't enjoy their lives the way a normal white person in South Africa does.

He could get a cold drink or coffee and a snack in the canteen at John Vorster but in the early evening when he knew he'd have to stay late, maybe all night, to work on this man with the Major, he'd had just about enough of the place. He took his break where he and his mates liked to go, the Chinese take-away and restaurant just down the street.

It had no name up and was entered through an old shopfront. There was the high sizzle of frying and the full volume of TV programmes, and the Chinese and his wife moved about very softly. Early in the day when there was no television transmission, a small radio diffused cheerful commercials at the same volume above their pale faces from whose blunt features and flat eyes expression seemed worn away as a cake of soap loses definition in daily use. They belonged to the ancient guild of those harmless itinerant providers, of all nationalities, who wheel their barrows close to the sinister scenes of life—the bombed towns, the refugee encampments, the fallen cities—providing soup or rum indiscriminately to victims in rags or invaders in tanks, so long as these can pay the modest charge.

Convenient to concentration camps there were such quiet couples, minding their own business, selling coffee and schnapps to refresh jackbooted men off duty. Perhaps the Chinese and his wife felt protected by John Vorster Square and whatever they did not want to know happened there; perhaps they felt threatened by its proximity; both reasons to know nothing. Their restaurant had few ethnic pretensions of the usual kind—no velveteen dragons or wind-chimes—but they had put up a shelf on the wall where the large colour television set was placed like a miniature cinema screen, at awkward eye-level for diners. In front of the TV they kept an area clear of tables and had ranged a dozen chairs for the use of policemen. The policemen were not expected to buy a meal, and for the price of a packet of chips and a cold drink could relax from their duties, so nearby. Although they were not supposed to take alcohol before resuming these, and the Chinese couple did not have a licence to sell it, beer was silently produced for those who, the couple knew without having to be asked aloud, wanted it. The young policemen, joking and kidding as they commented on the programmes they were watching, created a friendly enclave in the place. Diners who had nothing much to say to one another felt at least part of some animation. Family treats for children and grandmothers were popular there, because the food was cheap; children, always fascinated by the thrill and fear sensed in anything military or otherwise authoritarian, ate their grey chicken soup while watching the policemen.

Sergeant Chapman found a few mates occupying the chairs. He joined them. The hot weather left the brand of their profession where their caps, now lying under their chairs, had pressed on their foreheads. Their private smog of cigarette smoke mingled with frying fumes wavered towards the TV screen; he was in time for the last ten minutes of an episode in a powdered-wig French historical romance, dubbed in Afrikaans. It ended with a duel, swords gnashing like knives and forks.
—Hey, man, look at that!—
—But they not really fighting, themselves. The actors. They have special experts dressed up like them.—
—Okay, I don't say it's the actors; but it's helluva good, just the same, ay. To be able to do it so fast and not hurt each other.—

Then came the Prime Minister, speaking with his special effects (a tooled leather prop desk, and velvet ceremonial drape as backdrop) on reconciliation and total onslaught. Conversations started up among the young policemen while he was projected overhead and the dinner customers chewed with respectful attention. Two plainclothes men in their casual-smart bar-lounge outfits came in to buy take-aways, evidently pleased with themselves, and did not even seem to notice that their volubility was making it difficult for people to follow the P.M.'s voice.

Sergeant Chapman took the opportunity to phone Mariella, although she knew he would be home late, if at all tonight. He still had these impulses to talk to her about nothing, over the phone, the way you can ten times a day with your girl. The telephone was not available to ordinary customers but the policemen knew they could use it. Its sticky handpiece and the privacy of the noise that surrounded him as he dialled were familiar. But Mariella did not answer with her soft voice of flirtation. She was terribly excited. He didn't know whether she was laughing or crying. When she went into the kitchen just now to get herself some bread and cheese (she wasn't going to bother with supper if he didn't come) the venison was gone from the window. Gone! Just like that. She went outside to see if it'd fallen from the hook—but no.

—No, of course, man, I put that hook in fast.—

—But still, it could have fallen—no, but anyway, the hook's still there. So I saw the meat must've been pinched. I ran to the street and then I rushed round the yard—

—You shouldn't do that when I'm not there, they'll knife you if you try to catch them. I've told you, Mariella, stay in the house at night, don't open to anyone.—

But she was 'so cross, so excited' she fetched the torch and took the dog by the collar and looked everywhere.

—That's mad, man. I told you not to. Somebody could be tricking you to get you out of the house.—

—No wait, there was nobody, Marais, nobody was there, it was all right.—

—Well you were just lucky he'd already got away, I'm telling you, Mariella, you make me worry. There must be blacks hanging around the neighbourhood who know I'm often away late—

—No, listen, just wait till you hear—Buller pulled away from me and jumped over the fence into the lane, you know, there by the veggie patch, and he was barking and scratching. So I climbed over and there it was on the ground—only it wasn't the meat and everything, it was just the bone. All the meat was torn off it! You'll see, you'll see the places where big teeth pulled away! It must have been that baboon, that monkey thing, no dog could reach so high! And there was an item on the radio about it only this morning! You'll see, only a bone's left.— And now she began to giggle intimately.—Your poor Pa. He'll be mad with you for hanging it like that. We'll have to pretend we ate it, hay? Anyway, you'll be pleased to know my jam's okay. It set and everything. . .What should I do. . .send for the police? If it could be you that comes, I'll be already making the bed warm. . .—

Although she sounded so lovable he had to be serious and make her promise to keep all the windows locked. Apes were clever, they had hands like humans. It might even manage to lift a lever and get in, now that it had become so full of cheek. He came striding back to his mates with a swagger of sensation, a tale to tell.—You know that escaped monkey? Came to our place and swiped the Blesbok leg we brought from the farm yesterday! True as god! I hung it in the window this morning!—

—Ag, man, Chapman. Your stories. Some black took it. Hanging it in the window! Wha'd'you think you were doing, man?—

—No way, *boet*. It was that bloody thing, all right. She's just told me: she found the bone there in the lane where it et it. Even a black's not going to tear raw meat with his teeth.—

That one was a toughie, all right—the detainee. When Sergeant Chapman took over again, the bloke was so groggy —like a loser after ten rounds—but he wouldn't talk, he wouldn't talk. At about ten o'clock he passed out and even the Major agreed to call it a day until six in the morning. Sergeant Chapman told him about the venison. The Major thought it a great joke but at the same time suggested the Sergeant's young wife ought to learn how to handle a firearm. Next time it might be more than a monkey out there in the yard. Sergeant Chapman ought to know the situation.

There had to be some sign that the plot was being cultivated. That was what black men were for; so Eddie hoed the mealie patch. Vusi kept to the house. He sat in his armchair and read a thick paperback whose pages, top and bottom, were splayed and puffed by exposure to climatic changes or by much thumbing. *Africa Undermined: A History of the Mining Companies and the Underdevelopment of Africa*: sometimes he would borrow a ball-point from Joy, mark a passage. If he began to yawn and sigh this was a prelude to his suddenly getting up and disappearing into the back room. She would hear him tinkering there, the clink of small tools; she supposed it was to do with what was locked in the shed. She filled several hours a day with *Teach Yourself Portuguese*, but didn't have her cassettes with her, here, as a guide to pronunciation, so had to concentrate on the grammar. Vusi could have helped her with German—but Portuguese!

—How long were you there?— He had trained in East Germany. That much she knew about him.

—Two years and three months. We didn't learn from books. You just have to begin to talk, man, you have to make people understand you when you want something, that's the best way. But what d'you want to learn Portuguese for?—

—Mozambique. Charles and I thought of going there. To live.— She pulled her hair back down behind the arms of her glasses.—I might go, anyway. Teach for a while.—

—What do you teach?—

She made an awkward face.—I haven't much, yet. But I can teach history. The new education system there; I'd like to be involved. . .in something like that. One day.— The two words passed to him as a token that she was not deserting.

—Ja. You'd like it. It's going to be a good place. And Charlie, he's learning too?—

—He was. But not now.—

Vusi picked up her book and tried out a phrase or two, smiled at his poor effort.

—You *do* speak Portuguese.—

—Some words. . . I was only there a couple of months, everyone talks English to you.— He managed, with an accent better than hers, a few more phrases, as if for his and her amusement.

He sat in his chair again, waiting, his face as he himself would never see it, not in any photograph or mirror. He was possessed by an expression far from anyone's reach, so deep in the past of himself, a sorrow he did not consciously feel there in the watergleam of his black eyes hidden in the ancient cave of skull, in the tenuousness of life in the fine gills of the nostrils, the extraordinary unconscious settling of the grooved lips—lips that, when he was unaware of himself, not using them to shape the half-articulate communication of a poorly-educated black man's English, held in their form what has never been, might still be spoken.

Now when he did speak, on the conscious level of their being in the room together, it seemed to her he did not know who he was; she had to make the quick adjustment to his working perception of himself.—You not really married?—

She looked at his mystery, while he showed simple curiosity.

—No. Not really anything.—

He understood—was meant to understand?—she doesn't sleep with Charlie. If so, it was a confidence that licensed questions. —What's the idea?—

—Well. There's no other room for me, is there.—

He arched his head back against the chair, expelled a breath towards the ceiling with its pine-knots and pressed lead curlicues all four of them, at times, took tally of obsessively.

—We came to a sort of stop. About five months ago, after nearly six years. But we'd already accepted to do this, while we were still together, so we couldn't let that make any difference.—

—Hell, you're a funny kind of woman.—

It was said with detached admiration. She laughed.—You know better than I do what matters.—

—Sure. Still—

—It's *because* I'm a woman you say *still*—

He saw she jealously took his admiration as some sort of discrimination within commitment. He shied away. There came out of that mouth of his a careless response a city black man picks up as the idiom of whites in the streets. —That's one I can't handle.—

He escaped her, taking up *Africa Undermined* aimlessly and putting it down again on his way out of the room.

Charles returned from his daily run; part of the routine he had constructed for himself to support the waiting. His rump in satiny blue-and-red shorts rose and fell before motorists who overtook him and often waved in approval of his healthy employment of time. Eddie would have liked to come along (oh how long—five years—ago, as a seventeen-year-old in Soweto he had run in training, had ambitions as an amateur fly-weight) but a black-and-white couple would have been conspicuous. Panting like a happy dog, shaggy with warm odours, Charles was brought up short, in the room, as when one enters where some event is just over; but all that he was sensing, without identifying this, was that he had been talked about in his absence.

Although once she would have made a peg with fingers on her nose and so sent him off to shower, she did not now have the rights over his body to tell him he stank of good sweat; just smiled quickly and went on with her future tenses. He meant to go and get dressed but the need to know everything his colleagues knew, to follow their minds wherever they went, that would have made him a natural chairman of the board if he had grown up responding differently to propitious 'circumstances', led him to have a look at what chapter Vusi had reached in his book, and then, although he himself had read the book, to begin reading, again, wherever the other man had made his mark in ball-point blue.

Not suddenly—there must have been the too-soft impression before first Charles, then Joy became conscious of it—there was a voice never heard before, in the house where no one but the four of them ever entered, now. It was unexpected as the feeble cry of something new-born.

Vusi came into the room with an instrument from which he was producing a voice. He passed Charles and stood before Joy, playing a muffled, sweet, half-mumbled *Georgia On My Mind*—yes, that was it, identified as a bird-call can be made out as phonetic syllables humans translate into words. From those lips rippling and contracting round a mouthpiece, beneath his fingers pressing crude buttons, the song was issuing from an instrument strangely recognizable, absurd and delightful. Every now and then he drew a gulp of breath, like a swimmer. He played on, the voice gaining power, sometimes stammering (the peculiar buttons got stuck), occasionally squealing, but achieving the gentle, wah-wah sonority, rocket rise to high note and steady gliding fall out of hearing that belong to one instrument alone.

While what they had to do was wait, Vusi made a saxophone.

It was for this that he had collected the tabbed rings off beer cans. The curved neck was perhaps the easiest. It was made of articulated sections hammered from jam tins. Some of the more intricate parts must have required a thicker material. There might be a few cartridge cases transformed in the keyboard. He had worked on the saxophone shut up in the shed with the necessities stored there, as well as away down at the pigsties, where it was tried out without anyone else being able to hear it.

The white couple marvelled over the thing. An extraordinary artifact, as well as a musical instrument. Having played it to the girl that first time it was ever played for others, Vusi was unmoved by praise because no one would see what they were really looking at, as laymen enthuse over something that can't be grasped through their secular appreciation.

He didn't know Charles was reminded of the ingenuity of objects displayed in the concentration camps of Europe, now museums. These were made by the inmates out of nothing, effigies of the beautiful possibilities of a life to be lived.

The municipal art gallery owns a sacred monkey. A charming image, an Indian statuette copied by a Viennese artist in glazed ceramic, green as if carved out of deep water. It lives in a cupboard behind glass. The gallery is poorly endowed with the art of the African continent on which it stands, and has no example of the dog-faced ape of ancient Egyptian mythology, Cynocephalus, often depicted attendant upon the god Thoth, which she has seen in museums abroad and has been amused to recognize as the two-thousand-year-old spitting image of a baboon species still numerous in South Africa.

A set of pan pipes sticking up out of the bathwater: toes. A face reflected in the snout of the shiny faucet bulged into a merry gourd with a Halloween mouth. She can look at that but she doesn't want to see the distortion of her lower torso which is reflected if she leans her head, in its plastic mob cap, against the back of the bath. Her legs become gangling and bowed, joined by huge feet at one end and a curved perspective that leads back to a hairy creature, crouched. There is nothing beyond this vora-cious pudenda; it has swallowed the body and head behind it. She lies in the bath for relaxation. Nobody's told her she's dying, but they're being brought down all around her, as a lion moves into a herd, tearing into the flesh of his victims. A breast off here; a piece of lung there; a bladder cut down to size. She lies on her back and palpates her breasts dutifully. There are ribs, but no lumps. The nipples don't rise; that's good, she doesn't like the masturbatory aspect of what doctors advise you to do to yourself, as a precaution, in order to stay alive. These breasts don't recognize her hands; they've known only male ones. Her hands don't make them remember those.

Despite the fun-palace image in the faucet, her real thighs still have that firm classical roundness. They don't pile like half-set junket round the knees when she's standing. Not yet.

The delicately-engraved imprint of autumn leaves—a few varicosed patches—is more or less covered by a tan.

However she lies, her stomach rises like the Leviathan.

It was always there, waiting, flattened between the hip-bones, for its years to come! She doesn't take it too hard. These fantasies are the consequence of waking so early, and there's a simple scientific explanation for that: reduced hormonal activ-ity means you need less sleep. She nods her head in sage comprehension when this is explained to her; what it really means is you sleep eight hours after love-making. She feels them, other people, sleeping this sleep in other rooms. It's true that as you get older you suddenly know what happened in childhood. She understands quite differently, now, the family joke she used to be told about how she crawled over to her mother's bed at dawn, lifted her sleeping eyelid, and spat in her eye. Oh lovers, I envy you the sleep, not the love-making, but nobody would believe me. I am told to disbelieve myself. 'It's something a doctor can't really let himself prescribe. . .but you need to stop thinking you're not interesting to men any longer.'

Old stock; hers. She goes over it again, toes, thighs, twat (yes, put down the great notion it had of itself, temple of pleasure), nice breasts. The face can be left out of it, thank God, you can't verify your own face by looking down on it in the bath, wiggling it, spouting its flesh out of the water and scuttling it to sink to the belly-button again. This is not a bath with mirrors, far nicer, it has a glass wall that looks on a tiny courtyard no bigger than an airshaft where shade-loving plants and ferns grow, ingeniously and economically watered, in time of drought, by the outlet from the bath. They flourish in water favoured by this flesh as the Shi-ites buy grace in the form of bathwater used by the Aga Khan. She ought to contemplate the plants instead. She feels she doesn't want to, she doesn't want to be distracted from what she has to see, but she forces herself—she must stop watching herself, and this makes her feel someone's watching her, there's a gaze forming outside her awareness of self, it exists for a moment between the greenery.

Looking at the woman in the bath. Seeing what she sees.

She thought of it as having struck her, first, as the head of antiquity, the Egyptian basalt rigidity, twice removed—as animal and attribute of a god—from man, but with a gleam of close golden brown eyes like a human's.

No. A *real* baboon, Peeping Tom at large in the suburbs.

She had to think of it as that. If not (soaking herself groggy, seeing things), it would have to be her own visitation; a man.

Eddie came upon some droppings not far from the back of the shed. They looked human, to him. All four went to the spot to have a look. The Kleynhans place was so isolated, except for the passage of life on the road, to which it offered no reason to pause. They had felt themselves safe from intruders.

The hard twist of excreta was plaited with fur and sinew: Charles picked it up in his bare hand.—See that? It had rabbit for supper. A jackal.—

Joy gave a shivery laugh, although there was no prowling man to fear.—So close to the house?—

Vusi was disbelieving.—Nothing to eat there.— The converted shed with its roll-down metal door was just behind them.

—Well, they pad around, sniff around. I suppose this place's still got a whiff of chickens and pigs. It's quite common even now, you get the odd jackal roaming fairly near to towns.—

—Are you sure? How can you know it's jackal, Charlie?—

Charles waggled the dung under Eddie's nose.

—Hey, man!— Eddie backed off, laughing nervously.

Vusi was a tester of statements rather than curious. —Can you tell all kinds of animals' business?—

—Of course. First there's the shape and size, that's easy, ay, anyone can tell an elephant's from a bird's— They laughed, but Charles was matter-of-fact, as someone who no longer works in a factory will pick up a tool and use it with the same automative skill learnt on an assembly line. —But even if the stuff is broken up, you can say accurately which animal by examining food content. The bushmen—the San, Khoikhoi—they've practised it for centuries, part of their hunting skills.—

—Is that what they taught you at Scouts, man?—

—No. Not Scouts exactly.—

—So where'd you pick it up?— Eddie rallied the others. —A Number Two expert! He's clever, old Charlie. We're lucky to have a chap like him, ay!—

Joy was listening politely, half-smiling, to Charles retelling, laconically self-censored, what had been the confidences of their early intimacy.

—Once upon a time I was a game ranger, believe it or not.— That was one of the things he had tried in order to avoid others: not to have to go into metal and corrugated paper packaging in which his father and uncles held forty per cent of the shares, not to take up (well, all right, if you're not cut out for business) an opening in a quasi-governmental fuel research unit—without, for a long time, knowing that there was no way out for him, neither the detachment of science nor the consolations of nature. Born what he was, where he was, knowing what he knew, outrage would have burned down to shame if he had thought his generation had any right left to something in the careers guide.

—You're kidding. Where?—

—Oh, around. An ignoramus with a B.Sc. Honours, but the Shangaan rangers educated me.—

—Oh Kruger Park, you mean. They work there. That place.— Vusi's jerk of the head cut off his words like an appalled flick of fingers. Once, he had come in through that vast wilderness of protected species; an endangered one on his way to become operational. Fear came back to him as a layer of cold liquid under the scalp. All that showed was that his small stiff ears pulled slightly against his skull.

Charles wiped his palm on his pants and clasped hands behind his head, easing his neck, his matronly pectorals flexing to keep in trim while waiting. —One day I'd like to apply the methodology to humans—a class *analysis*. (He enjoyed their laughter.) The sewage from a white suburb and the sewage from a squatters' camp—you couldn't find a better way of measuring the level of sustenance afforded by different income levels, even the snobbery imposed by different occupations and aspirations. A black street-sweeper who scoffed half a loaf and a Bantu beer for lunch, a white executive who's digested oysters and a bottle of Fleur du Cap—show me what you shit, man, and I'll tell you who you are.—

That afternoon a black man did appear in the yard. He was not a prowler, although he probably had been watching them, the Kleynhans place, since they'd moved in. He would have known from where this could be managed delicately, without disturbing them or being seen.

He was a middle-aged farm labourer dressed in his church clothes so that the master and the missus wouldn't chase him away as a *skelm*. But he needn't have worried, because the master and the missus never appeared from the house. He found the two men who worked there at Baas Kleynhans's place now, as he had done, farm boys. He had come to see how his mealies were getting along. Yes. Yes. . .There was a long pause, in which the corollary to that remark would have time to be understood: he had been circling round the Kleynhans place, round this moment, to come to the point—an agreement whereby he could claim his mealie crop when it was ready for harvest. These other two, his brothers (he spoke to them in Sesotho and they answered in that language, but when he asked where they were from they said Natal) were welcome to eat what they liked, he was only worried about the white farmer. Could they claim the patch as the usual bit of ground for pumpkins and mealies farmers allowed their blacks? He would come and weed the mealies himself very early in the morning, before the baas got up, he wouldn't bring his brothers any trouble.

But the young men were good young men. They wouldn't hear of *baba* doing that. The one in jeans and a shirt with pictures all over it (farm boys dressed just the same as youngsters from town, these days) said he was looking after the mealies, don't worry. Gazing round his old home yard, the man admired the new garage with the nice door that had been made out of the shed and asked why this new white man hadn't ploughed? What were they going to plant? And what was his (Vusi's) work, if this white man wasn't going to have any pigs or chickens? They explained that farming hadn't really begun yet. First they'd built the garage, and Vusi—Vusi had been working inside. Helping the farmer fix things up. Painting the house. Ah yes, Baas Kleynhans was sick a long time before he died, there was no one to look after the house nicely.

The three black men talked together in the yard for more than an hour. They drifted towards a couple of boxes that still stood there, from Charles's deliveries, and sat on them, facing one another, gesticulating and smoking, sometimes breaking the little knot with a high exclamation or a piece of mimicry, laughter. When the man took off his felt hat a lump at the centre of his dusty hairline was polished by the sun. The white couple got a look at them from the bathroom window. It was an opaque glass hatch that opened under layers of dead creeper. What was happening in the yard could have been seen and heard more clearly from the kitchen windows, but the white couple also would have been visible, there, and they could not understand what was being said, anyway.

At first they felt only anxiety. Then they began to feel like eavesdroppers, spies: those who have no commune, those on the outside. The slow accretion of past weeks that was the four of them—a containing: a shell, a habitation—was broken. Eddie and Vusi were out there, yet it was Charles and Joy who were alone. They had no way of knowing what it was they were witnessing.

The man wobbled away on an old bicycle, calling the dying fall of farewells that go back and forth between country blacks. Both the pair in the house and the pair outside waited, just as they were, for about ten minutes. Vusi was silent but Charles and Joy (still in the bathroom, with its snivelling tap) could hear the continuing murmur of Eddie in monologue.

They all met in the kitchen. The girl looked ridiculously breathless, to the two coming in from the yard, as if she had been climbing.

—He used to work for the man who owned this place before. He wants his mealies.—

Charles's emotions, like his blood, flushed near the surface. He was testy when anxious; now, impatient with Vusi. —It took the whole afternoon to say that! Christ, we've been going crazy. You seemed to know the man. We thought—God knows what— that you were having to give explanations, that you were cornered—I don't know? And what could we do? You seemed to be *enjoying* yourselves, for Christ' sake. . .—

As anxiety found release his tone drained of accusation; he ended up excited, half-laughing, rolling tendrils of bright beard between thumb and finger. Like a fragment of food, at table, a shred of leaf from the dead creeper round the bathroom window clung to the hairs.

Eddie went to the fridge and took out beer.—We should have given him something to drink, but I couldn't come into the white baas's kitchen and just take. He must've wondered why we didn't have any in his old room, man; I was scared he'd ask to go in there, and see no beds, nothing. I was already thinking could I say we had girl-friends somewhere, where we sleep. But he knows everybody for miles around this place.—

They discussed the man and decided there was nothing they could do except hope he would not come back too shortly. Soon it would not matter anymore if he did.

Joy did not look at Charles but directed a remark at him: —If we have to stay much longer I'll have to start wearing a pillow. When I met our friend the estate agent's wife at the chemist's last week she had a good look at me. 'You don't show yet, do you, dear?'—

—Oh my god. You'd better stop going to town.—

She did not complain. Her hair was put up in an odd knot on the side of her head—she was a woman, after all, she played about with her appearance, waiting. The way of doing her hair was very unattractive; on the side from which it was pulled over, the bone behind her ear was prominent and her skull looked flattened.—And what was that Cyclops eye on his forehead?—

Eddie winced, puzzled.—That what?—

—Some lump I could see in the sun, quite big and shiny.—

Charles tossed the remark absently at her, no one was interested. —A cyst, I suppose. I didn't notice.—

—Like a bulging eye in the middle of his head. Or one of Moses's horns growing.—

Vusi had no need of ring-tabs any longer—he dropped his in his emptied beer can and gave it a shake, sounding a rattle for attention.—Kleynhans paid him fifteen rands a month. He worked for him for twelve years. When Kleynhans died, the daughter told the agent Klopper he could stay on without pay in that room in the yard until the place was sold. His son works at the brick-field and lives with his wife and kids with those other squatters near there. They've been chased off twice but they built their shack again. Since we came, the old man's living with them. No job. No permission to look for work in town. Nowhere to go.—

—Yes.— Charles dragged all five fingers again and again through his beard.—Yes.—

A habitation of resolve, secreted by their presence among one another, contained them again, the four of them: waiting. They were quiet, not subdued; strongly alive. There was no need to talk. After a while Vusi fetched his saxophone and it spoke, gently. There was a summer storm coming up, first the single finger of a tree's branch paddling thick air, then the land expelling great breaths in gusts, common brown birds flinging themselves wildly, a raw, fresh-cut scent of rain falling somewhere else. So beautiful, the temperament of the earth. Waiting, they saw the rain, dangling over the pale spools that were the power station towers.

Ms Dot Lamb, chairperson of the Residents' Association of the suburb where, if an outlaw can be said to have taken up residence, this one seemed to have a base, since it kept returning there, requested an interview with the town councillor whom the residents had voted into office to protect their property and interests. The promise given by him produced no result—as if to show how little it felt itself threatened by the councillor, the creature 'cleaned up' as a resident put it, an entire bed of artichokes cultivated from imported seed for table use as an elegant first course. Ms Lamb called a meeting of the Association. She was a woman who got things done; the residents were people who wanted things done for them, without having to take the trouble themselves. It was she who had rallied them to contest the plan to build a home for spastic children among their houses. She had won (for them) the battle to stop toilets for blacks being built at the blacks' suburban bus terminus, making a strong case that this convenience, far from promoting public decency, would merely encourage the number of blacks who gathered to drink among the natural flora of the koppies that was such a treasured feature of the suburb. Now these koppies were being used by an escaped ape as well. Was it for this that ratepayers had been notified of increases in property taxes envisaged for the coming year? Valuable pets, loved companions of children, had been killed. People feared to leave small children to play in their own gardens.

The residents authorized Ms Lamb to take further steps. She wanted no more shilly-shallying with the so-called proper channels. She went straight to the local police station, kicked up a fuss, and actually got the superintendent to send two armed white policemen and a couple of black ones to mount a search along the ridge of koppies behind some of the finest homes in the suburb. They rounded up several illicit liquor sellers and arrested fifteen men without passes, but did not find what they had been instructed to.

The SPCA protested that an animal should not be hunted and shot by the police, like a criminal. Zoo officials offered to try and dart it. If, as a number of people insisted, it was an ape, it would find a safe home in the new ape-house, where at 3 p.m. every day the inmates perform a tea-party for the amusement of children of all races.

Eddie went to the road and thumbed a lift in the African way, flagging a whole arm from waist level as if directing a motor race. He was wearing his Wild West jacket. Vusi and Charles were still asleep—some people can pass the time, waiting, by sleeping more—but Joy saw him go. Her hands tingled with anguish, as if she were going to be sick. She did not wake the others and did not know if she was doing what was right. She did not know whether, when they woke up, she would pretend she had not seen Eddie.

Eddie got a lift with a black man in a firm's panel van. They talked about soccer. He did not ask to be let down at the local dorp where Joy and Mrs Naas Klopper shopped. He went all the way—to Johannesburg.

Eddie had nothing to leave at the entrance to a supermarket where you were asked to deposit your briefcase or carrier bag in return for a numbered disc. He did not uncouple a trolley from the train against the wall, or pick up a plastic basket. He walked the lanes as if at a vast exhibition, passing arsenals of canned fruit, yellow mosaics of pickles in jars, flat, round and oval cans of pilchards, sardines, anchovies, mussels in brine and tuna in cottonseed oil, bottles of sauces, aerosol cans of chocolate topping, bins of coffee beans, packets of rice and lentils, sacks of mealie-meal and sugar, pausing now and then, as if to read the name of the artist: *Genuine Papadums, Poivre Vert de Madagascar*—and then passing on to pet and poultry foods, detergents, packaged meat like cross-sections of viscera under a microscope, pots, Irish Coffee glasses, can-openers, electric pizza-makers, saws, chisels, light bulbs, roundabout stands of women's pantyhose, and greeting cards humorous, religious or sentimental. White women pushed small children or small dogs in the upper rack of trolleys. Black people turned over the packages of stewing meat. Other blacks, employees, wielded punches that printed prices on stocks they were replenishing. The piped music was interrupted by chimes and a voice regularly welcoming him (in his capacity as a shopper) and announcing today's specials. At the record and tape bar he spent half-an-hour turning over the decks of bright neat tapes the way others did meat packs. There were no facilities for listening to tapes or records, but he knew all the groups and individuals recorded, and their familiar music sealed within. A supermarket wouldn't have anything that hadn't been reissued in cheap mass pressings—you'd need a record shop for really good, new stuff. Going through these was just looking up what hadn't changed.

He queued at one of the exits holding a set of transistor batteries and a snuffbox-sized tin of ointment he hadn't seen since his mother used to put it on his sores as a kid. A *mama* ahead of him, turning to speak Setswana, at home here in this city in her slippers, outsize tweed skirt and nylon headscarf from some street-vendor's selection, assumed his support, as one of her own, in an argument over change with the aloof almost-white cashier. From the stand beside him he took, as a tourist picks up a last postcard, one of the pairs of sunglasses hooked there.

In the streets there were thousands like him. He crossed at traffic lights and walked pavements among them. Young ones loping in loose gangs of three or four, out of work or out of school, going nowhere. When you are that age, the city, where there is nothing for you, draws you from the townships, to which you always have to go back. Others, his own age, carrying their employers' mail and packages to the post office, daringly

173

shaving their motor-bikes past traffic, delivering medicines and film, legal documents, orders of hamburgers. Older ones in those top brass peaked caps and military tunics with which white people strangely choose to dress the humblest of their employees—doormen and commissionaires—like their military heroes. The city was blacker than he remembered it. Down the west end of Jeppe and Bree Streets, the same long bus queues making an accompanying line of fruit skins and coke cans in the gutters, the same Portuguese eating-house selling pap and stew, the same taxi drivers using Diagonal Street as the backyard where they groomed their vehicles like proud racehorse owners, the same women crowded round the alley exit of the poultry wholesaler's to buy sloppy pails of chicken guts. But in the white part of the city, where there were no street stalls but banks and insurance company blocks, landscaped malls, caterpillars of people being carried from level to level—into what used to be the white centre of the city, his own kind seemed to have flowed. It was Saturday and there were light-coloureds, painters and carpenters of the building trade, dressed in pastel safari shorts and jackets, straw hats with paisley bands, like the Afrikaners who grandfathered them. Black kids of respectable families had dazzling white socks half-way up their small legs. Lovely black girls tilted the balance of their backsides to counter the angle of the high-heeled sandals it was apparently fashionable this year to wear with jeans; the nails of their crooked toes and beautiful hands signalled deep red as they approached and passed him. All would have to go back to the places for blacks, when they had spent their money; but there was no white centre to the city, anymore (he had forgotten, in five years, that this was so, or it had happened in those five years). They came in and surged all over it, it lived off them and for them. The male office-cleaners, tiny, bare-chested figures looking down, in the wind and dust blown from the mine dumps, from the tops of skyscrapers where they washed their clothes and drank beer, must be able to see their own people far below, flowing all round the company headquarters of the white race.

He spent a long time looking in windows filled with pocket calculators of all sizes and kinds, video equipment, cameras and the latest in walkabout tape players, which, as watches once had been, were being reduced to smaller and smaller format. Inside a shop he had this marvellous precision of workmanship demonstrated to him by a young Portuguese who probably had fled to this country from black rule in Mozambique just about the same time as Eddie had fled from his home, here in Johannesburg, eluding the political police from the handsome building with touches of blue paint, John Vorster Square, a few blocks from the shop in which he was now trying on headphones. —S'wonderful, 'ey? You don't 'ardly feel them, they so light.— The young Portuguese was willing to show every feature of each shape, size and model. When Eddie left without 'making up his mind', he gave Eddie a card with a name written large and curly below the shop's printed title—*Manuel.* —H'ask for me, I'll look after you.—

In an outfitter's Eddie was shown a range of casual trousers by an Indian employed there. —This's what all the young chaps are wearing, man. Bright colours. What are you? Twenty-eight?— He sized up Eddie's waist with a frisker's glance. He admired Eddie's jacket: that certainly wasn't locally-made! When Eddie didn't see anything he liked, he was reassured:—Just look in next week, say, after Tuesday. We getting fabulous new stuff all the time. Whenever you passing. . .—

He roamed again towards the West end, to the queues from which he could catch a bus to get him part of his way back. He bought a carton of curried chicken and ate as he went along. Outside a white men's bar a black girl singled him out with a sidling look, and approached. He smiled and walked on: no thanks, *sisi.* With the prostitute's eye for the stranger in town, she was the only one in the city to recognize him: someone set apart in the crowd of his own kind from which he appeared indistinguishable.

Stanley Dobrow entered his photograph for the 'Picture of The Year' competition held by a morning paper.

Old Grahame Fraser-Smith—the 'old' was an epithet of comradeliness on the part of his colleagues, he was only forty-eight—got the idea in his head that although short-sighted, he had seen into the eyes of the creature. In the operating theatre, during those intervals between putting together broken faces with a human skill and ingenuity more miraculous than God's making of a woman out of a man's rib, he told the story differently, now. It seemed to him that as he bent down for the golf ball, he saw the creature bend first, just as he was doing, but farther off. And they looked at each other. You know how arresting eyes can be? It was hardly necessary to point this out where everyone around him was reduced to eyes above masks. No, true, he couldn't describe the body, certainly not the gait, as van Gelder insisted he could. Yet the eyes—you know how it is sometimes, in a room full of people, you see really only one person, you look into that pair of eyes and it's as if you are face to face, alone, with that person? It was like suddenly meeting someone seen many times on a photograph; or someone he'd been told about as a child; or someone people had been telling one another about for generations. He stopped there. He didn't want the assisting surgeons, anaesthetist, nurses, the medical students who came to watch the beauty of his work (about which he was genuinely modest) to reduce that encounter to something fanciful, and therefore funny. But if van Gelder was a bone-man, so was he, a Hamlet who had contemplated and reconstructed with his own hands the living maxillo-facial structure of a thousand Yoricks. To himself he secretly continued: he had looked back into a consciousness from which part of his own came. There were claims from within oneself that could materialize only in these unsought ways, in apparently trivial or fortuitous happenings that could be felt but not understood. He thought of the experience as some sort of slip in the engagement of the cogs of time.

Eddie was there before dark.

Vusi and Charles were playing chess and Joy was burning rubbish in the front garden. So she was first to see him come as she was first to know he had gone. She had a broken branch and went on poking at whatever was burning until he had to pass her on his way up to the house. She put up a folded hand with her usual effacing gesture, smiling, not aware that she smeared the cobweb of flying ashes that had settled on her forehead. —Hullo.—

If she wouldn't ask any questions, he would.

Eddie stopped.—What's that for?—

She was better-looking with the waves of flame melting the narrow definitions of her face, colouring and rounding it. —A rat came into the bathroom. They're breeding in that pile of junk we threw out of the shed. I had to lug everything round here.—

He nodded. He had been away, but at once was together with her, with the others, again, in the knowledge that no fire could be made near what was behind the new garage door.

He went on to the house.

They must have heard him talking to Joy. They must have decided to talk it out calmly, but Charles struggled up from under his own self-control, the chessmen rolled over the floor. —Are you bloody mad?— He was gone from the room.

Vusi did not seem to see Charles; opened his mouth dryly and closed it again.

Eddie dribbled one of the chessmen with the toe of his running shoe. He went out to the kitchen, and came back with a beer. Charles was there, gathering up the chessmen.

The release of gas from the beer can as he pierced it was like an opening exclamation from Eddie.—Well, nothing happened. I went to town, I'm back.—

Vusi was silent, withholding his attention.

Charles had his big body safely chained down on a stool.—I'm sorry. But it's clear you know what you did, what risk you took for us all.—

—There's nothing to worry about. *Nothing happened.*— Eddie spoke to Vusi. He had to reach Vusi. It was Vusi to whom they were all responsible, even in collective responsibility; Vusi, not Charles, to whom Joy had had to say she had seen Eddie take a lift, on the road, early in the morning. —I didn't go to see anyone. You can believe that.—

Vusi gave a slow blink to dismiss any suggestion of mistrust.

Eddie's presence was acknowledged.—That's not the question, man. You could have been picked up.—

—Well, I wasn't.—

Joy came in and saw they were not quarrelling; it was no more possible for them to dare quarrel than for her to have made her bonfire near the shed. Discipline was the molecular pattern that attracted them back to their particular association. If Eddie had been picked up, even if he had not been recognized as a banned exile who had infiltrated, and had got away with being jailed as an ordinary pass-offender (the papers he had been provided with described him as a farm labourer and did not permit him to look for work in an urban area), the pattern would have been distorted. Vusi could not function without Eddie, Eddie and Vusi without Charles and Joy, Charles and Joy without Eddie and Vusi. The entity reconstituted itself irresistibly, there among the sofa covered with the conch-design cloth, the armchair that had become Vusi's, the fake ox-wagon wheel with its fly-haloed pink hats; there was no sending it flying apart, from within, by attacking (with the sort of open reproaches any ordinary relationship would withstand) the component—Eddie—that was once more in place, at the Kleynhans place.

The white pair later heard Vusi talking for a long time in his and Eddie's language in the second bedroom. Each made a mental translation, according to what they themselves would have been saying to Eddie, of what Vusi would be saying in the low cadence that seemed to vibrate the thin walls of the house like some swarm settled under the tin roof. Charles was giving him the hell he couldn't, aloud; above all, how could the kid Eddie risk *Vusi*, Vusi who had been operational before, who knew his job, who was needed to stay alive and had managed to survive four times the near certainty of imprisonment and death his job carried. Joy was asking why: if Eddie really knew why he was here—the reasons of his own life, of the lives of all his people for generations—then how could he have an impulse to drop back into the meek or loud-mouth compliance of the streets, still under that same magisterial authority of someone's long-dead white grandfather? Poor Eddie. It could only be because he had not understood properly why he had to be here and nowhere else; not taking advantage of slowly-evolving opportunities to advance himself in the black business community, or to avail himself, at newly-established technikons for blacks, of what, after all, were necessary skills for the service of his people, or to join the elite of black doctors allowed to practise only in black areas or black lawyers barred from taking chambers in white areas where the courts were. She could testify, in herself. She would not have been here if she had not found her own re-education, after the school where she had sung for God to save white South Africa. Without that re-education she would not have come to know for herself, for certain, that she could not now be bearing classified children (white) while living in a white suburb like that of the house with a view where she had grown up. She could not be anywhere but on the Kleynhans plot with a view of the power station.

That evening there was the rather prim atmosphere in the house that surrounds someone who has been drunk and now has slept it off. Eddie appeared, sobered of his single repetition, *Nothing happened.* Vusi must have told him that if he couldn't stand the Kleynhans place any longer, that was all right, because from tomorrow the three men would be out every night from midnight until just before dawn. It had been Charles's turn to cook (they had solved the problem of which sex was suited to the kitchen by having a roster) and, in spite of what sort of day it had been, he had made a mutton stew. Eddie loved mutton; but of course it had not been made with a treat for him in mind.

After they had eaten, the men went out into the yard. The moon was not yet risen. The light from the kitchen window touched shallowly the zinc glint of the garage door as it rolled up sufficiently for them to duck in. It rattled down behind them. Eddie didn't think it was working smoothly enough.—Better get us some oil, Charlie, or it's soon going to rust.— Charles raised eyebrows, opened nostrils, swallowed a yawn, a man without tenure. While they were checking the heavy picks, the spades and black plastic sheeting Charles had laid in ready for the end of waiting, Joy didn't mind doing the washing-up on her own for once. If there was something practical to plan, the men liked to do it behind the outhouse door, where they were in tactile reach of the means by which what they were discussing was to be realized.

They were gone a long time. She took a beer from the fridge with her to the livingroom and turned on Eddie's tape player, which was always beside his end of the sofa as a pipe smoker will have his paraphernalia handy on a chair-arm. After she had told Vusi about seeing Eddie hitch a lift, she had made it possible for herself to keep out of everyone's way, all day. In order not to be with Vusi and Charles, not to sit around with them in that same room, or to be in the bedroom which was, after all, Charles's room as well, she had dragged cardboard boxes, rags, old bones, torn Afrikaans newspapers the black man who used to live in the yard had collected, to the front garden and made her bonfire among the broken poles of the pergola. Now she felt the comfort of being together with them once more—all three of them, Vusi, Charles and Eddie, although they were not in the room with her. The music was whatever Eddie had left in the player; a tape with a strong beat. All on her own, she began to dance, smiling to herself as if to others dancing towards and away from her. She worked off her sandals without pausing, and danced on the nap of the ugly rug Charles had bought along with the job-lot 'suite' to make a show to the Naas Kloppers of the district that the house was meant really to be lived in. Rhythm tossed her head and the knot of hair loosened and slowly unravelled, then swung from shoulder to shoulder. She threw her glasses onto Vusi's chair. At night, moths circled in place of flies above the lop-sided pink shades, falling singed; her bare feet trod one now and then. Her small breasts rose and fell against her chest like a necklace; she swooped and shook, swayed and softly sang.

Vusi's dreaming face, that had so little to do with the temporal level of his thoughts and actions, took the wash of crude 60-watt light from the chandelier, suddenly in the doorway. The face appeared to her as a wave of phosphorescence in the dark wake of the house around her movements might reveal a head from a submerged statue. Eddie and woolly Charles came up behind him.

She had no breath left, her mouth was open in a panting smile.

—Come on.— It could only be Eddie she summoned.

She went on dancing.

Eddie was standing there.

Slowly, Eddie began to stir to life, first from the hips, then with this-way-and-that slither and stub of the feet, then with the pelvis, the buttocks, the elbows, the knees, and as his whole body and head revived, moved to her.

Eddie and Joy were dancing.

Charles could dance only when drunk; a performing bear, round and round; sometimes some girl's teddy bear. He stretched out on the sofa, occupying Eddie's end as well, and smiled at them encouragingly. He might have been a father happily embarrassed to see a neglected daughter coming out of herself.

Before the tape ended Vusi fetched his saxophone. That voice that was strangely his own entered the room ahead of him, playing along with the beat, speaking to them all, one last time.

When signs were not noted for a week or so in a suburb where the fugitive had been active, residents there at once lost interest in having it trapped. So long as it attacked other people's cats and dogs, frightened other people's maids—that was other people's affair. Indignation and complaints shifted from suburb to suburb, from the affluent to the salaried man. The creature was no snob; or no respecter of persons, whichever way you cared to look at it. The policeman's venison in a lower-income-group housing estate, a pedigreed ShihTzu carried away when let out for its late-night leg-lift in an Inanda rose garden—each served equally as means of survival. And the creature never went beyond the bounds of white Johannesburg. Like the contract labourers who had to leave their families to find work where work was, like the unemployed who were endorsed out to where there was no work and somehow kept getting back in through the barbed strands of Influx Control; like all those who are the uncounted doubling of census figures for Soweto and Tembisa and Natalspruit and Alexandra townships, it was canny about where it was possible somehow to exist off the pickings of plenty. And if charity does not move those who have everything to spare, fear will. All the residents of the suburbs wanted was for the animal to be confined in its appropriate place, that's all, zoo or even circus. They were prepared to pay for this to be done.

(But the owner of the largest circus that travels the country said it was unlikely an ape that had learned to fend for itself in a hostile environment would be ever again psychologically amenable to training.)

Almost two months had passed since a thirteen-year-old schoolboy had been the first to sight the creature while playing with friends in the family swimming pool. Arriving as a result of somebody's lack of vigilance, it seemed to some people the menace might be trapped for ever in refuge among them, as an eel may fall by hazard into a well on its migratory nocturnal wriggle towards a suitable environment and survive for many years, growing enormous, down out of reach. It was inevitable that when it was worth a line or two in the papers, now, the creature was facetiously dubbed King Kong, and sometimes even King Kong of the mink-and-manure belt, although it had been seen only once, and then first by a horse, causing the horse to bolt with owner-rider, in the country estate area of the far Northern Suburbs. Former wife of the chairman of a public relations company, the rider was known to her friends as quite a gal, and typically she wheeled the horse and rode after the thing through a eucalyptus plantation, but never caught up or caught more than a glimpse of something dark. Anyway, that was no King Kong; what she'd chased was about the size of the average dwarf.

In the opinion of a zoologist, a monkey, baboon or ape may survive on the koppies round about Johannesburg, in summer, yes. But when the Highveld winter comes. . .*Simiadae* suffer from the common cold, die of pneumonia, like people—just like people.

One day, they disappeared.

The back bedroom was empty and nobody slept on the mattresses or read *Africa Undermined* by the light of the goose-neck lamp between them. Joy tugged the badly-hung curtains across the windows and closed the door quietly as she went out. She could have moved in there, now, but didn't. She and Charles kept each other company, lying in the dark in the front bedroom and thinking in silence about Vusi and Eddie. He said to her once:—One thing—you and I have been closer to those two than we'll ever be to anyone else in our lives, I don't care who that might be.—

It might be the lovers they once were, the lovers to come; wife, husband, children.

Once or twice in the following nights Charles went to Vusi and Eddie in the small hours.—They say I shouldn't, anymore. It's right; there's danger that might lead someone to them.— Only then did he add the conclusion—his conclusion and hers— to what he had said in the dark. —And most likely we'll never see them again.—

There was not much to tidy up. It was just a careful routine matter of making sure there was nothing by which anyone could be identified. Neither to have it lying about nor in one's possession or on one's person: he stopped her from folding up her conch-printed cloth, now familiarly wrinkled from its use on the sofa. —Well, I'll just let it stay where it is, then.— —No you won't. Haven't you got some kind of dress or something of that stuff? Your preggy outfit? You've been seen wearing the same material.—

During the last few weeks, she had taken the precaution of making herself a loose shirt to disguise her lack of belly when she went shopping and might meet Mrs Naas Klopper. So there was another bonfire, this time down at what had once been the Kleynhans piggery. The cloth burned in patches; pieces, eaten into shapes by the flames, kept escaping destruction. Again, Joy had a branch with which to poke them back into the furnace heart of the fire. It served her right for carrying unnecessary possessions with her into a situation too different, from anything known, to be imagined in advance.

—But if you can't go to them anymore, will they have enough food to last out?— And she, in what she thought of as her stupidity, her left-over dilettantism of austerity, not realizing you eat while you can, had started off by buying them cheap sausages!

Charles was tearing apart the spines of a few books, with marginal notes in Vusi's handwriting, they had left behind.

Feeding a fire with books was something he could not have believed he would ever do.

He stopped, with the peculiar weight of helplessness big men are subject to, when they must hold back.—Eddie says he'll manage.—

She looked, in alarm.

—Vusi has his mind on only one thing. I don't think he cares whether he eats or not, now.—

The cotton cloth gave off the smell of its dye as it smouldered—the natural dye made from the indigo berry, she had been told like any tourist when she bought it in the other African country where she had received her new surname and passport on her way back to where she had been born. Now Eddie and Vusi, who were not known to her then, even under those names, were somewhere she had never seen. Charles had tried to describe it; she marvelled that it could have been adapted and wondered if it could possibly be maintained long enough. Charles explained that Vusi and Eddie would have to wait until the day, the hour, in which the exact coincidence of their preparedness, contingency arrangements, and the gap in the routine Vusi had studied, arrived. Vusi had this charted in his head as precisely as an analemma on a sundial.

Charles and Joy could sit on the front stoep, now, in the evenings, like any other plot owners taking the air. They sat drinking beer and she tried to visualize for herself where she had never seen, gazing way off, as to an horizon of mountains, at the only feature of the Kleynhans place view, the towers of the power station whose curved planes signalled after-light back to the sunken sun, and above whose height toy puffs of smoke were congealed by distance.

And then the man came on his bicycle to see how his mealies were doing. Charles and Joy were helping themselves to bread and coffee, in the kitchen, at seven in the morning; even Charles had not slept well. They saw him cautiously wheel the bicycle behind the shed, and then appear, sticking his neck out, withdrawing it, sticking it out, like a nervous rooster. He went up to the door of his old room and called softly, in his language. They watched him.

—Oh Christ.—

—I'll go.— Joy slept in an outsize T-shirt; she put her Indian skirt over it and went out into the yard with the right amount of white madam manner, not enough to be too repugnant to her, not too little to seem normal to the former Kleynhans labourer.

—Yes? Do you want something?—

Mild as her presence was, it clamped him by the leg; caught there, he took off his hat and greeted her in Afrikaans. —*Môre missus, môre missus.*—

She changed to Afrikaans, too. —What it is you want here?—

He shook his head reassuringly, he wanted nothing from the missus, he asked nothing, only where was her boy? He wanted, please, to speak to her boy.

She was like all white missuses, she knew very well whom he meant but she suspected him, they always suspect a strange black man at the door. And she refused to understand because she knew he had something he wasn't telling—like his mealie patch he'd left on what was now her property.—What boy? Which boy d'you mean? What's his name?—

No, missus, he didn't know the name—those two boys that work for the baas on the farm, now. Could he please see those boys? They were (in an inspiration, they had suddenly become) his wife's cousins.

Now the white missus smiled sympathetically.—Oh those. No, they don't work here anymore. They've gone. My husband has finished with the building, he didn't need them any longer.—

Gone?

He knew it was no use asking where. When black people leave a white man's place, they've gone, that's all; it's not the white man's business to know where they'll find work next. Then he had another sudden idea, and again he saw in her face she knew it as soon as he did.—Does the baas need a boy for the farm? Me, I'm old Baas Kleynhans's boy, I'm work here before, long time.—

She was smiling refusal while he pleaded. —No, no, I'm sorry. We don't need anyone. My husband's got someone coming—next month, yes, from another farm, his brother's farm—

They knew exactly how to lie to each other, standing in the yard in which she was the newcomer and he the old inhabitant.

She said it again: she was sorry. . . And this gave him the courage of an opening.—When I'm here before—after Oubaas Kleynhans he's die, I'm look after this place. Those mealies (he pointed behind him) I'm plant them. And then the other baas he say I must go. Now those boy—your boy—I'm tell them it's my mealies and they say they can ask you, I can come for those mealies.—

—Oh the mealie patch? No, I don't know anything about that. But there are no mealies yet— Both her hands turned palm up in smiling patronage.

—Not now. But when the mealies they're coming ready, that boy he's say he going ask you—

—You can have the mealies.—

He grinned with nervous disbelief at the ease of his success. —The baas he won't chase me?—

She must be one of those young white women who tell their men what they must do. She was sure:—The baas won't chase you.—

—When the missus and the baas like to eat some of those mealies, when they coming still green, the missus must take.—

—Yes, thank you.— And then, the usual phrase from white people, who are always in a hurry to get things over, who don't seem to know or take any pleasure in the lingering disengagement that politely concludes a discussion:—All right, then, eh?— And she was gone, back into the kitchen, while, since he hadn't been chased away, he took this as the permission he hadn't asked for—to go through the white people's property to look at his mealies.

Charles and Joy kept checking on whether the bicycle was still there, behind the shed. Half-an-hour later it was gone, and so must he be, although they had missed witnessing him ride away.

Charles heated up the coffee. He had not appeared before the man; the man would not be able to describe the baas, only the missus and the two boys who had worked for them. Joy blew on her cup.—I really think he's harmless.—

But that was exactly what made him suspect—his humble pretext for having kept an eye on them for weeks, now, his innocent reason for trying to find out where Eddie and Vusi were: perfect opportunities for someone in plainclothes to have picked up a poor farm labourer out of work and offered him a few rands simply in return for telling what and whom he saw on a farm where nothing was growing but his trespassing patch of mealies.

—And if I had chased him away?—

—That'd've been much worse. For pete's sake!—

Once approved, she had natural grounds for pointing out her forethought.—I told him someone else was coming to work for us, but only next month. To hold him off and at the same time make the set-up not seem too unnatural.—

Charles opened his hands stiffly, doubtingly, and then made fists of them under his bearded jaw again.—Next month.— That part of the proposition was good enough. The day after you have left a country it will be as remote, as a physical environment in which you may be apprehended, as it will be in a year. Next month would be no more able to reach them than the time, months ahead, when the mealies would be ready for eating. —But now he'll be hanging around. He'll be arriving every day with his hoe and whatnot. He may bring friends with him.—

—So it would have been better if you'd gone out and played the heavy baas scene.—

—I've told you, you couldn't have done anything else.—

The occasional lapses of confidence in herself, that had roused his tenderness when they were lovers, now irritated Charles. You had no business to have gone this far, to be the back-up for Vusi and Eddie—all that meant—if you were still at the stage of allowing yourself self-doubt. But they were alone; no Vusi, no Eddie, and there they had to stay until Charles, on one of his outings in the combi, learnt that arrangements were ready for them to get away, as arrangements, at the beginning, had brought them successfully to Klopper's Eiendoms Beperk to look for a place in this area. They had only each other, even if it was in an awareness very different from that of the lovers they had been. They had lost the scent of one another's skin; but the house held them together, this place which they had occupied, not lived in, as in old wars soldiers occupied trenches and stuck up pictures of girls there. Neither said to the other what both felt while going matter-of-factly through this stage of what had been undertaken: some days, a desolate desire to get away from the house, the shed with the shiny roll-down door, the veld where except for the mealie patch, khakiweed filled in the pattern of rows where beans and potatoes had once grown; some hours, a sense of attachment to the room under the ox-wagon wheel chandelier and the curlicues of the pressed lead ceiling where the four of them had spent time that could never be recorded in the annals of ordinary life; to the outhouse they had bricked up together, and even to an aspect neither of them would ever have of any landscape again—the presence of the towers of the power station, away over the veld. This sense of attachment was so strong there seemed, while it lasted, no other reality anywhere to be found.

The ape family is not exactly omnivorous. Like the human animal, it is able to adapt its eating habits to changes of environment. If the creature had been a pet, or kept in any other form of captivity normal for a creature whose needs must be subordinate to the dominant human species, the diet supplied to it would have been fruit, vegetables and some cereal, probably stale bread. It also would have developed, as creatures do in mournful compensation for what they cannot tell those who keep them caged or secured by a chain to a perch, yearnings transformed into addiction to certain tidbits. Although members of the ape family are generally vegetarian in their wild state, in times of drought, for example, they will eat anything their agility and the strength of their hands equip them to catch; and in captivity this atavistic (so to speak) memory can be seen to rouse from quiet masturbation a perfectly well-fed blue-bottomed baboon in the Johannesburg zoo, whose prehensile bolt of lightning strikes down any pigeon who flies through the cage on the lookout for crumbs—he tears it apart instantly. The instinct must have been what returned to the fugitive when, in early weeks on the run, it killed or maimed dogs and cats. This surely was a period of great fear. Humans are the source of the terror of capture; a dog or cat is an intermediary who represents the lesser risk. To kill a suburban dog or cat is to destroy the enemy's envoy as well as to eat.

But after a while the creature changed its tastes. Or became more confident? Sergeant Abel van Niekerk and Constables Gqueka, Mcunu and Manaka had not been able to catch it. It had feasted on venison.

Now it lived by raiding dustbins; if not carelessly bold, then desperate. It still frequented the affluent suburbs where first seen, although now and then a sortie into the working-class white suburbs was again reported. Most likely it was from that class of home it had escaped (though no one was admitting any responsibility) because along with racing pigeons, rabbits etc., an ape is a lower-income-group pet, conferring a distinction (that man who goes around with his tame monkey) on people who haven't much hope of attaining to it as a company director or television personality.

A left-wing writer, taking up a sense of unfortunate duty to speak out on such paradoxes, wrote a stinging article noting sentimentality over a homeless animal, while—she gave precise figures—hundreds of thousands of black people had no adequate housing and were bulldozed out of the shelters they made for themselves. Some people of conservative views had a different attitude which nevertheless also expressed irritation with animal lovers and conservationists, who were more concerned about the welfare of a bloody ape than the peace and security one paid through the nose for in a high-class suburb well isolated from the other nuisances—white working-class, black, Indian or coloured townships. The monkey or whatever it was was in self-imposed exile. If it had been content to stay chained in a yard or caged in a zoo, its proper station in life, it wouldn't have had to live the life of an outlaw. If one might presume to do so without making oneself absurd by speaking in such terms of something less than human—well, serve the damn thing right.

Charles had found the cave. He had searched the veld within three or four kilometres of the power station, carrying a mining geologist's hammer and bag as the perfectly ordinary answer to anyone who might wonder what he was doing.

And he had found it. They called it 'the cave', right from the first night he took them there to see if it would do, but it wasn't a cave at all. It was the end of a rocky outcrop that sloped away underground into the grassland of the Highveld, sticking up unobtrusively from it like part of the steep deck of a wreck that is all that remains visible of a huge submerged liner of the past. Some growth had huddled round for the shelter of the lion-coloured rocks in winter, and the moisture condensed there in summer. In daylight, they saw the covering of leathery, rigid, black-green leaves, with a rusty sheen of hairs where the backs curled; to Charles, whose taxonomic habit would always assert itself, no matter how irrelevantly, wild plum in a favourite quartzite and shale habitat. Another muscular rope of a tree with dark thick leaves had split a great rock vertically but held it together; the rock fig. All this tough foliage, exposed to heat and frost without the protective interventions of cultivation, more natural than any garden growth, looked exactly like its antithesis —the indestructible synthetic leaves of artificial plants under neon lights. Hidden by it was a kind of shallow dug-out which Charles thought to have been made by cattle (who will easily form a depression with the weight and shape of their bodies) at some time when this stretch of veld had been farmed. But when, those nights between midnight and dawn, he and Vusi and Eddie had used their picks to dig a pit, they had fallen through into what was (Charles saw) unmistakably an old stope. There were rough-dressed eucalyptus planks holding up the earth that sifted down on their heads as they tunnelled on a bit. Eddie found a tin teaspoon, its thickness doubled by rust. Vusi's pick broke an old liquor bottle; there was a trade name cast in relief by the mould in which the bottle had been made: *Hatherley Distillery*.

Charles had never heard of it: must be a very old bottle. —Ja. . . So somebody worked a claim here, once. . . Long ago. I'd say round about ninety years. They came running from all over the world, and worked these little claims.—

—White men.— Eddie confirmed what went without saying.

—Yes. Oh yes—Germans and Frenchmen and Americans and Australians. As well as Englishmen. After the discovery of gold they poured into the Transvaal. Digging under every stone, sifting gravel in every river bed. But in the end only the financiers with capital to buy machinery for deep-level mining had a chance to get rich, eh.—

Eddie, by the hooded light of one of those lamps truck drivers set up when their vehicles break down on a freeway, patted the dust out of his thick pad of hair.—D'you think there's still gold in this stuff?—

—Not in commercially viable quantities.— Charles wore a mock-shrewd face. —Looks more like iron-ore, to me, any-way. . .—

—Man, I never thought this thing would end up landing me working in the mines.—

Vusi stopped digging and grinned slowly, over Eddie's charm, gave an applauding click of the tongue.

As their brothers had for generations carried coal and sacks of potatoes, they unloaded and stowed in the pit they had dug the AKM assault rifles and bayonets, the grey limpet mines with detonators and timing devices, the defensive and offensive hand-grenades. The pit was lined and covered with plastic sheeting and covered again with earth, grasses and small shrubs uprooted in the dark. The shelter for the two men was far less elaborately constructed. The stope was there; with Charles they hitched a sheet of plastic overhead to hold the loose earth and put down a couple of blankets off the mattresses in the back bed-room, some tins of food and packs of cigarettes. The entrance to the stope, already concealed on all but one side by the rocks, was covered with branches cut from the single free-standing tree that grew among them. (With another part of his mind, Charles identified, while hacking away at it, the Transvaal elm or white stinkwood, which would have grown much taller near water.)

They could not make fires. But before Vusi decided that his night visits should cease, Charles brought them a very small camper gas-ring, which was safe to use well back in the stope and during the day only, when any light from its tiny crown of blue flame would be absorbed in the light of the sun. That light had never seemed so total and shadowless, to them. It laid their silent

rocks open like a sacrificial altar to a high hot sky from which
even the faintest gauze of cloud was burned away. It surrounded
them with a clarity in which they were the only things concealed, the only things it couldn't get at. At first they could not
come out at all into the sun's Colossus eye, a fly's a million times
faceted, that revealed the minutely-striated smoothness of one
tube of grass, the combination of colours that made up a flake of
verdigris on a stone, the bronze collar on the carapace of a beetle
working through a cake of cow-dung. Then they found a narrow
cleft where, one at a time, they could lie hidden and get some air
through the overhang of coarse dusty leaves. Impossible for
anyone straying past to see a human figure in there. If cows had
used the shallow dug-out to rest in, herdsmen, the boy children
or old men who couldn't earn money in the cities, must have
rested here, too. Both Vusi and Eddie had grown up in the black
locations of industrial cities and had never spent days whose
passing was marked only by the movement of cattle over the veld
and the movement of the sun over the cattle. Eddie lay, in his
turn, on the shelf among the rocks, in this—crazy—peace: *now*.
What a time to feel such a thing; how was it possible that it still
existed, with what was waiting, and buried, there in the pit.

Vusi used that peace to go over behind wide open eyes (again
unable to smoke, this time because the trail would hang as
marker above the deserted rocks) every detail of what he had
learned from his contacts, planned on that basis, and planned
again to provide for any hitch that might upset the timing of the
first plan. He knew from experience that nothing ever goes quite
according to any plan. The wire that should be cut like a hair by
an AKM bayonet turns out to be a brick wall, the watchtower
that should be vacant for two minutes between the departure of
one security guard and the arrival of the next is not vacant because the first guard has lingered to blow his nose in his fingers. Vusi's concentration matched the peace. A lizard ran softly
over his foot as if over a dead body dumped among the rocks.

They played cards in their cave. They slept a lot. They had
bursts of discussion; indiscriminately, about trivial matters—
whether athletes lived longer than other people, whether you
could stop smoking by having a Chinaman stick needles in your
ear—and about segments of experience that somehow were not

integrated into any continuity that is what is meant by 'a life'. Vusi told, as if something dreamt, how in Russia in summer when it was stuffily hot he had lain on the ground, like this, lain on some grass in a park and felt the terrible cold of the winter, still iron down in the earth; and Eddie was reminded of a sudden friendship with a guy in exile from the Cameroons he'd got to know in Algeria, for two weeks they'd argued over political groupings in Africa—and now it was a long time since he'd thought of the conclusions they'd been excited over. The silence would come back, broken by some floating reflection from Eddie (—It's true. . .they say in these very cold countries the earth stays frozen deep down—); and then holding once more.

After Charles, a white man and conspicuous, couldn't come to them, Eddie went at night across the veld all the way to the main road to take water from the backyard tap of an Indian store. He went there during the late afternoon and bought sugar and cigarettes, returning when it was safe, after dark. Vusi could have done without both, but said nothing to stop him. Since he had taken the liberty of wandering about the city that time, it was as if Eddie assumed it was accepted he had a charmed life. Anyway, smelling of earth and unwashed clothes, now, he was only one of the farm labourers who crowded the store for matches and mealie-meal, soap and sugar, and were given a few cheap sweets in lieu of small change. He brought back with him chewing-gum, *samoosas*, and some magazines published by whites for blacks—smiling black girls opened their legs on the covers. Vusi did not pass time with magazines and did not miss the books he had carried with him, hidden, across frontiers. He needed nothing. If the girl, Joy, could have seen him she would have seen that he had become one with that face of his.

Eddie amused himself, opening with a thumb-nail some tiny white ovoid beads he found in a crevice of warm rock. Out of them the two men saw come transparent but perfect miniatures of the adult lizard. Their tender damp membrane could scarcely contain the pulse of life, but under the men's eyes they slid away to begin to live.

Mrs Lily Scholtz was hanging on the line the lilac nylon capes the clients of 'Chez Lily', her hairdressing salon, are given to wear, and which she brings home to pop into the washing machine every Sunday. Her husband, Bokkie, former mining shift-boss turned car salesman, was helping their neighbour with the vehicle he is building for drag racing. Mrs Scholtz heard the dustbin lid clang and thought her cat, named after a TV series Mrs Scholtz hadn't missed an episode of, some years back, was in there again. The dustbin is kept between the garage and the maid's room where Bokkie Scholtz does carpentry—his hobby; Patience Ngulungu doesn't live in, but comes to work from Naledi Township weekdays only. Mrs Scholtz found the lid off the bin but no sign of Dallas. As she bent to replace the lid, something landed on her back and bit her just below the right shoulder. Out of nowhere—as she was to relate many times. First thing she knew, there was this terrible pain, as if her arm were torn off—but it wasn't; without even realizing that she did it, she had swung back with that same arm, holding the metal lid, at what had bitten her, just as you swat wildly at a bee. She did not hit anything; when she turned round there it was—she saw a big grey monkey already up on the roof of the garage. It was gibbering and she was screaming, Bokkie, Bokkie.

Mr Bokkie Scholtz said his blood ran cold. You know what Johannesburg is like these days. They are everywhere, loafers, illegals, robbers, murderers, the pass laws are a joke, you can't keep them out of white areas. He was over the wall from his neighbour's place and took the jump into his own yard, God knows how he didn't break a leg. And there she was with blood running down and a big grey baboon on the roof. (His wife refers to all these creatures as monkeys.) The thing was chattering, its lips curled back to show long fangs—that's what it'd sunk into her shoulder, teeth about an inch-and-a-half long—can you imagine? He just wanted to get his wife safely out of the way, that's all. He pushed her into the kitchen and ran for his shotgun. When he got back to the yard, it was still on the roof (must have shinned up by the drain-pipe, and to come down that way would have brought it right to Bokkie Scholtz's feet). He fired, but was in such a state, you can imagine—hands shaking— missed the head and got the bastard in the arm—funny thing, almost the same place it had bitten Lily. And then, would you believe it, one arm hanging useless, it ran round to the other side of the garage roof and took a leap—ten feet it must be—right over to that big old tree they call a Tree of Heaven, in the neighbour's garden on the other side. Of course he raced next door and he and the neighbours were after it, but it got away, from tree to tree (their legs are like another pair of arms), up that steep little street that leads to the koppies of Kensington Ridge, and he never had the chance of another shot at it.

The Bokkie Scholtzs' house is burglar-proofed, has fine wires on windows and doors which activate an alarm that goes hysterical, with noises like those science fiction films have taught come from outer space, whenever Dallas tries to get in through a fanlight. They have a half-breed Rottweiler who was asleep, apparently, on the front stoep, when the attack came. It just shows you—whatever you do, you can't call yourself safe.

On a Saturday night towards 2 a.m. there was an extensive power failure over the Witwatersrand area of the Transvaal. A number of parties were brought to an end in rowdy darkness. Two women and three men were trapped in an elevator on their way up to a nightclub. There was a knifing in a discothèque stampede. A hospital had to switch over to emergency generators. Most people were in bed asleep and did not know about the failure until next morning, when they went to switch on a kettle. But clocks working off household mains marked an hour exactly: 1.36 a.m.

The early morning news mentioned the failure. The cause remained to be established. Alternative sources of power would soon be linked to restore electricity to affected suburbs in Johannesburg and peripheral areas. The midday news reported sabotage was not suspected. On television in the evening, no mention, but the radio announced from official sources that in the early hours of Sunday morning several limpet mines had struck a power station causing severe damage. There was no information about loss of life.

Something Out There

The newspapers, prohibited by Section 4 of the Protection of Information Act of 1982 and Section 29 of the Internal Security Act of 1982 from publishing anything they might learn about the extent of the damage, how and by whom it was caused, and not permitted to take photographs at the scene itself, titillated circulation with human interest stories (Bouncing Baby Boy Delivered by Candlelight) and, keeping the balance of a fine semantic nuance above the level where words break the law, recalled the number, nature and relative successes of similar acts of urban sabotage in the current year as compared with those of the two preceding years. It was all analysed academically, the way military strategists fight past wars on paper. There were maps with arrows indicating point of infiltration of saboteurs from neighbouring states, and broken lines in heavy type culminating in black stars: the conjectured route taken from point of entry to target. Sometimes the route by which the saboteurs probably made their escape, afterwards, was marked. Others had been caught, killed while security forces were giving chase, or put on trial. The sentence of death by hanging was passed and executed, in one or two cases.

The Prime Minister had been scheduled to make a major speech in a farming constituency where a by-election was to be held. Instead of having to counter dissatisfaction with his agricultural policy, he was able to call upon support from all sections of the community to meet the threat from beyond our borders that was always ready to strike at our country. He did not need to, nor did he mention this latest attack on its vitals, which had happened only three days before the speech; his face, composed somewhere between a funeral and a *stryddag*, was enough to put complaints about beef and maize prices to shame.

The release of official statements lags behind what people in the know come to know. A good journalist must have his contacts in both the regular police force and the security police. A manhunt was on, routine road-blocks and a close watch on all airports and border posts were being maintained: there was to be no further information supplied to the public while important leads were being followed. The important leads—everyone knew what those were. Another routine in such cases: a number of people, mostly blacks, had been detained even more promptly than normal power supplies could be restored, and were under interrogation, day after day, night after night, during which a name extorted by an agony of fear and solitude, and if that didn't bring results, by the infliction of physical pain, might or might not be that of someone who would attempt to blow up a power station. John Vorster Square and its suburban and rural annexes were working at optimum capacity. But Sergeant Marais Chapman had been taken off interrogation duty and sent with a couple of black security men to question people within a cordon of the area in which the towers of the power station were the veld landmark. One of the good journalists knew, without being able to publish a word in the meantime (the story was on file) that the police had been to the Indian at the store, who did not recognize any of the photographs they showed him, and that they had visited all plots and farms, questioning black labourers. It was in the course of these visits that they found an empty house, a deserted yard, at Plot 185 Koppiesdrif, where an old man with some story about being there to weed his mealie patch told them this was Baas Kleynhans's place but the oubaas was dead and the boys that worked there now, they had gone away two weeks ago, and the white people who were living in the house, last week he saw the missus but now this time when he came to weed his mealies, they were gone, too. The old man gave the name of the baas who looked after the farm now Baas Kleynhans was dead. So Naas Klopper—out of nowhere!—found the police sitting in Klopper's Eiendoms Beperk, waiting to ask what he could tell them about the Kleynhans place.

The journalist interviewed him shortly after. He wanted to talk to Klopper's wife, as well, because Klopper let slip that the white couple had 'taken us for a ride', they'd even had (the refreshment grew in proportion to the deception) a meal at the house—his wife had felt sorry for the girl, who was pregnant. But Mrs Naas did not want to give an interview to the English press; they would always twist in a nasty way something innocent that Afrikaners said. She did, however, talk to a nice young man from one of the Afrikaans papers, serving him coffee and those very same buttermilk rusks she'd baked and taken along to the young couple just after they'd moved in. She described again, as she had to the police, what the black looked like who had come from the yard, for a moment, with a tool or something (she couldn't quite remember) in his hand. Just like any other black—young, wearing jeans that were a bit smart, yes, for a farm boy. He hadn't said anything. The white girl hadn't spoken to him. But she was flustered when Mrs Naas— out of kindness, that's all, the girl said she was a foreigner— remarked she hoped the boy wasn't some loafer who'd come to the back door. Rosser their name was. They seemed such polite young people. Whenever she got to that point in her story, Mrs Naas was stopped by a long quavering sigh, as if somebody had caught her by the throat. She and whomever she was telling the tale to would look at one another in silence a moment; the journalist was not excepted. Something alien was burning slowly, like a stick of incense fuming in this room, Mrs Naas's split-level lounge, which had been so lovingly constructed, the slasto fireplace chosen stone by stone by Naas himself, the beasts whose skins covered the bar-stools shot by him, the tapestry made stitch by stitch by Mrs Naas in security against the rural poverty of the past and in certainty that these objects and artifacts were what civilization is.

Mrs Naas—being a woman, being artistic—notices things more than a man does, Naas Klopper advised the police. It was Mrs Naas's description of the girl and the young man that they took back to compare with their files and photographs at John Vorster, and to use in the interrogations that, if they couldn't always wring words from the obdurate (and sometimes you couldn't get a sound out of these people, no matter what you did to them) might reveal an involuntary change of expression that made it worthwhile to press on for recognition, names, evidence of collusion. So it was the police had in their files, the journalist had in his article (biding its time for a Sunday front page), a description of the wanted white couple as a blond bearded man in his twenties and a young pregnant woman. The journalist had no description of any blacks who had taken part in the sabotage attack, although it was known that the actual job was done by blacks. It was the involvement of whites that was the newsworthy angle; one white revolutionary was worth twenty blacks.

If it was detrimental to State security to allow publication of

any details about the saboteurs, it was useful to use certain
details of the attack to impress upon the public evidence of what
threatened them. Let State Information pick up the saboteurs'
weapons and hold these at citizens' heads: that's the way to shut
any big mouths asking awkward questions about why they had
come to be threatened—everyone'd be quick enough to agree,
then, they must give the Prime Minister, to save their skins,
anything he demanded. A photograph of a cache of arms was
released to all newspapers; AKM assault rifles, limpet mines
with detonators and timing devices of the type it had been
established had blown up part of the power station, defensive and
offensive hand-grenades with detonators, several hundred
rounds of ammunition. Some Dragonov sniper rifles, actually
from a different, earlier cache, were thrown in for added effect,
as a piece of greenery gives the final touch to a floral arrangement. The sites on which these arms were discovered were not
shown, but it was stated that some had been buried in the veld at
a hideout among bushes where the saboteurs appeared to have
lived prior to the attack, and some had been stored in the garage
of a house on a plot. The 'reinforced' outhouse was thought to be
an arsenal on which more than one group of saboteurs had
drawn. A biscuit tin displayed in a corner of the photograph
contained ammunition. When Mrs Naas Klopper saw it she gave
a cry of recognition. There was the child with the puppy and the
roses; her own biscuit tin, in which she had made the offering of
rusks.

A baboon has been found dead in a lane.
The stench of decay led some children to it while they were
roller skating. Its right arm was shattered and its fur tarred with
blackened blood. Now somebody got a photograph of it, before
the Baca municipal street-cleaners' gang were persuaded by a
fifty-cent *bonsella* to take the carcase away on Monday morning.
Nobody wants to publish the photograph. The dead baboon
was found the Sunday an attempt was made to blow up the

power station. The sabotage attack filled the newspapers and has given people other preoccupations; after all, some of the suburbs the creature had made uneasy were without electricity for eighteen hours.

It has been identified as a young, full-grown, male Chacma Baboon. Only a baboon, after all; not an orang-outan, not a chimpanzee—just a native species.

The Kleynhans Place has now been photographed by newspaper-men for papers published in English, Afrikaans and Zulu for specific readerships, black, white, and in-between, and for the international press. It has acquired a capital 'P' to distinguish its ominous status as a proper noun, the name of a threat within the midst of the community of law and order. If the Kleynhans Place can exist, undetected, a farming plot like any other on the books of Klopper's Eiendoms Beperk, what is left of the old, secure life?

Investigating the Kleynhans Place attack the police found two mattresses on the floor in the house, as well as two beds; old newspapers going back many weeks to that story about a monkey seen by some kids while they were swimming. Nothing there to work on. The only thing the white couple seemed to have forgotten was a home-made musical instrument, a sort of saxophone. (That was not ranged along with the exhibit of arms in the photograph released by the Security Chief to the press.) The Security Branch has searched its files for a political suspect known to have been a former musician. It is obvious the instrument was made by a black—a certain naïve ingenuity, the kind of thing blacks manage to put together out of bits of junk in a mine compound or while serving long prison sentences. Contact with the Prisons Department in charge of Robben Island has brought the information that similar objects are sometimes made by the long-term politicals held there. This particular piece of work incorporated tin rings from beer cans (plenty of those found in the kitchen) and cartridges that match those in the cache of live ammunition.

Quite early on in their investigations the police released the information that one of the four people—two whites and two blacks—it has been established were responsible for the Kleynhans Place attack, was apprehended on the Swaziland border and killed in a shoot-out with the police. No policeman was injured in this incident. A guard at the power station lost two fingers but no other personnel were injured by the explosion, and there was no loss of life among personnel or public. The old man who had visited the Kleynhans Place to watch the progress of his mealie patch was brought to the police mortuary to look at the corpse of the dead black man. The face was in a state to be recognized although there wasn't much left of the body. He identified the face as that of one of the farm boys who had worked for the white missus he had seen on the Kleynhans Place; this old man was therefore the key link in the investigation, proving beyond doubt that the white couple had set up house for the purpose of providing cover and a safe place for all four to plan the attack, and to store the weapons and ammunition required. (Mr Naas Klopper has testified that an open shed had been audaciously turned into a magazine with a steel door.) The two black men posed as farm labourers until a few days before the attack, when they moved to an old, abandoned mine-working near the power station. Blankets, the remains of fast-food packets, marked their occupation out there in the veld.

Nobody knows who the saboteurs, alive or dead, really are. There are names, yes—as the investigation has proceeded, as the interrogations at John Vorster yield results, there have been names. On the wrist of the dead man there was a cheap chain bracelet with a small plaque, engraved 'Gende', and it has been established that this was one of the names of a man known as 'Eddie', 'Maxwell' or 'David Koza'. He had been among thousands detained in the riots of '76, as a schoolboy. He had left the country uncounted, when released; no one knew when he had gone and no one knows when he came back.

The white pair were not married. There is no such couple as Mr and Mrs Charles Rosser, who sat there shyly in Mrs Naas's lovely home. The Afrikaans first name, 'Anna', was not the girl's name. A Mr and Mrs Watson, living quietly in Port Elizabeth, who haven't seen her for years—she changed 'out of all recognition' through political views they couldn't tolerate

—named her twenty-nine years ago 'for joy' at the birth of a little daughter. So far as they are aware she has never been to Australia. 'Charles' was christened Winston Derocher—one of those sentimental slips these politicals make, eh, coming as close as to call himself 'Rosser', when he must have known informants in England would supply John Vorster with a file on him!

The second black man, the survivor, has been identified as Zachariah Makakune, also know as Sidney Tluli. He is believed to have infiltrated from exile several times, and to have been responsible for other acts of sabotage, none of which involved loss of life, before the Kleynhans Place attack. But his luck must run out some day; he will kill or be killed. It was hoped that he had died in one of the South African Defence Force's attacks over the borders on African National Congress men given asylum in neighbouring countries, but it was discovered that the Defence Force was misinformed; he had moved house, and it was new tenants, a building worker and his family, citizens of that country who had never been beyond its borders, who had been machine-gunned in their beds in his place.

So nobody really knows who he was, the one who died after the Kleynhans Place attack, nor whom they believed themselves to be, the three who survived and disappeared. Nobody really knows which names mark the identity each has accepted within himself. And even this is not known fully to himself: all that brought him to this pass; this place, this time, this identity he feels. 'Charles', sometime lover of Joy, 'Charlie', brother of 'Vusi' and 'Eddie'—Winston Derocher, given his father's hero's name as first name, does not know that his distant French ancestor, de Rocher, founding a family too confused by the linguistic and cultural exchanges of treks and intermarriage to keep records, was a missionary who, like himself, lived by assertion of brotherhood—another kind—outside the narrow community of his skin. 'Vusi' does not know that the rotgut liquor bottle he found with the trade name *Hatherley Distillery* came from *Die Eerste Fabriek*, approved by President Paul Kruger, the prototype factory on the veld where 'Vusi's' own great-grandfather worked for the little money that was to become the customary level of wages for blacks, when the mining camp was proclaimed a town, a city, a great industrial complex.

Dr Grahame Fraser-Smith, looking back in fancy into the eyes of hominid evolution on a golf course, was ignorant of a more recent stage that had gone into his making. He doesn't know he is descended, only three human generations back, from a housemaid, Maisie McCulloch, who was imported by a mining magnate to empty the slops in a late Victorian colonial mansion now declared a national monument, and who left this position to be taken over by blacks, herself opening a brothel for all races in Jeppe Street.

No one has ever found out who let the baboon loose.

The sacred member of the ape family, the work of art in the municipal art gallery, has both a known and a hidden provenance. It is authenticated as an eighteenth-century European copy of a seventh-century statue from Māllapuram, India. The old lady who donated it had migrated to South Africa to escape racial persecution in Europe. She was not aware of the rarity of her gift, and thought she was making a display of generous patronage of the arts without sacrificing anything valuable in the private cache of European culture she had saved, along with her own life, from destruction.

The mine-working where Eddie and Vusi hid, that Charles identified as belonging to the turn of the 19th century, is in fact far, far older. It goes back further than anything in conventional or alternative history, or even oral tradition, back to the human presences who people anthropology and archaeology, to the hands that shaped the objects or fired the charcoal which may be subjected to carbon tests. No one knows that with the brief occupation of Vusi and Eddie, and the terrible tools that were all they had to work with, a circle was closed; because before the gold-rush prospectors of the 1890s, centuries before time was measured, here, in such units, there was an ancient mine-working out there, and metals precious to men were discovered, dug and smelted, for themselves, by black men.